Secrets That Find Us

Sahar Abdulaziz

Cover Design by Greg Simanson
Edited by Candice Barnes

PRINT ISBN: 978-1-5331-2068-7
EPUB ISBN: 978-1-5137-0558-3
Library of Congress Control Number: 2016901092

TABLE OF CONTENTS

"Add a few drops of venom to a half truth and you have an absolute truth"
- Eric Hoffer

PROLOGUE

You know you want me, he said.
You can trust me, he said.
Don't be frightened; I won't hurt you, he said.
But if you dare tell anybody—anybody—I. Will. Kill. You,
And then he proceeded to rape me.

FOR YEARS, I'VE REPLAYED his threats in my mind with the same stomach-turning intonation. I never dared to allow myself to forget, or worse, to allow time to soften the blow.

I remain haunted by the sound of his raspy smoker's voice, mumbling a litany of incoherent and menacing grunts. How at one point during the rape, his clammy, meaty hands clumsily groped and pawed at me, while his breathing became labored—short, sporadic bursts turned to uncontrollable coughing fits. His ugly face with large, greasy pores contorted in the strangest grimace. His tongue slithering in and out of his panting mouth. I enjoyed watching him unable to catch his breath. I wanted him to die.

Just when I thought he'd taken his last gulp of air, he somehow cleared the back of his throat, gurgling thick globs of phlegm, only to unceremoniously spew one sloppy, goopy hurl right over my shoulder. He was disgusting and classless.

Make no mistake—I crave to feel the bitter, vile sting of each sadistic memory. The day my youth was stolen and my body desecrated, shattering any hopes and dreams I might have kept stashed away.

Regardless of what happens today, I refuse to forget or let what he did to me, become shadowed by either time or circumstance. I am neither sorry, nor will I ever regret what transpired. If that makes me his equal, a monster, so be it. But God in all His wisdom will be my judge and jury, not you. Now, you twelve strangers, my so-called peers, as I sit before you in judgment, you study me closely, in search of any sign of deception in my dead eyes or my refined body language.

Now, as I am forced to wait, I laugh at you. I despise you. Nothing more than a pack of worthless sheep, summoned by some chosen moral imperative while you judge me by my actions based on what you think were my intentions.

Am I that easily understood?

I dare say, I think not, and this whole affair is a sham.

* * *

The embittered monologue never had a chance to be delivered. Just one of the many angry pages laboriously printed on backs of accumulated legal papers tucked safely away in her folder; one of only a few incidental belongings now callously jammed into a state-issued plastic bag, jumbled together, waiting for pick up.

A guard making his routine evening rounds discovered her unresponsive body. At first, he assumed she was just asleep, but something didn't look quite right. Her head slumped, shifted into a crooked, unnatural position with her tongue protruding out to the side, limp and hanging.

They immediately activated the alarm. Confusion and commotion within the prison walls ensued. A small unit of heavy-laden boots could be heard stomping down the corridor, onto the tier. The medical team dispatched at once to the scene, but there was nothing left to do. She was dead. The initial ruling was suicide, although until the completion of the autopsy, the cause of death would be marked off as pending.

CHAPTER 1

THE PHONE CALL

KNEE-DEEP IN THE MIDDLE of power scrubbing the tub with her nose encased in deadly chemicals, Raven's phone rang. She despised cleaning, particularly bathrooms.

"Hello? I'd like to speak to Ms. Grant. Ms. Raven Grant."

"Who's calling?" she asked, tugging her grimy plastic gloves off. Raven crooked her neck, trying to balance the phone between her shoulder and chin without it dropping.

"Superintendent Williams from the Beckman Correctional Facility. Is this Ms. Grant?"

"I'm Raven Grant." He had her full attention.

"Ms. Grant, I am calling next of kin about former inmate Terri-Ann Stone. I am not sure if you have been notified, but I need to inform you that inmate Stone… um, your sister? Am I correct?

"Yes, Terri's my sister—"

"Well, your sister was found unresponsive in her cell. The coroner has ruled her death as an apparent suicide."

"My *sister? Terri?* Dead? I don't, when did this—"

"Yesterday evening. Approximately eleven p.m.," he answered, correctly anticipating her question.

"What do you mean by 'apparent' suicide?"

"Until the autopsy is officially complete, the coroner will not confirm death by suicide, but we are pretty confident she will come to the same conclusion. There was nothing to lead us to believe anything to the contrary."

"I see." Raven plopped down on the bathroom floor.

"From her paperwork, we ascertain that you are her executor, and therefore, you are permitted, should you wish to do so, to pick up her personal property. However, while her personal belongings will continue to be stored here, any belongings of a deceased inmate which remain unclaimed after one year will be disposed of in accordance with procedure 401.19."

Oh, dear Lord, he must have a script to read off of. She cringed. *This can't be happening. Terri can't be dead.*

"If the personal property of the former inmate is not claimed by the end of the specified period, a special board designated by the Commissioner will convene, myself included, to decide if any, or all, of the items being stored have any sale value. If it is determined to have a sale value, then the same special board will solicit offers for purchase from at least three reputable dealers, granting sale to the highest bidder. Any and all proceeds from such sale will be paid to the State Treasurer by the Superintendent, which in this situation, would again be myself."

"What if Terri's belongings don't have any value?" Raven was tired of Terri being referred to as "former inmate." "I mean monetary value, not personal, of course because I'm sure it has personal value to me..." When nervous, Raven babbled.

"If such a person—in this case you, Ms. Grant—wishes to claim these belongings, they will be required to sign a receipt for property received, so please make sure to bring proper and adequate photo identification with you, such as a driver's license, passport, or any other legal identification card. If you decide not to pick up the former inmate's property, and it is deemed to have no monetary value, it shall be disposed of."

"I understand." *Not really...* Raven thought.

"Additionally, the property officer has recorded all items approved for storage on the inmate's inventory log. You will be given a copy of this. Any and all items deemed contraband shall be disposed of in accordance with 103 CMR 403.14, Disposal of Inmate Property." He hesitated a second before continuing.

"Um, okay?"

"And what would you like to do about the final arrangements?" he asked.

"I have no idea... You mean the burial?"

"Yes, ma'am."

"Did my sister have anything written down anywhere about what she wanted to be done, you know, like, in case of...her wishes?"

"Not that I am currently aware of... But unfortunately in matters such as these, we, the State Department of Corrections, require a decision from you quickly. Should you not have the funds or the ability to cover these costs, mainly due to the sudden, unexpected nature of your sister's death, the state can and will take care of your sister's funeral arrangements if you so desire."

"I don't know... I'm not sure what she would have wanted, but you said the prison would take care of all the final arrangements? I wouldn't know where to begin."

"That's fine. All we will need from you is a signed burial order as soon as possible."

"I can come tomorrow to sign the paperwork. Can I pick up my sister's things at the same time?"

"Yes, ma'am. I will make sure all your sister's belongings are ready for pick up tomorrow, as well as any and all paperwork in regard to her burial. Do you have any other further questions?" he asked, sounding preoccupied, ready for the call to come to an end.

"I can't think of any." *Only a million*...she again thought.

And with that, his presentation was delivered, as it must have been delivered countless times before. The call ended abruptly, and Raven was shaken back to her reality of smelling like cleaning solution, left holding the phone, bewildered.

* * *

One plastic brush missing a slew of teeth, one small tube of used toothpaste, one yellow toothbrush, one bottle of shampoo and conditioner in one, two hand towels, three black hair bands, one bottle of baby oil, an almost empty container of deodorant, and one pen.

Also in the bag were a pair of cheap, state-issued flip-flops, one set of reading glasses, and an old worn-out pair of white, tube socks. The only clothing in the bag included a single, well-worn, green sweatshirt with one matching pair of sweatpants, neither with strings or hoods. Either Terri never owned much, or perhaps she might have given the rest away. *People do that sometimes, giving away prized personal possessions before they commit suicide,* Raven mused.

Shoved into the bottom of the bag were ten softcover novels—the maximum allowed, rubber banded tightly together, now permanently boasting bent bindings, tattered pages, and extensively highlighted passages. Terri appeared to have been a voracious reader, although by state regulations, all her publications had to have come directly from a book publisher, a pre-approved distributor, or an actual book company. Curiously, Raven noticed how all the books shared a common theme: depression and death. A tattered public defender's business card stuck out of the first book's pages, appearing to take the place of a bookmark.

The property officer unceremoniously handed over the entirety of all of Terri's meager belongings to Raven. A thick mound of accumulated legal documents—all for naught—were inside a legal-sized brown folder with Terri's name boldly typed on the front label. Raven accepted the folder, not entirely sure what she was supposed to do with it. It probably included some of her legal paperwork from her defense case. No matter what defense her attorney had tried to perform for Terri, she'd adamantly refused to plead innocent, readily admitted to the murders, and had outright refused to disclose the motivations behind her actions.

The correctional officer then handed Raven the promised paperwork. "Sign here for the burial. By the *X*, ma'am."

Overwhelmed and a tinge flustered, Raven glanced over the form, eyes scanning quickly without actually absorbing the fine print. Quickly signing off on it, Raven observed how the officer glanced back down once again at his paperwork to confirm everything designated for next of kin was properly delivered. Satisfied, he had Raven sign once again on the dotted line to confirm receipt of all personal possessions. As soon as she was done, he slid the bulletproof, plastic window shut.

And that was it.

Raven collected Terri's belongings in her arms the best she could manage. She balanced the bag and folder trying not to appear as clumsy and shaken as she felt. She mouthed an inaudible *thanks* to the property officer who had already comfortably perched himself back on a chair. He watched her with a strained, bored expression plastered across his bored face. Through the plastic window, he gave a curt nod and silently moved his lips to indicate, "*No problem.*"

Visitors to the maximum-security prison were often taken aback at the stark coldness of the menacing structure—high cement walls with towers strategically placed at each corner, and an equally high barbed wire fence coiled like a gigantic toy slinky outlining the entire perimeter. The prison noticeably lacked any visible windows from the outside, yet as Raven headed to her car, she couldn't shake the feeling she was being watched. Paranoia?

While only inside the visitors lounge for less than an hour, time had stood still for Raven, making it feel more like an eternity. Thousands of impoverished souls survived behind these massive concrete walls, countless years lost revolving around the mundane and tedious days spent here. Raven could only imagine each of the thousands of stories and dire circumstances that brought each person to this place.

The sun had begun to withdraw, declining back into the winter darkness. Heading out to the parking lot, Raven managed to almost trip twice. As much as the crisp, cold air felt refreshing, the sharp chill cutting her face served as a bleak reminder to get her butt in gear and back home before the expected storm arrived. She despised driving in the snow.

Before embarking on the day's trip, Raven had taken the initiative to clear her trunk of all the useless crap she usually drove around with, making sure she had enough space for her sister's belongings. Opening the now empty trunk, she chucked everything of her sister's inside. Drawing in a deep breath, a knot formed in her throat at how little space Terri's stuff actually took up. Almost forty years of a beleaguered existence now stuffed into one single, clear plastic bag, and one flimsy, overstuffed old legal folder. Surreal.

Safely nestled in the confines of her Jeep. Raven shuddered, beyond grateful to be leaving the imposing structure Terri had been forced to call home for her final last years.

CHAPTER 2

RAVEN

RAVEN BARELY KNEW her half sister growing up. Their separate worlds and Terri's absence, limited any discernable interaction. Sifting through the jumble of convoluted stories Raven heard from the Grants and Terri, she came to believe the mother she and Terri biologically shared wanted nothing to do with either girl. Terri's father had left shortly before she was born. His reasons for leaving had been lame half-truths interwoven into half-baked lies. Terri never had much of a chance to get to know her father, but that was no great loss. He turned out to be just another loser, never looking back, never caring about anyone but himself.

Unable to dictate the direction of her destiny, Terri had become subjected to the haphazard whims of others whose farce of a life forced upon her a collection of sordid mishaps and hardship. Grasping for any level of control, Terri remained tight-lipped about most of her past, despite Raven's adolescent attempts at prying during their infrequent heart-to-heart chats on the phone. When pushed, Terri would share only the most insignificant tidbits, often in tight-fisted portions, wanting to move on with the conversation as quickly as possible.

To this day, Raven's collection of childhood memories starts and centers on the life she spent with the Grants. As much as Raven racked her brain, trying to piece the puzzle of the missing years together, there wasn't a whole lot more in her memory about Terri. Raven knew even less about her biological parents. Whatever she thought she remembered came mostly from random stories heard from, or relayed by, predominantly the Grants and occasionally, Terri. Most of the genuinely accurate recollections existed solely in the protection and confines of Raven's subconscious, which was probably for the best. All else remained word of mouth.

Raven was just shy of two years old when Social Services became involved, removing her from her parents' home due to "severe neglect" and sent her to live with a local foster couple. Mr. and Mrs. Grant fell in love with the little girl at first sight, raising her as their daughter, and subsequently adopted her. Together, the couple provided Raven with a childhood anyone would be envious of, and a life full of choices and freedom. Both promoted resiliency and security. Raven would not have been privy to this normalcy had she been left to wallow in her real mother's lack of care.

Upon arrival at the Grants', Raven's possessions were limited to a few old, grainy photos worn down at the corners where supposedly they had been clipped to an official file folder, issued to her adoptive parents. Raven never saw the file itself or read its contents, nor had she been curious enough to care. After the Grants passed away, Raven remembered hearing about the file and decided to keep a watchful eye out for it while packing up and clearing out various dressers and drawers. So far, nothing had shown up. Besides the one set of pajamas she arrived in, and the swaddled handmade blanket, Raven owned next to nothing from that brief period in her past.

The Grants had been generous, yet firm in their opinion not to spoil Raven. Their self-contained world consisted of only right and wrong—ambiguity was seldom entertained. Keeping Raven in the dark about her birth family would have been morally wrong in their eyes, so without hesitation, they encouraged Terri and Raven to stay in touch. From time to time, Raven would receive mail from Terri, usually in the form of a cryptic postcard or small mass-produced card. Communications remained one-way, spotty, with never a return address. Nothing fancy or overly detailed was written, just a simple, "Hi, how are you doing? All's fine with me. Hope you're listening to your new parents," kind of message.

Occasionally before signing off, Terri would include some unimportant detail about her life, more as a filler than anything. "The weather here in Texas is hot and humid. I hate feeling sticky." Or "Have you ever eaten a falafel? Those things are delicious—I can wolf down two easily!" Sometimes funny anecdotes that would offer Raven a giggle. "Hey, did I tell you I'm learning how to belly dance, but so far, my hips aren't cooperating."

Oddly enough, Terri habitually signed off on her communications with, "Love you, Ladybug." Raven never understood the reference, but it felt nice all the same. Genuine. Uncharacteristically sentimental. Out of all the written communication, that one simple turn of phrase held some connection and meaning to her past. A past Raven had no personal recollection of.

Raven never heard a single word from either of her birth parents.

* * *

Unlike Terri, who never seemed to settle, Raven's entire childhood and youth consisted of living in the same modest dwelling, in the same quaint and familiar neighborhood, amidst the same recognizable faces. To some, Raven's life may not have been exciting, but for Raven, she had thrived on and yearned for consistency as a young girl. The predictability of her days fit her personality to a *T*, and she was more than content existing amongst familiarity and comfortable mediocrity. She'd felt safe. To this day, change frightened Raven.

Inevitably, and especially around her birthday, Raven would obsess over her sister's whereabouts, wondering what she was up to, what she looked like. As anticipated, a card or short note from Terri would arrive, sometimes a few days late. The contents of the letter predictably remained devoid of any concrete conversation, purposely written to avoid addressing many of Raven's youthful curiosities.

"Why doesn't my sister just come visit me, Ma?" Raven recalled asking Mrs. Grant.

"I don't know, dear," admitted Mrs. Grant consolingly. "It could be any number of reasons, but you shouldn't worry yourself about all of that right now."

"I could go visit her."

"Maybe one day... Now enough. Go set the table; it's almost time to eat."

The avalanche of questions dissipated over time, until one day they all but disappeared. Eventually, preoccupation with the natural demands of childhood helped Raven give up dwelling on the "why doesn't she come visit me" mantra, at least until the next postal tease from her sister arrived. For their part, the Grants prayed for the day when the unfiltered adolescent third degree would come to a halt, and they could at last tell Raven the entire truth. They abhorred lying, even by omission, but the truth wasn't theirs to dispense. The Grants had made a solemn promise to respect Terri's wishes until told otherwise.

The colorful, often gaudy postcards and letters that arrived each year, including all special occasions, were postmarked from all over the country. Raven, too young to take any notice, never gave the envelopes or their origins much thought until her twelfth birthday. That's when a peculiar, official-looking stamped envelope arrived. Contained inside the rather plain envelope was a short, handwritten note with an aged, finely folded newspaper clipping.

> *Hey, Ladybug!*
>
> *Are you too big for me to call you that now? I know it's been a while since I last wrote. Okay, I admit, more than a long while. Sorry about that. I won't bother to make up an excuse since I have nothing but time to write to you. Anyway, I've put this awkward conversation off long enough. Now that you've reached the ripe old age of twelve, I think it's about that time you were given the truth about where I've been hanging out, or should I say, cooped up. Perhaps the truth will clear up a few questions for you.*

The attached clipping, while not overly detailed, contained more than a sufficient amount of disturbing information, perhaps a bit too much for a twelve-year-old mind. Nevertheless, it had captivated Raven.

Shortly after Terri's twenty-first birthday, she had been arrested outside of a church. The police converged on the scene like a clip out of the movies after receiving a frantic call from the resident minister. Sirens blared as growing crowds of onlookers gawked from a safe enough distance, unable to pull away from the lurid drama playing out around them.

Terri later referred to the scene as almost having an "out of body experience." The reporter observed how the horde of police, in their haste to corner the suspect, pulled up over the curb, creating a barrier to hide behind. Then, with guns drawn, they logistically began surrounding her, yelling out commands that Terri simply ignored. Guarding themselves, the police remained back, hesitant to approach any further.

Seasoned officers didn't know what to make of the macabre scene before them. The bizarre young lady remained seated on the cement stoop of an old ornate church in town. She was covered head to toe in dry, caked blood, uncontrollably shivering and despondent. After a short while, realizing the suspect didn't appear willing to put up a fight, they quickly apprehended her. The medics, with the assistance of the police, strapped Terri onto a waiting gurney, and although technically in police custody, she was brought to the local hospital for examination.

Terri was subsequently charged with the murder of her mother and stepfather, who were found lying dead in the family home. Police reports indicated the two bodies were discovered face up in a pool of their own blood. Both were shot in the back. The stepfather was said to have been also shot in the groin. Their bodies were plastered in dog feces, twigs, leaves, ketchup, and maple syrup. One detective at the scene was quoted as saying, "We walked into a grotesque and nauseating mess."

The .38 caliber revolver at the scene, suspected as being the murder weapon, had been found placed squarely between the two victims, barrel facing toward the ceiling. Inside the barrel of the pistol, a small, thinly rolled piece of paper read, "When you lay down with dogs, you get up with fleas." The gun encrusted in blood and feces, had Terri Stone's fingerprints clearly marked, and the note was subsequently determined by forensics to be Terri's handwriting.

Raven cringed, but kept reading.

I have decided to include a newspaper clipping in the letter. This old news clipping should make explaining certain issues easier. Oh—and, by the way, so that you know, I was impressed. The reporter had been surprisingly accurate in his description of the crime, except the part where he wrote, "the motive for the grisly murders is still unknown." Now that was some bullshit! An outright lie! I knew exactly why those two miscreants had to die—the reporter just never asked me. If he had, he would have found out that I never had a doubt. On the other hand, I'm not entirely sure what I would have told him if he had given me the opportunity to answer, I guess he was stuck writing his story with what he had. I don't blame him.

Here's the deal, Raven—I'm sharing all of this with you so you won't find out what happened from anyone else. That's the least I can do. Sending you postcards from places I've never been won't cut it anymore. I apologize for the deception, but you were too young to drop this crap on, but you have to admit, it was pretty sweet how I did that. I bet you're wondering how letters and cards had postmarks from all over the country? Right? It's simple. Other inmates, people who owed me favors, asked their visitors to mail them off for me. Apparently I come cheap—one stamp.

Anyway, I wanted you to know, you can ask me anything you'd like, but here's the thing—I won't promise to answer you. I will, however, promise to tell you the truth whenever I do decide to share anything important moving forward. That you can be sure of, you have my word, whatever that's worth. The rest of it, well, that's going to have to wait for another time, another discussion, or maybe even another life.

Stay the good girl I know you are for your folks. They are respectable, kind people. Not like those two sacks of shit that got shot up.

Love you, Ladybug

- Terri

* * *

Now that the cat was out of the bag, Terri felt comfortable writing fairly regularly.

Terri began by first writing about safer subjects. Soon enough, the two sisters settled comfortably on discussing books, recipes and occasionally, politics or current events. Raven, still only a child, was unsure how to respond to her sister's sudden interest in her life or the wacky jailhouse tales she'd disclose. After sending the clipping, Terri never again mentioned or spoke about her case or what drove her to murder their parents, and Raven simply never asked.

Over time, Raven's growing collection of letters and cards from Terri became unmanageable. They quickly outgrew the top shelf of her closet, so instead, she graduated to a hand-me-down travel case she'd found in the attic, pleasantly surprised by how so many letters could fit so easily into one of those things.

Raven hated to admit it, but she suspected she suffered from a mild case of self-diagnosed OCD. She couldn't seem to help herself. She liked—no, make that *needed*—order. Everything had to be in its designated space exactly the way she left it and expected it. Any deviation from that caused her stress and anxiety. Therefore, as a way of compartmentalizing her relationship with Terri, whatever Terri sent over the years went directly into that suitcase—chronologically, of course. Letters, cards, a few old photos, everything, that is, except Terri's newspaper clipping. Raven stuck that in her wallet, tucked securely behind her driver's license. She wasn't entirely sure why, she just did it.

On occasion, as Raven began working part-time jobs, she'd send her sister a few funds in the form of postal money orders. Nothing much, just a little something to add to Terri's inmate commissary account, money she could use to purchase a few incidental, state-approved items of her choosing. Terri never once asked Raven for the money, nor did she ever see fit to acknowledge it, either. Raven thought that a bit strange, but decided it was best to intentionally leave the topic out of their already marginal and strained discussions. Safe subjects only.

Once every other month, Terri called Raven collect. A five-minute phone call filled mostly with forced small talk, bordering on the predictable. Nevertheless, Raven looked forward to those calls if only to reconnect with the unknown part of her previous life.

Between calls, Raven's mind would elaborately plan out what she'd like to say or ask her sister, but inevitably, when the time came, she'd fail to follow through. So many questions rattled around in her head, and not enough answers, but Terri deliberately made having those kinds of conversations uncomfortable. Terri was a pro at discussing only those topics she wished to discuss. She relied on her uncanny ability to draw her listener into her world instead of the other way around. She would slice through the weight of pending details and particulars while all along, cleverly disclosing nothing. During most of their phone calls, Terri did the majority of the talking while Raven tended to do most of the listening.

Once in a blue moon, if the timing was just right and Terri seemed open to having a real discussion, Raven would throw out a question to see where it would land. Sometimes, she'd surprisingly get back a fairly candid yet heavily condensed answer. Most other times, though, mainly when Terri was being terse or combative, not so much.

"What was our mother like?" Raven asked.

"She was a product of her environment," Terri shot back flippantly. Raven was never sure what Terri was implying with her monotonous tone and quick wit.

"Okay, meaning?"

"Meaning she was a screw—a royal piece of work. The environment that helped mold her into who and what she became was just as screwed up, i.e., she was a product of her environment." Terri's flat voice indicated that this subject was best left alone and off limits.

Only on one other occasion did Raven work up the nerve to pose to her sister a question that needed asking. "Are you sorry you, um, you know, that they are dead?"

"Never," Terri replied with a stark, cold finality that left Raven with the chills.

The surprising part was that after all Terri had gone through and experienced—which for the most part, remained primarily speculative on Raven's part—she was remarkably upbeat for someone serving life in prison. Raven strongly suspected her sister's moods were maintained synthetically through the use of drugs, despite being in a maximum-security prison and locked up in her cell for over twenty-three hours a day. Occasionally slurring her words, Terri would forget mid-sentence entirely what they had been chatting about, or she'd just become dead silent. Lost among scattered thoughts, blathering on about absolute nothingness, laughing hysterically at her jokes, sarcastic and cutting.

Raven's relationship with Terri existed outside of her normal life. She kept Terri's existence private, on the edge of her carefully guarded and constructed world, controlled by her incessant need to catalogue. Therefore, most people who knew Raven knew her only as Raven Grant, never Stone. Raven purposely refused to disclose to any of her friends anything about her notorious half sister, or who her real parents had been. Most of Raven's friends just naturally assumed the Grants were her biological parents, except for school officials of course, and that was more than fine with Raven.

CHAPTER 3

BACK HOME

WHILE HEADING BACK HOME, the impending weather threatened to quickly turn ugly. The ominous sky cast a dark umbrella weighted with gray clouds, ready to dump wet, heavy snow mixed with ice. Although the winter had just begun its reign of tyranny, the season had already become miserable, terrorizing the East Coast weekly with one disruptive storm after the other. In preparation for the next weather event, icy, hazardous roads and highways were already inundated with globs of rock salt and grime, coating every available surface, including her Jeep. Perhaps this time, in some small way, the weather was a godsend, allowing Raven's mind to shift from dispiriting thoughts of Terri to her immediate undertaking: driving safely back home, preferably in one piece.

Raven, a fair-weather driver, tended to panic or become overly anxious behind the wheel if she anticipated being in any danger of getting caught out in hellish driving conditions. To stay focused and keep relatively calm, she used music to soothe her nerves, often turning the radio on full blast. Anyone else in the car would have physically agonized over the pounding decibels.

Partial to folk music, in particular the oldies from the late sixties and early seventies, Raven would sing along at the top of her lungs. Raven's voice wasn't necessarily horrible, only increasingly grating after the second stanza. The Grants had been a musical couple. Back then they had tried to introduce Raven to many of the same songs that were now considered classics.

Clicking through station after station in an attempt to find anything remotely familiar or soothing, Raven finally settled on the local news, hoping for an updated weather report. Instead, after a few moments, she was slapped with this gem:

Convicted murderer, Terri-Ann Stone, held in the Beckman Correctional Facility for Women for the past seventeen years, was found dead in her cell from an apparent drug overdose on December 9th. A state investigation has now revealed Stone had most likely been hoarding her antidepressants months before her death. However, there will be further investigation as to how Stone managed to procure an excessive amount of various pills.

The New York Department of Corrections' report indicated there was also the possibility that Stone had been supplied with additional pills each week from another inmate. According to the report, the unidentified inmate admitted that Stone told her she was anxious and having difficulty sleeping. The inmate further confessed to officials she helped Stone procure pills, but claims she never thought Stone was stockpiling them to commit suicide. The Foxboro County Medical Examiner's Office has now officially ruled Stone's death a suicide.

Stone, only twenty-one years old at the time, was found guilty back in 1999 of the brutal murders of her mother and stepfather. Although the prosecutor at the time initially sought the death penalty for both murders, Judge Harrison handed down two concurrent life sentences instead.

New York State had been without a death penalty since June 2004 when the state's highest court in People v LaValle ruled that the death penalty "violated the state constitution of New York."

While subsequent legislation has been introduced to either replace or fix the statute, all succeeding legislative attempts have failed. As a result, capital punishment has not been used in New York State since 1963 when Eddie Mays was electrocuted while in Sing-Sing Prison.

Stone was forty years old.

And now for the weather. Bill, how is that snowstorm looking out in your neck of the woods?"

Raven's fixation on listening to the newscast instead of paying attention to her surroundings almost caused a major accident. She was caught completely by surprise when a semi, driven by a lunatic with a death wish, barreled down the highway speeding past her. His massive tires shot gloppy brown slush at her Jeep. Small, embedded pebbles pelted her windshield. Shrieking, Raven death-gripped the steering wheel, trying with all she had not to let panic take over as the road ahead became increasingly trickier to navigate.

Once the truck had passed, she fought to regain her bearings while simultaneously screaming a torrent of profanities. Raven struggled to maintain control of her vehicle, thankful not many other cars were on the road. Most folks were smarter than her and had obviously heeded the state's warnings to stay off the highway and remain safely at home. With heart racing and eyes bulging out like a deer in headlights, Raven shut off the radio, deciding it was wiser to concentrate in silence for the remainder of the trip home.

Outside, the cold, blustery winds howled. Temperatures continued to plummet drastically. Water, already puddled on the roadways, began to freeze into patches of black ice. Newly formed layers of crystallized, light snow blanketed the roadways, making for a tough ride home. As the intensity of the gusting winds picked up, their combined strength and power forced snow to drift across the highway, severely impairing Raven's already limited visibility. It took all she could muster not to careen off the road, and she anxiously struggled to prevent her vehicle from spinning out or sliding into an embankment.

Normally no more than a one-hour ride, Raven's trip took over four stress-filled hours. Once back on home turf, she found herself struggling to block the swarm of intrusive thoughts racing back and forth in her head. A barrage of wandering uncertainties poked and prodded, demanding to know exactly who Terri had truly been. Unanswered question after question taunted her, and now, with Terri's death, hidden answers most likely permanently expunged.

Minus the searing headache coming on hard and fast, Raven felt grateful to finally be back, safely at home. Mentally drained and physically exhausted, she made yet another solemn promise never to drive voluntarily in the snow again, no matter what was asked of her. All the way home Raven had cursed herself, furious that she hadn't just picked a totally different day to go up to the prison. The phone call from the superintendent had given her a sense of urgency, though, making her fearful that if she hadn't hurried, they would have thrown away Terri's belonging before she was able to retrieve them. For whatever reason, which Raven couldn't fathom, she wouldn't have allowed that to happen.

She dragged the bag and legal folder into the house and dumped everything in the hallway. Next, she stripped off layers of sweat-drenched clothing and headed straight to the bathroom. One more second and her bladder would have burst. She'd been holding it for ages, too chicken to veer off the highway to find a bathroom or take the chance of getting lost, or worse, stranded.

Raven cranked up the heat to full blast and slowly began to calm down. She swallowed a few ibuprofen, gulping them down with a large glass of room-temperature cream soda. For now, all she wanted was to park her tired, frozen butt in front of the television and devour something deliciously fattening, preferably a bag of chips. However, after rummaging through the pantry and cabinets, they were nearly empty—par for the course. She'd forgotten for the zillionth time to buy bread, along with a myriad of other groceries and goodies. Grumpily, she settled for leftover sliced salami rolled into a lettuce wrap, a bag of stale potato chips, and a refill of soda on the side. *Hail to my acid reflux. I salute you.*

Somewhat satiated, Raven laid back, propping herself up with pillows, relaxing on the couch, and staring ahead. Not exactly paying attention to the television screen, Raven's eyes drooped. The tenseness between her shoulder blades had morphed into one hell of a stiff neck. Gripping that damn steering wheel for dear life can do that to a person.

Today had proven to be a difficult day all around. Not two days before, Terri had been no more than a letter, a casual phone call, or a postcard. But in death, she had become so much more real. A bona fide person whose life had been rife with frayed experiences, regardless of where she had lived her final years.

Now, unrepentantly, Terri decided to reach out from the grave. The morbidity made Raven's head spin with confusion and chills went up her spine. While alive, Terri couldn't have been bothered to connect, but as Raven's life became systematically embroiled with uncertainty, Terri upped the ante and had decided now was the time to acknowledge her as family. None of this made any sense—not her parents dying so close together, or Terri killing herself; none of it made any damn sense. Despite her increasing misgivings and building resentment, Raven strove to imagine what life had been like for her sister year after year in that cement dungeon—each day filled with the monotony of the last, and the last the same as the promise of tomorrow, with no future or guarantee of ever getting out alive.

But unlike the majority of inmates, grateful for a chance to leave the tier and spend time with loved ones, Terri purposely never welcomed Raven into her world. Terri had adamantly refused all requests for visits, no matter who the person was, except one time, and that was only to sign off on legal papers. Terri's position confused Raven.

"Why continuously write to me if you don't want to ever see me?" she once wrote her sister.

"I would love to see you. More than you'll ever know, Ladybug," she wrote back, "but not here, not in this place, and don't be upset with me. One day you'll understand. That's a promise."

Frankly, Raven never thought she'd understand, but she found staying angry with Terri impossible. The truth was, it had been hard to stay mad at or miss someone she never genuinely knew. There were times Raven felt exceedingly disconnected, as if someone had pulled the plug out of her past life, casting her in the part of a nobody without a history. There now wasn't a single familiar soul to call, write, visit, or break bread with. All that had disappeared in what felt like a flash.

* * *

Unlike some children forcibly removed from their parents for whatever reason, Raven knew her new family truly wanted her and admirably cared about her. She never felt like she'd been dealt a raw deal. In fact, it was just the opposite. The Grants were an older, childless couple. From day one, the couple had poured all stored-up devotion and affection into Raven, and she greedily had slurped it all up, a starving, willing partaker.

From the start, whatever Raven did, tried to do, or wanted to do, was always good enough in the Grants' eyes. Gentle souls who cherished their new addition to their family, the Grants had selflessly made room for Raven into their already comfortably settled lives. Through unfettered devotion, they bestowed upon their young charge an admirable opportunity to create a positive life. To say Raven loved and adored the older couple would have been an immense understatement. When her elderly parents recently died, only weeks apart from one another, Raven's heart shattered into a thousand pieces. Her sudden expulsion from the safe, predictable, protective world she was raised in temporarily pushed her off-kilter, saturating her with indecision.

The Grants unwavering kind-heartedness in life matched their benevolence toward Raven in death. Monetarily, they'd taken every precaution possible to ensure Raven would be properly provided for. The modest mortgage-free house and the land around it had been gifted to her in their will, along with a more than substantial sum of life insurance funds—more than enough to pay bills, attend a local college if she so chose, and then some.

Still, beginning her new life alone felt daunting. Raven couldn't figure out why life decided to abruptly exact punishment from her for a crime she had no idea she had committed. Learning to successfully plot a course through the murky adult world left her overly cautious and a tad bit anal. Overwhelmed, she simply didn't know how to pull it together.

Raven's mind ordered her to take charge: own her space, make do with what she had available in the here and now, and retreat once again by turning the house she happily grew up in into her safety net. She began completing simple, no-brainer chores—anything she could find that would wear her down, including reorganizing the house and all of its contents. Each figurine held a story, a history. Anything superfluous, or a duplication, or unnecessarily ornate, was immediately boxed up to give away. Each day, she battled against herself, while sorrowful thoughts annoyingly tagged along, urging her to stop for a moment and wallow.

She would never have thought to touch or invade the sanctity of her adoptive parents' personal belongings while alive, but now, all that changed. By legal decree and final request, the sorting turned into a solemn duty, a grim obligation she was ill prepared to complete.

Losing both loving parents was a huge adjustment. The fact that her real parents were also dead, and now her half sister, as well, made her feelings even more bizarre. Oddly enough, despite the fact that Terri was personally to blame for murdering Raven's parents, and in all probability had been a certified psychopath, Raven didn't feel fazed, which was real ground for concern. Why didn't she flat-out hate Terri? That was the real question.

Lethargy invaded her tired muscles. Raven glanced over with listless eyes toward the hallway where the pile of Terri's belongings remained, a pile reminiscent of a quest of sorts—the Holy Grail of past damage and answers. An encapsulated litany of long-lost questions beckoned her to search, and to discover.

But not tonight.

I'll tackle this mess tomorrow. No matter what I find out, it's better than this not knowing fog I've been living with all these years.

* * *

Terri

Six months earlier…

Terri slowly shuffled back to her "house"—her six by four cement, gray cell. Without resistance, she stepped inside. The heavy metal door slammed shut securely behind her. She never gave the guards a hard time about anything. What was the point?

"You know the drill, Stone," shouted the correctional officer accompanying Terri back to her cell.

She lived on a maximum-security level floor. Whenever Terri was permitted into the exercise yard, she had to be chained up in a four-piece suit, inmate jargon for a full set of restraints—handcuffs, leg irons, waist chain, and a security box to cover the restraints' key holes. On the tier, however, she was allowed to roam the pod more freely during certain hours. Although she knew the other women in her pod, Terri made sure to stay pretty much to herself, never getting involved in either prison politics or schemes.

As a "lifer" and notorious, violent murderer, the other women intentionally stayed out of Terri's way, considering her the sort of person one did not deliberately want to cross. Since she wasn't a pain in the ass, never giving lip or trouble, most of the seasoned guards also left Terri alone. Once in a while, a newbie correctional officer—also known on the tier as a "cowboy"—would try to assert some authority Terri's way. To Terri, it wasn't worth a response. She'd play it cool and remain quiet until the C.O. tempered down or got drilled by one of the other guards. Either way, Terri didn't give a rat's ass.

Terri knew the drill all right. She bent over, squatting low enough, wincing as she pushed her still-cuffed hands through the metal flap so the guard could unlock and remove the cuffs. Heaving an audible groan, she kicked off her state-issued flip-flops and plopped down on her thin cot. *Alone again.* Terri's eyes scanned the small space, making sure nothing had been disturbed in her absence. She had memorized every solitary inch of the cell. Each single thin, jagged crack, every chip in the peeling paint, and every groove or inconsistency. *The monotony of being in this windowless, godforsaken cell is going to kill me, just not fast enough,* she thought to herself miserably.

Shivering uncontrollably, Terri threw on an old, worn sweatshirt. She practically lived in the damn thing all season long since the piped-in, warm air felt more like air-conditioning half the year—and not the half when she needed it. The stale, stagnant air remained icy cold. All the inmates complained, but nothing ever changed.

Besides a few standard toiletries, Terri never bothered much with her personal appearance. In the corner of the cell above the metal toilet hung a miniature mirror. Adamantly refusing to own a wristwatch, which was just another form of torture for a lifer, Terri instead marked her time using a mirror—her only timekeeper. The mirror denoted increasing aging lines, sagging jowls, hollow cheekbones, and growing creases on her sallow face. Much like the rings of a tree revealed its age and the kind of seasons the tree witnessed and battled through, the mirror was the only scale left to measure her dwindling appearance. It never masked her or tried to deceive her, no matter how abhorrent or appalling the reflection staring back at her had become.

Terri plopped down at her desk across from her metal cot. Stacks of books were neatly lined up in alphabetical order alongside papers, pens, and pencils meticulously organized and treasured. Her infamous legal folder lay flat on the single shelf over her desk. She'd given up reading those papers years ago, and when feeling especially embittered, she became half tempted to rip the contents up into smithereens and flush them down the toilet.

Over the past decade, to keep the little sanity she had left, Terri had become quite the proficient reader and writer, radiating a touch of surprise and anger all at the same time. *I could have become somebody if I'd only been given half a fair shake. Instead of being here, locked up in a cell, and languishing for the rest of my life, kept alive while waiting to die.*

As much as Terri took pleasure in the process of writing, she had to think long and hard before putting a pen to paper. She never intended to share the gory details of her life with anyone, much less Raven. However, something inside Terri changed, or perhaps she felt she needed to leave some mark or testimony, indicating to the world that had thrown her away, that Terri Ann Stone did, in fact, once exist and matter. For now, she'd place her decision to end her life sentence on hold until she could finish telling her story on her own terms.

Inhaling deeply with a steadfast determination and purpose she hadn't felt for ages, Terri made her decision. She reached up and pulled down her legal folder. She lifted up the lip, took out the first page, turned it over, and bowed her head with tenacious concentration.

And Terri began her excursion back in time…

CHAPTER 4

PANDORA'S BOX OPENS

RAVEN'S STIFF NECK throbbed every time she tried to turn her head in either direction. *I knew I should have gone to bed, but no, I had to curl up on the couch, "to sleep the sleep of the dead."*

Dawn arrived, still serving bitter temperatures coupled with dull, heavy gray clouds. It made the thought of going outside unappealing. Instead, Raven stood up, yawned, and stretched. She sluggishly staggered upstairs to the bathroom to get cleaned up. *A hot shower should do the trick.*

Downstairs, the television continued blaring. Since the Grants' passing, Raven had developed the terrible habit of sleeping with the television blaring in the background. Yet the constant background noise never left Raven feeling fully rested. Now, the weather report on the local news began to filter through her subconscious.

"Although the temperatures are at the freezing mark, the wind chill factor today will make it feel more like five degrees below zero. More snow is heading this way with approximately two to four inches expected later on today…"

Well, if I have to stay inside, I might as well attempt sifting through Terri's pile of crap. Wish I had gone food shopping…

Within an hour, Raven was cleaned up and feeling more human, especially after downing two strong cups of instant black coffee and a toasted Pop-Tart. She was half tempted to throw another one in the toaster for good measure, but lately she had put on a few extra pounds. Her jeans were becoming noticeably tight when she attempted to button them. Instead, Raven grabbed a handful of dried fruit from the jar on the counter and headed for the living room, chewing her latest lame attempt at making healthier food choices.

Outside, gusty winds began picking up and the temperature continued to plummet. The farmhouse had seen better days, but thankfully, for the most part, it still had decent enough insulation. When the gas heat wasn't enough to keep the temperatures inside toasty, the fireplaces in each of the main living areas, including the bedrooms, certainly did the trick. Ice storms and heavy winds were known to knock out electricity, sometimes for days, so Raven made sure to keep all of her mobile devices and laptops fully charged, just in case.

Mr. Grant had kept his family well supplied with wood. Of course, as a younger man, he'd chopped and stacked the cords himself. Roaming the expanse of his property, scouting for fallen, dead trees, had kept him hard at it most of the spring and late into the summer. It was backbreaking work, however, and as he'd aged and become less mobile, he'd have several cords delivered each fall instead. Gratefully, Raven continued to be more than well stocked.

Courtesy of the Grants, Raven had become the proud owner of over fourteen acres of beautiful farmland, four cleared, most still dense with forest. The quaint late-1900s farmhouse she'd grown up in was located almost directly in the middle of the plot. The woods surrounding the house normally remained dark and thick, and since there weren't any other houses close enough to see or been seen by, the seclusion felt deliciously absolute. Since they were the only residents in the immediate area, this meant the township never bothered to give the Grants a physical mailbox, but instead had an address assigned to them. That meant all mail got delivered to the small town post office about four miles away as a P.O. box.

As a youngster, Raven loved to walk the grounds, pretending to be an explorer from far away exotic lands sent to discover new and unchartered territory. Part of the game of exploration included finding hidden treasures. Raven turned into a consummate collector of small trinkets, whether it was a thimble, an old movie ticket stub, or an exceptionally beautiful ribbon from a birthday present. Anything that fit her fancy or caught her eye.

She'd also write short poems or stories in each of her dime-store journals, and when filled up, they too were placed in a plastic, sealed bag and then locked in a metal container to be buried in the ground. On occasion, Raven would sneak a few used, tossed glass jars from Mrs. Grant's canning cupboard. In those, she'd keep post-it-notes full of wishes and dreams, written and folded as small as she could muster. Raven buried many a secret treasure on that land, but like the pirates of the past, she'd had the forethought to draw a map with painted, plastic location markers hammered into the ground and used as visual reminders of where everything was hidden.

The home remained situated on a well-worn dirt road off the larger, more traveled main road. The road connected to yet another wide dirt pathway that was, in fact, her driveway. Both the dirt road and pathway were privately owned by the Grants, so the township never bothered to plow them during snowstorms. Thus, Raven made certain to own a four-wheel-drive Jeep instead of a car. Even when it rained, as opposed to snow, the gullies and trenches in the malleable ground leading up to the house made for a constant driving hazard. While growing up, each summer it was her chore and responsibility to patch up the worn-down areas of the road with dirt from the property that she'd dig up and shovel into a wheelbarrow.

Working with her hands gave Raven a real sense of accomplishment. She loved the smell of fresh-cut grass and the feel of rich dirt. Since Mrs. Grant canned, Raven never indulged much in store-bought fruits or vegetables unless in school or at a friend's home, and she could taste the difference immediately. The vegetables from their garden were the best. Buckets full of vine-ripe tomatoes, cucumbers, and strawberries were all bursting with the sun's true, delectable flavors. In the cellar, a vintage collection of seeds awaited her attention. Keeping up with the garden chores alone come spring was going to pose an issue. She'd have to decide on a plan of action soon. Living on a farm held so many assets, including a legacy towards self-sufficiency. From an early age, Raven had been taught to be independent—don't look to others if you don't need to, and above all, make do with what you have instead of ungratefully wishing for more. One prime example was, despite the Grants' owning a dryer, clothes were hung out to dry on the line throughout the spring until winter. Towels and socks became a bit stiff, but the fresh scent of her clothes and bed linens after being hung to dry in the sun, more than made up for that inconvenience.

In school, Raven did well enough, bringing home solid b's, occasional a's, but hardly ever a C. Unfortunately, school never held much of an attraction, as she preferred learning kinaesthetically. Raven and Mr. Grant spent many hours toiling the soil together, and while they rarely spoke while working, once in a while, if the timing was just right, Raven would inevitably drop a line.

"Pop? Would you and Ma ever think about selling this land and moving away?"

"Moving?" he asked incredulously. Then he muttered, "Selling my land and moving? Hmm, no, Raven. Never. This land is a part of us now. If we did that, it would be like cutting off one of our limbs, like an arm or leg."

"But wouldn't you like to move someplace warm, with palm trees and no snow?"

Mr. Grant just guffawed and stopped what he was doing to take a closer look at his little girl. Raven had grown into such a beautiful little thing. Sweet, always helpful… She made him and his missus extremely proud to be considered her parents. "I'm just not the palm-tree kind of man, Raven. Neither is your ma. I need mountains and trees—these kinds of trees," he listed while waving his hand around his head, gesturing at their surroundings. "These trees tell a history. One day—not now, because I can't expect for you to understand at your age—I hope you will come to love and appreciate this little corner of heaven as much as we do. Now, enough chitchat. Grab that shovel and let's head into the house. It's about time for dinner, and we need to get ourselves cleaned up before Ma will let us sit at her table."

* * *

Raven gave it her best effort, trying to organize the kitchen her way after Mrs. Grant's passing, but once she began the task, she soon realized she had little need to buy anything new. She already had all she needed, except of course the two people she cherished who had made this house a home and a real family. They could never be replaced, and missing them had overshadowed whatever else she tried to do.

Not being much of a cook, despite Mrs. Grant's endless attempts to teach her, Raven began relying mostly on takeout and frozen meals, quick sandwiches, and junk food galore. It gave her little cause to spend a great deal of time in the kitchen. Mourning, combined with sheer laziness, had begun taking its toll on her. However, this brought with it another whole set of dilemmas—the fast food was far from satisfying; it was expensive and unhealthy, and she had begun feeling sluggish and bloated. Even her thick hair showed signs of malnutrition. Eventually, all the garbage she indulged in would have to be put to a halt. For now though, one more change felt tremendously overwhelming and beyond reach.

Mrs. Grant, much like her husband, had run a tight ship. Although the house revealed a style not revisited since the early 1950s, it was eclectically delightful, invitingly comfortable, and easy to keep clean. While the home enjoyed no visible clutter, once Raven began to sift seriously through the contents of the house and attic, it became apparent it was time to get rid of some stuff. Raven began carting off or giving away to the local charities much of the older furniture, clothes, and other knickknacks that just needed to go and find them a new home. The task of packing and sorting through her parents' clothing and personal belongings had been heartrendering and took a miserable few weeks.

By and large, most of her parents' bedroom decor had consisted of mementos and photos about her. There was one photo in particular of the three of them taken at a county picnic, framed and mounted on the wall. Her favorite. Raven unhooked the frame from the wall, positioning it above the fireplace in the living room instead.

After removing the bulk of their clothing and other knickknacks, Raven decided to keep her folks' bedroom door shut until she could muster up the energy, both physically and mentally, to clear the rest of their belongings out properly. Once enough time went by, since supposedly *time heals all*, she'd keep the furniture, but for now it was too painful to figure out. Not surprisingly, she opted to remain in her childhood bedroom.

The semi-monumental task of sifting through Terri's plastic bag took all of five minutes, if even that long. Out of respect for her sister's death, Raven wanted to prolong the "unraveling," to study each item individually to see if it held a deeper, hidden meaning, but other than the ten highlighted novels, nothing else seemed important or personal. There's only so much sentiment one can attribute to an old toothbrush and a few other miscellaneous items. Raven assumed Terri would have probably tossed them all out on her volition, but doing something like that would have only drawn unwanted suspicion, the kind of unnecessary attention that would have certainly caused her intentions and plans to be thwarted if discovered.

Despite the uselessness of most of Terri's stuff, Raven just couldn't bring herself to throw any of it away, old toothbrush and all. So, back in the plastic bag it all went, and into the closet until she could figure out her next move.

By midmorning, Raven was nestled back on the couch. Her mind began to wander, replaying the discussion she had had about the burial, and whether or not she had handled the call from the prison correctly. Did she make the right decision about having the prison take care of Terri's burial, or would her sister have wanted to be cremated? *How am I supposed to know? Maybe Terri mentioned it somewhere in her belongings, or in a last will or testament? Something! But where?* Raven made a mental note to keep an eye out for anything indicating Terri's last wishes, but in all likelihood, it was probably too late to change what she had already signed away.

Then she had a thought. Raven leaped off the couch, raced back across the room into the hallway, and grabbed her handbag to search for the copy of the burial paperwork she had been given. Maybe there was some leeway or procedure for changed minds and hearts, just in case a cremation turned out to be Terri's actual choice. Scanning quickly, then reading more slowly, what Raven read made her want to puke. "Oh, man… How could I have been so stupid?" she groaned aloud. "*Shit*-shit-shit-shit-shit!" And then she kicked the closet door. Reading further, her stomach began to knot up. *I really did it this time.*

Essentially, by consenting and signing off for the prison to "handle" all of the funeral arrangements, Raven had lost all legal rights to the deceased body, and now all decisions moving forward would be by the discretion of the Department of Corrections. Furthermore, signing that form meant Raven no longer had to be informed about where the department decided to bury her sister.

She continued to read the document, bits and pieces swimming before her eyes.

"Should the Anatomical Board decide not to claim the remains, which would be at their discretion, this facility will usually arrange within one working day the cremation contracted through the department's cremation facility."

Now, she'd never be able to visit Terri's grave, nor would she be informed about where they'd eventually decide to put her! And that was *if they actually buried her*. They could just as easily decide to donate her body to research or science or something, doled out part by part as an "anatomical donation," or just cremated.

The form also stipulated that "within thirty calendar days of an inmate's death, the next of kin must claim the residue of the remains. Please note, as next of kin, in claiming the remains you will be responsible for any and all expenses at the fair market value, as determined by the facility contracted through the New York State Department of Corrections."

Raven shivered. Its final notation seemed so…cold and businesslike.

"Should you, as next of kin, wish not to claim the residue of remains, the medical services unit will ensure a proper burial container is provided, and all graves will be marked for identification purposes only. Visitation of said graves by the public at this time will not be facilitated."

Now, even in death, Terri remained State property, forever, thanks to Raven.

Raven leaned against the wall and slid to the floor defeated, seconds away from bawling her eyes out, more out of sheer frustration than anything else. *How could I be so damn stupid? After two funerals in the past year, you would think I would have been smarter than this! But no, instead, I signed off and ran away—letting someone else handle what I should have taken care of.*

And then she remembered the legal folder. Perhaps Terri had written her wishes in there. It was worth a shot.

She grabbed the folder out of the bag, careful not to spill the precariously overstuffed contents out, and headed for the sofa so she'd be able to spread out the papers more easily. She slowly unwrapped the thin cord from around the folder and pulled out another, more compact folder tucked inside. To her bewilderment, her name was written on the front in bold, black marker in the recognizable handwriting she knew so well.

For Raven's Eyes Only.

What the hell?

Raven couldn't help herself. Filled with hesitation, mixed with a heavy dose of excitement, she peeked inside. Just a bunch of old useless documents from her case. *But why would Terri want me to have these? What's so secretive about this stuff? Even the courts keep a copy.* Her heart sank.

Disappointed, Raven pulled the stack of papers out, but when she did, she could immediately sense how the papers in her hands felt different, pressed and crinkly, not the smooth feel of stacked copier paper. Somehow used. Turning the pile over, she let out a deep groan… —*holy shit, Terri!*

Terri, Terri, Terri, you sneaky woman, you! Terri had used the backs of her legal documents to write Raven, probably knowing full well that a notebook or even a journal had the potential to become confiscated after death, but never her legal papers! Guards could shake Terri down, strip search her, and even look inside her body in places that left nothing to the imagination. But they were not legally permitted to read the contents of her folder without permission, nor could they take it away.

Raven cautiously stacked the papers on the small side table then pulled the first page off the top. She snuggled into the soft, old sofa, wrapped the quilted comforter around her body like a tent, and began to read.

* * *

Dear Ladybug,

I suppose by now you have read or heard all you can bear about the monster I supposedly am—or was. If you're reading this, it means that I'm dead. I pulled it off, ended my personal nightmare and swallowed my destiny. It also means that you are now in possession of the last few most important items I had left to bestow upon you. Not too impressive, sorry about that. I wish it could have been more. I wish I could have left you money, or a car, maybe a nice necklace, or even a nice photo of me without numbers plastered across the front of my chest. Instead, I will leave you the truth. Since truth in our society is a hot commodity, I suppose, in a small way, you're about to be rich beyond your years.

A big part of me wants to tell you my side of the story, while the other part, the less selfish part, thinks that I should just let you believe whatever you've heard so you can despise me and put me out of your thoughts; go on with your life without my baggage hanging over your head. And, perhaps after reading this, you will despise me, maybe even resent me, but at least then you'll know why. Unquestionably why.

Nothing happens in a bubble.

For years, you've had a million questions swarming around that head of yours, apprehensively trying to wait for the right time to ask, but I never actually gave you that break. You probably didn't think I knew that, did you? Well I did, but I had my reasons; but I'll get to all that in good time.

First off, I'm sorry you got dumped with all this. You didn't deserve having to be the one and only person I left my 'legacy' to, but I had no one else, and, well…that made you the top pick.

Secondly, despite all of what you've heard, even monsters have their raison d'être, which is fancy talk for 'motivation or justification for existence.'

Lastly, if you should decide not to read any of what I have written to you, please, just do me one simple last request: burn everything. Don't throw it away. I don't want anyone else knowing the truth. If you can't handle it, that's fine, I can completely understand that; and frankly, I don't blame you. Honestly Raven, it's not like I will know anyway, being dead and all, but everything contained in this legal folder has been written to you and for you only. I'd like you to honor that.

CHAPTER 5

TERRI

HOURS TICKED BY and the sun dimmed, but Raven couldn't tear her eyes away from the documents. The fact that Terri had written the letter solely for Raven made reading it all the more daunting and demanding, forcing her to pay attention to every innocuous nuance and sordid detail. Quite a few times, with strained eyes and heart, Raven had to stop, unable to continue. From the flow of the passages, it was apparent Terri hadn't written in one, or even ten sittings, either. It was obvious that whatever needed to be revealed, was finally pouring out in passages. Terri's exacting language was a plethora of amassed pain; a miserable story too complicated to ingest in large doses.

I wasn't born a murderer, far from it. When I was small, I too had dreams and aspirations, but sadly, they quickly became deflated and replaced—dismantled by the totally insane mother I was saddled with. I could also equally lay blame on my father for my less than stellar childhood, except that he graciously got himself incarcerated before I popped into the world. As life sometimes does, karma decided to fly in for a stopover. Before daddy had a chance to re-enter the free world, another inmate sliced him up in the yard over another male inmate they both evidently wanted to bang. Apparently dear old dad lost. 'C'est la vie', or in his particular case, death.

Terri's handwriting made reading a laborious task. Her print was naturally on the small side. Precise. Limited by the available amount of paper in her possession, writing tiny was her method for trying to save space. The indents from Terri pushing down hard on the pen also caused the pages to become difficult to read. They strained Raven's already tired eyes; she'd often lose her place, forcing herself to re-read each page over at least twice before moving on.

I think I would have become an excellent writer, but I never knew how much I enjoyed writing until I set out writing you this letter. For all intents and purposes, I would have been one hell of a late bloomer and a single hit star. But life is like that sometimes, Raven...it holds back secrets and makes you work hard to find the answers, only dropping subtle hints for you to follow—if you have the courage to search for them. I never had that courage.

Being a deliberate reader, Raven soon realized that Terri's letter was going to involve more time and energy than first assumed, but she was captivated, tense with guarded expectation, and hungry for the promised truth. Some of what Terri wrote was contemplative and thought provoking, while a good portion sounded purely cold-hearted and angry, making Raven wince and shudder, like in her description of her fellow inmates.

Life behind bars isn't what you see in the movies. On more than one occasion, after watching some of these fools go at it, I think to myself, "Thank God there are prisons."

Honestly, some women in here just take up space. Not a redeeming bone in their entire bodies. Those are the types of people I wish got snuffed out in their sleep—their lungs pressed closed until the last breath in their worthless souls seeped out and became absorbed into the atmosphere

Then there are a few of the others who just made a mistake, a big mistake, or perhaps even many big mistakes rolled into one, but their basic humanity is still there, hanging on for dear life. I can see it. Regardless of how this place tries to wear a person down and hammer the humanity out of you, this rare breed of people still hold on to who they innately are. I honestly admire people like that, Ladybug. At one time, I tried to be like them, but life wore me down and I folded. Maybe I just didn't have the ability to fight everyone and everything around me all the time. I don't know. But just when I had the chance to grab my share of happiness, it got whisked out from underneath me, and I gave up trying to fight back for it.

Sometimes I wonder to myself what kind of person I would have become if I had been born to different parents, given the chance to live a different life. Would I have been the same type of person and still squandered my existence, or would I have become somebody? Would I be working in a place like this, opposed to dying in it?

I know it doesn't do me any good to sit and lament about a bunch of what ifs, but sometimes I can't help it. My mind just goes there, and being locked up day in and day out, my mind tends to win.

Anyway, I guess I'm sharing this because it's my way of telling you to think long and hard about the choices you make in life, so you don't wind up in a place like this, and trust me—you never want to be in a place like this.

I also don't ever want you to take life for granted—or the people in it who care about you. No telling how long any of us will be around. And don't let fools push you around either, Raven. Never let your guard down with people who haven't earned your trust, but once they do, don't ever let go of them or let them down either.

I never shared this with you, but a long, long time ago, I knew the Grants. Kind-hearted people raised you.

Hold up—*Terri knew the Grants? How is that possible? Why am I only finding this out now? What was the big secret?* This annoyed Raven, who chucked the paper on the sofa table. How could they have kept this from me, and why? What was the point? What else am I going to find out?

Raven needed fresh air. A long walk through the woods would help clear her mind. She stood up, ready to grab her coat, but one peek outside quashed any desire of going hiking anywhere. The storm remained ominous. Resentfully, she slumped back down on the couch, inexplicably hungry, aggravated, and still physically exhausted from yesterday's ordeal.

While contemplating her next unhealthy culinary indulgence, her phone rang; it was Padraic McMahon, fondly referred to by all who knew and loved him as Paddy. Paddy was Raven's high school pal turned steady boyfriend. The forever-dependable Paddy drove a pickup truck and worked at his family's business. However, since the funerals, he'd been pulling double duty, hauling, packing, and carting away at Raven's bequest.

"Hey, Rave. Called to see how you were holding up."

"I'm fine I guess, thanks. Just annoyed."

"Why's that? What happened now?"

"Nothing… Everything, I don't know. It's this whole thing about Terri. I picked her stuff up yesterday, and in the bag she had an entire long-ass letter written to me on the back of her legal papers. I only found it by chance, trying to look for anything that might tell me how she wanted her remains handled after death."

Paddy whistled. "Are you kidding? That's weird, right? I mean, she never wrote to you much—that's what you told me, anyway."

"Exactly. Weird. And the more I read, the more I get aggravated, like there's a complete part of my life that was attached to hers somehow, that I never knew about. For example, did you know she knew the Grants?"

"Ah, no. Why would I know that?"

"I meant figuratively, Paddy." Raven laughed. "In her letter she admitted she knew them, and that they were good people. Why wouldn't they have told me all those years that they knew my sister?"

"Maybe they only knew each other in passing. It's not the biggest community here, Rave. Everybody pretty much knows everybody and their business. I wouldn't get so worked up about it."

"Maybe." Raven wasn't quite sure.

"So were you able to find out anything about how she wanted to be, um, buried?" Paddy asked warily. Raven had been through so much recently, that he didn't want to stir the emotional pot too much more, now that her half sister was also dead.

"No, not yet. I'm going to finish reading through this letter. Hopefully something will be mentioned. If not, oh well. Not much I can do about it now. Anyway, enough of me, how are you doing? Did you work today?" She wanted to change the topic.

Paddy and his three younger brothers worked with their dad at the family-owned business, McMahon & Sons. Coming from a large family and being the oldest sibling seemed to have trained Paddy on how best to be useful, mindful of others, and not annoyingly needy. Of all emotions, Raven couldn't deal with needy, but then again, she wouldn't have to with Paddy, whose broad shoulders were hers to lean on.

"I worked half a day. With the storm coming in and making a mess out of the roads, we closed up early. Do you need anything? Let me know before the brunt of this storm hits."

"No, I have what I need."

"Oh, really? When was the last time you did any grocery shopping?"

"Stop it, you! I'm good. As a matter of fact, I'm about to raid my chocolate supply now," Raven jested, chuckling.

"Yeah, well, okay. Give me a ring if you need me, and Rave…Try not to totally drown yourself in junk food."

Raven half-heartedly promised while crossing her fingers, toes, and legs. Hanging up, she hauled herself off to the kitchen to grab some M&M's from the fridge. She loved her chocolate cold.

CHAPTER 6

GROWING UP

***BEFORE I CONTINUE**, I want to apologize for always being so vague about my past, but after you read all of this slop, you'll understand why. But whatever you do, for God's sake, Raven, do NOT feel pity for me. I did what I had to, the way I had to, whether or not you, the State or the Lord above agrees.*

So with that little ditty understood, let's start.

My mother was an alcoholic from the time she came out of the womb, which probably is not much of an exaggeration. If she wasn't drinking, she was sleeping. In fact, growing up, I distinctly remembered our fridge filled with more beer bottles than it ever was with milk or juice. Food, when there was any, was of the instant variety. The acne I endured and struggled with most of my young life was proof of that. I can't imagine what she fed me when I was too young to feed myself.

Never calling one place home for too long, Mother preferred to stay relatively close to her family. So while we moved around a lot, we never moved far away. Even so, most of the places we lived in were dumps in rundown areas, popular for their pubs more than their libraries.

But just like me, Mother wasn't totally to blame for being a worthless, wretched, hot-tempered bitch. She had a whole lot of help and training along the way. As I said, nobody is born that way. She was a 'product of her environment', and more.

Grandpa was known to be a mean drunk, and when he drank more than his fair share, he got loose and fancy-free with his hands, usually on Mother. As an abused and neglected child, she had no choice but to keep out of her father's way and raise herself, along with her younger brother, who turned into another worthless piece of shit the state had to be accountable for.

My grandmother by this time had already passed away. I personally think she ran away, but who knows for sure. That left my grandfather to raise a wild girl and a precocious boy alone. Gramps had no clue what to do—because most of the time, his contemptible ornery ass was either intoxicated or passed out somewhere.

When my mother reached the tender age of fourteen, she had already become pregnant by my worthless father. Daddy dearest was quite a few years older than mom and blatantly unconcerned of my mother's jailbait status. A real creep.

My mother had no choice but to drop out of school. As a result, she had no skills to make ends meet since grandpa drank away most of the family money, so soon after she had me, she began selling herself to buy food, pay the rent, and support her acquired drug and alcohol habit. My father never stuck around long enough to see me born, but instead spent most of his adult years in and out of the penitentiary until his demise. Together, these two special people made me.

All in the family, huh?

It was hard for Raven to imagine what it had been like being raised in the dysfunctional environment Terri had described. All Raven had known growing up with the Grants had been nothing short of gentle kindness and love. Together, the older couple had made her feel as if she had truly been their daughter. Besides, Raven couldn't recall one instance of either of them ever raising their voices at one another, much less *at her*. Thankfully, alcohol, and certainly never drugs, had ever been permitted in the house.

Raven wanted to stop reading, but she was glued to her seat, feeling like a rubbernecker at the scene of her own accident, and so she continued.

Need I say more? But, of course, I must continue! What fun would there be if I left my sad, pathetic story at just that? I have a whole bunch of legal papers to fill up before I meet the man upstairs… Or downstairs. I'm deathly afraid of heights, so downstairs might be a better alternative for me anyhow.

I wonder…do you keep a journal? And if you do, what are your dreams and aspirations? Are you the disciplined type of person who always writes down every thought, or are you like me—whenever the mood or necessity dictates?

I wish I could have written all my thoughts down on something nicer than legal papers, which up to this point, were completely and utterly worthless. So many times I wanted to throw this stack of legal shit in the garbage. I hated and despised the way it just sat on my shelf for years, taunting me, a constant reminder of the day my life became meaningless, but I couldn't toss it, and now I'm thankful I didn't. They've finally become useful.

You'll also have to try and forgive me, Raven, if I digress or go off on a tangent here and there. I can't help it. I've never had any formal literary training, and since I'm not writing this to get published or graded, I think I can take certain liberties where and when necessary.

Now, getting back to my story.

So… I wasn't even two years old before my less-than-maternal mother, a kid herself, left me with my inebriated grandfather and the ever-so-worthless philandering uncle, her brother. She didn't return until I was close to eleven. As a matter of fact, I didn't even recognize her when she came back home. My uncle had to tell me who the hell she was when I saw her one morning in the kitchen making something to eat as if she belonged there all along.

"Good Morning, Terri-Ann," she droned flatly as if we knew one another.

"Morning, Miss."

"Miss?" She laughed. She found it funny that I didn't know who my mother was.

"This is your mother, Terri," announced my uncle, hunched over, nursing his cup of lukewarm coffee, still in the same clothes from the night before, only more wrinkled and stale smelling. "Say good morning to your mother."

"Good morning… Mother," I mumbled, but it hadn't mattered a bit. My mother, by this time, was already mixing her coffee with a bit of whiskey, and any attention she afforded me moving forward was going to have to wait until she was good and intoxicated. Then the mouth plug would pop, and then she wouldn't shut the hell up even if she had wanted to.

A few minutes later, a scruffy, ultra-thin man who smelt like urine came into the kitchen and sat next to me. The stench was appalling. It took all I had not to grab my nose.

"Say hello to your new daddy, Terri-Ann," instructed Mother in her gravelly voice.

My new stepfather was a real piece of work. Mean, sneaky, and always lurking around. Mother, of course, never noticed, and if she did, I doubt she cared.

They were a quarrelsome couple and always in each other's faces arguing about something, usually drug related. Then, once high enough, their tempers reverted to being peachy keen, and their demented love blossomed forever more. It was the weirdest relationship. Almost parasitical in the way they fed off one another's need to stay high.

Mother and I had a difficult relationship from the very beginning. She resented having to involve herself in my daily affairs, so she didn't—left me basically on my own, to fend for myself. Luckily, I was resourceful, smart enough to stay out of her way when she was smashed. When she drank, she became a mean drunk—exceptionally unpredictable and particularly volatile, she'd aim for my face and head the most when lashing out.

Despite my crumbling home life, in school, I tried. I enjoyed English class the most when we were reading literature. Some of the stuff we were forced to read was unquestionably dry, but I found that if I took the time to listen to what I was reading, the language used could become surprisingly interesting, even intriguing. I'll tell you what though—Shakespeare was one sick pup!

Without any stability, my home life continued to deteriorate. As a tween, I began trading my body to the boys for cigarettes and favors. I was not a teenager yet, maybe 13, but an old soul. I saw how my mother conducted her business and gleaned what I could for my own. Surprisingly, for a fairly homely girl, I was able to build an enterprising business for myself.

Now, don't go on thinking I'm just being unduly harsh on myself, or looking for underhanded praise—I'm not that humble. Remember, I have no reason to embellish the truth. The fact was, I was unsightly. Not hideous, just not overly attractive. Always so unkempt, but the boys didn't give a damn, and their exuberant boyish attention made me feel wanted. At the same time, most of the boys I let touch and grope me weren't much to brag about either, so I guess it was a fair exchange.

To tell you the truth, I can't remember most of their faces any longer. Not like I haven't tried, though. Sitting in my cell these past years, I'd play a host of mental games in my head, but for the life of me, trying to count all the boys I ever fucked has eluded me. I get to a certain age and period and it all goes fuzzy. Blank. I lose count around age fifteen. Then everything becomes more of a blur.

Am I too raw? Too graphic? I don't mean to be vulgar, but I told you from the beginning; I'm going to tell you the whole raw, ugly truth, so buckle up, baby cakes.

From occasional prostitution, I ventured into occasional petty larceny and moderate drug use. Stealing here or there to cover the costs of the drugs had become a necessity. In hindsight, I probably should have just made do and stuck to abusing alcohol like my slush of a mother. Much cheaper to buy and easier to get a hold of than half the crap I was into, but I couldn't get past the putrid smell or taste of it. It's hilarious if you think about it. Here I was, a drugged-out, thieving child prostitute, but I still had standards.

Despite the absurdity of what Raven just read, she had to laugh. Terri had a point. Raven also never cared for the smell of alcohol, either. Chalk that one up to something they had in common. She kept reading…

I wasn't the smartest thief for sure, but I got away with a ton of stuff. Being fairly unappealing as a child can be hard enough, but when you are a thief, it makes everything doubly difficult if you get caught. Nobody feels compassion for unattractive thieves, but if you are a beauty, then society becomes abundant with rescue intervention programs, which launch into gear by the time the first forced tear slides down your pretty face. I had no such luck.

On the other hand, being, so "ultra regular" also had its perks. People tended not to pay me any attention, which usually worked exceedingly well in my favor when stealing from local shops. After the first glance up to see who entered the store, their contemptuous eyes inevitably never made eye contact again.

My shoulder-length, mousy-brown hair stayed greasy, and my less than pristine teeth were spaced too far apart, giving me an impish smile at best. My skin stayed sallow from the lack of nutrition. Later on in my teens, I remained in a constant battle against a beastly case of acne. My nails weren't much better, always excessively brittle and constantly chipping or peeling. I fell into the revolting habit of biting them, and to this day, I still chew them down to the quick.

Eventually, I began to take care of myself more, and while still not necessarily what you would describe as pretty, I was fairly attractive and, at long last, clean. By the time I was sixteen, I was motivated to quit the drugging and partying. I began to settle down. I had a steady boyfriend that I really liked, and I was starting to feel better about myself. I won't lie; I finally grew into my body and sported a pretty fine figure, until of course when I got pregnant at the ripe old age of eighteen. I chose to drop out of school before I visibly blossomed, not exactly feeling like being known as the school Prego.

What a happy little dysfunctional family we made, huh? Mean-drunk Grandpa and the Johnny-Apple-seed-dropping Uncle Fenny. We called him Fenny, but his name was, in fact, Fillmore. Don't ask, I have no idea why anyone would name a kid some ridiculous name like Fillmore, but all I know is, nobody ever called him by anything but Fenny.

Fenny was known in the area as "a player." He loved women, and for some ungodly reason, the women loved him, along with his infinite gift of the gab. In particular, Fenny saw himself in the role of local dispenser of wisdom. Folks in the area all knew he was full of shit, but enjoyed listening to him pontificate. Boy, could he tell a tale, particularly when he jumped on his political soapbox. As bizarre as it may have seemed at the time, and practically to anyone else who knew anything about him, old Fenny was a self-described "conservative," except of course, where his own moral values were concerned. He would then conveniently take a wide array of liberties, qualifying his less than pristine behavior when challenged with, "My morals and my political leanings are not polarized," he'd benevolently explain. "They are what I like to call a creative blend, which produces a distinct and unique balance. In life, one should always aspire to be balanced." Even when Fenny was boldface lying, he lied with flair.

But alas, Uncle Fenny's so-called "unique and creative blend of balance" was coarsely interrupted one day when the irate husband of one of his female admirers decided to permanently put an end to his shenanigans. Poor stupid Fenny was caught hanging around outside the Bar & Grill in town one night. He was found with his throat slit, and private parts jammed with a hunting knife. The local news rag, never one to miss an opportunity to enjoy a play on the word, dubbed his death, "Fillmore Stone's Stones Get Cut Short!" It was never discovered who executed the deed, but whoever pulled it off now had a double set of balls!

And then there was my mother, also known as Wendelin. Winnie, for short, not to be confused with "whiny" unless for whatever reason you desired to have your teeth bashed into the back of your skull. Anyway, Mother survived her life by participating in it as little as possible, which meant spending little to no energy on anyone but herself. Her drug and alcohol habit would have eventually gotten the best of her had she not been prematurely snuffed out. When forensics did the autopsy of her after the murder, they reported her liver and kidneys would have killed her shortly had she lived long enough to die naturally.

And, of course, last but not least, the stepfather from down under—and I don't mean Australia. Carl. No use in shortening his name, it was already one syllable too long.

Carl was a certifiable piece of work. A down-and-dirty predator. Rumor had it he was kicked out of his girlfriend's house when she caught him with his zipper open, diddling her 18-month-old daughter—still in a damn diaper! From what I gathered, after trying to claw his eyes out, the girlfriend threatened to have Carl arrested and thrown into jail if he didn't agree to leave and never come back. Homeless, Carl took off to the only place left on earth that would still welcome him—the bar, and there he met Winnie the Wino. Together they became the dynamic drunk duo. This meathead made my life a living hell, and ultimately, it was those same perversions that were the cause of all that transpired... But I'm getting ahead of myself.

Life with this motley crew wasn't easy, Ladybug. As much as I wanted to better myself, the dysfunction had too strong of a pull to numb myself out of existence with drugs. I didn't see myself having any quantifiable future to hold out for, and the immediate demands of each day's needs outweighed good common sense. Not an excuse, just me trying to keep it real with you. Which is why I'm writing this letter, right? No use lying, even by omission now.

Carl took it upon himself to deflower me the same day his wretched, worthless ass officially moved back into the house after one of many heated rows with my mother. That snake had the nerve to try and justify the rape, claiming I was already sexually active. Somehow, in his convoluted head, that meant I was available to him.

Carl was able to get away with this shit while my slovenly drunk mother lay on the couch snoring herself into a stupor, and he continued to do so on and off until eventually I turned up pregnant. That's when his fun came to a screeching halt.

Five months into the pregnancy, even my mother, the queen of unconsciousness, began to notice my protruding belly, and when she did, all hell broke loose. She went on the warpath. Not necessarily because I was pregnant, don't kid yourself; but because she suspected, correctly, who the father of my child was—her slimy husband, Carl.

Knowing better than to entice Winnie's unpredictable wrath, I never denied or confirmed a damn thing, unlike Carl, who thought he was super sharp by explaining to my mother how my pregnancy was a result of my being a bitch. "She laid down with dogs, and see, that bitch got up with a belly full of fleas…serves her right," he proclaimed self-righteously.

Like I told you, I wasn't beautiful, but I wasn't stupid either, yet in the end, it hadn't mattered. When Winnie got something in her head, on the rare occasion when that happened, it stuck like epoxy glue. She wanted me gone and was out for blood. Mine in particular. Not Carl's, just mine. That's when I knew I had to get out of that loony bin as soon as possible if I wanted to stay alive. I write this without any hyperbole or exaggeration. Winnie wouldn't have batted any eye or missed a beat if she decided to cut me up.

So, I left home. As soon as my mother and stepfather headed out to wherever they were trying to score for the day, I hightailed it out of there as quickly as I could. Packed up the little I owned and bolted. My only objective at the time was to survive, but I remembered feeling frightened, because although I clearly lived in dysfunction junction, it was all I had ever known. Leaving meant change, the unknown, and I wasn't sure if I had what it took to survive. I also had no idea where I was going, but that didn't stop me. I just knew I had to keep on moving, too deathly frightened to stop or be stopped.

I remember at the time thinking I had better stay out of sight and off the main roads as much as possible. No use in drawing any attention to myself, possibly placing myself in further danger with some wandering, axe-wielding murderer or escaped convict or something.

I think I know what you're thinking, because I'm thinking it as I write too—the irony; I'm in a maximum-security prison serving two life sentences as a murderer, and there I was, afraid of bumping into somebody like myself. I'm sure the absurdity wasn't lost on you, Ladybug. Nevertheless, this was what I remember thinking.

Where we lived at the time was not exactly the suburbs. Upstate New York has its pockets of towns and small cities, but we lived in a more rural, thick-forested area with mountains, a few lakes, and streams. I remember convincing myself I could fish to eat. Make a fishing pole out of a stick and twine like Huckleberry Finn.

I must have legged it a good few hours, stopping periodically to sit and rest. I was lost in the woods, going in circles. The late afternoon air was becoming chillier as the sun started to set. This was in the beginning of October. I can remember because a nice portion of leaves were still hanging on the trees and in the most incredible vibrant colors, akin to a postcard. I suppose all of the scenery would have been even more beautiful had I not been currently homeless, pregnant, and scared shitless.

Bottom line, by hook or by crook, I had no choice but to find shelter before nightfall. Eventually, I stumbled upon a path that, although covered with leaves and other debris, still appeared more cleared out than what I had been previously hiking on and over. Finally, my luck began to change. Up ahead in the same direction I was traipsing, I caught sight of a small rustic cabin embedded farther back in the woods.

Just as I glanced up, I also clearly saw a sort of small, rocky footpath leading up to the cabin's porch, covered mostly in dried leaves and pine needles, but still visible enough.

Eager to finally be someplace other than outside in the cold, I trudged closer to the cabin, trying to formulate any half-viable-sounding excuse to use if anyone answered when I knocked on the door. By this time, Ladybug, I was beyond hungry and chilled to the bone. I began making up ridiculous scenarios and excuses, but nothing I thought up came close to sounding right.

"Um, excuse me, but I just ran away from a nut house. Oh, and I'm almost five months pregnant with my stepfather's child. Can I stay with you?"

"Oh, hello. I just ran away from home and I am starving and freezing. Can I live with you, or at least use your bathroom, and possibly have something to eat?"

"Hi, my name is Terri. I need help. Please help me."

I knocked. "Hello?" From the outside, it appeared abandoned or not much lived in. A small portion of the porch at the far end, away from the stairs, had rotted away, but most of the wood planks were still surprisingly solid. The vacant structure held a certain charm, as if at one time, somebody had cared about it, but now, although sturdy, the cabin boasted desolation, as if there hadn't been a single soul living in it for a long, long while, and I was grateful.

No, answer. I knocked again, but this time louder and bolder.

"Hello? Anybody home?"

Still no answer.

"Ready or not, here I come!"

The cabin was blissfully empty.

The front door had no lock, just a door handle, and with not a person to be seen or heard, I invited myself in. Called out one last feeble "hello" for posterity, as I stepped inside and was beyond relieved when nobody answered back or met me at the door with a shotgun pointed in my face.

The wood floor of the cabin was clear of debris, unlike a few of the shelves, which still held a few trinkets and somebody's discarded keepsakes. The inside certainly wasn't large, but I didn't care; it was perfect. No more than one big room with a sink area, and a wooden table with two handmade wooden chairs, but already cozy and welcoming to me, despite being fairly sparse. The door closed behind me, becoming a blessed buffer from the chilling night winds outside, but the best part was the fireplace. One wall, about the length of the cabin's entire side, was completely made out of brick. Mimicking something out of the colonial period for sure.

In hindsight, I should have been more cautious, but youth and ignorance seemed on my side for once as I stomped my way about the cabin. Then I saw another door and cautiously opened it thinking it might lead back outside, but instead, it was an empty room, possibly used as a bedroom at one time. It was small, but certainly large enough for a full-size bed, a dresser, and a trunk.

The place needed a thorough cleaning, mainly the floors, which were covered by a nice layer of thick dust, but nothing I couldn't take care of. Then I looked closer and saw little animal droppings, and my stomach lurched at the thought of coming face-to-face with a raccoon or mouse. I had a hell of a wild imagination, but it was tempered by my need to rest.

Outside, the cold winds were picking up intensity, and since I didn't own a flashlight, I needed to secure some light, and preferably, heat. The only possible thing left to do was to ignite a fire in that big pit of a fireplace. Hopefully, the chimney had nothing living in it, but I was too worn out and cold to think intelligently. I might not have had a flashlight with me, but I always carried a lighter in my bag—a habit I got into for my friends who smoked, but not a habit I personally got into. Again, I had standards.

Determined to become warm, I reluctantly trekked back outside to gather anything I could burn, despite not knowing exactly what it was I was collecting. Just as long as it was wood, I was game. This included twigs and even a few handfuls of dried leaves I hoped would ignite quickly. I brought my pile back inside and began for the next half hour, which felt like a flipping eternity, to try and light the damn fireplace up. Eventually, it lit, and I was able to feed the fire periodically through the night with the little I collected, until eventually, drifting off into a deep sleep on the bare floor…

Gloriously content and safe, for the first time in years.

CHAPTER 7

RAVEN

DARKNESS BROUGHT even colder temperatures. The farmhouse imparted the kind of chills Terri had described her first night in the abandoned cabin. However, Raven felt completely unmotivated to build a fire. Grudgingly, she put down the page of Terri's legal sheet of paper she was reading and cranked up the heat. *'The electric bill this month is going to be ghastly.'*

Then, with stomach grumbling and demanding immediate attention, Raven used her lack of culinary skills to whip up two over-easy eggs, which promptly turned into scrambled. She buttered up some saltine crackers and made a fresh cup of dull instant coffee. *I seriously need to do some food shopping. This is getting utterly ridiculous.*

After eating, Raven wasn't quite ready to continue reading Terri's letter, so she opted for some channel surfing and mind-numbing TV. After an hour of unsuccessfully flipping through the same channels, making her seriously question the reason behind paying such a steep price for cable, she finally settled on a random comedy show to watch. Within the first few minutes, it became disappointingly clear the show was neither funny nor worth wasting her time on. Instead, Raven reached over and grabbed the next page in the waiting stack. Just as she picked the papers up off the table, something fluttered out from the back of the stack and onto the rug, making Raven leap.

"Ahhh! What the heck?" At first Raven recoiled, not sure what that thing was, but assuming it consisted of the insect variety. Quickly realizing it was only a piece of paper instead of some insectoid, she coolly bent over and picked it up, curiously wanting to take a closer peek.

A poem?

TREASURED RAVEN

Out of the grasp of the wicked winds
In your nest made of discarded timbers
You rest your gentle wings
Your black silk feathers adorn your precious head
Like a crown fit for an angel
A treasure you are, so beautiful and innocent,
Conceived by the darkness, but trusted into light,
Shine your blue glass eyes upon my shrinking breath
As time demands payment for the wretched
As evil comes to call
But you my darling, Raven, will never trip or fall.

What is this? Raven wondered. *Did Terri write this? Is it about me, or am I projecting too much? But it's my name.* Still, it left Raven puzzled, reading it repeatedly over while trying to ascertain the poem's innuendos. She felt as though the prose may have been speaking to, or about, her. It always baffled her as to why she had been given a name like Raven. She just assumed it was because of her jet-black hair. Now, she wasn't so sure.

In your nest made of discarded timbers,
You rest your gentle wings

Maybe this is the cabin Terri wrote about? But that made no sense. The implication would have placed her in the cabin with her sister, but why would she have been there?

Conceived by the darkness, but trusted into light,
Shine your steel blue glass eyes upon my shrinking breath

My eyes are a sort of baby-blue, hazel-ish color, but conceived by darkness? What could Terri have meant by that? Trusted into the light? Whose light? What the heck is shrinking breath? Poetry is too dark for me. This doesn't make any sense.

Raven was honestly too agitated to figure out some convoluted poem, but the words were compelling, and for Raven, they held some significance beyond what she was able to grasp at this point. On the other hand, if the poem had been somebody else's and Terri had kept it, the question remained—why?

Raven began to deliberate. *Okay, Terri had been pregnant by this time. Did she lose the baby? If not, where did this other Raven go? Maybe this poem had been my mother's and not Terri's at all, and she just stuck it in the book. But then, why would she have kept it? A keepsake? Maybe… Well, here's to hoping this letter eventually reveals answers, or at least a few clues to help me piece this mess together.*

* * *

Terri

Six months earlier

The noise level on the tier drove Terri batty. Metal doors clanging shut, orders being barked by irate guards, and a host of loud sirens or bells indicating either upset in the yard, or a shift change, made it hard for Terri to concentrate. Add to that, the noise level of dozens of screaming women trying to hold a conversation through thick plastic and glass windows, and it became an absolutely tragic cacophony.

Most of the women on this particular tier were serving long sentences. The old-timers and lifers rarely had the inclination to get into it with new arrivals. Most of the newbies were by and large, filled with an enormous amount of displaced anger and denial. Some of the addicts became particularly hostile and combative, primarily because going to prison meant getting "clean" or drug-free for the first time. In actuality, acquiring junk to get high on in prison wasn't impossible, just harder, and it took added ingenuity and funds.

On the opposite side of the pendulum, there were the few inmates who spent their existence locked in despair, not intending to hurt anybody but themselves. Guards had to constantly rush to the cells when despondent inmates began banging their heads on walls and doors, cutting their arms and wrists, or refusing to eat. Some tried to hang themselves with man-made ropes from strips of fabric they were able to misappropriate directly from the underside of a mattress cover. The level of the ingenuity of some of these people proved mind-bending, bringing into question why they hadn't used those same smarts before landing their asses in prison.

Quite often, some of the newbies, unable to fathom facing a long stretch of time behind bars, were placed on *suicide watch* for good reason. Any indication a prisoner was willing to take her life would be cause for increased security and attention—which is exactly what Terri did not want.

The third cell down from Terri was the pod's makeshift beauty salon extraordinaire, spearheaded by the ever-resourceful Martina Krumf at the helm. Martina was every inmate's go-to gal when it came to beauty and prison fashion. If caught plying her trade, Martina could face disciplinary action, but nobody dared snitch; and in all honesty, most guards looked the other way, as long as it kept the tier relatively drama-free.

"Knock-knock," called Terri, pretend knocking on the cell door. Inside, Martina was busy with her "client"—lining another female inmate's eyes to mimic eyeliner and mascara. To get the pencil to smear, she'd repeatedly dip the point into a jar of Vaseline.

"How's it going, Terri? Coming to get hooked up, or just a friendly visit?" Martina asked, knowing full well it was the latter.

"You know me, just checking in."

"I hear you," answered Martina. "Let me finish up here and I'll be by your 'house'. We'll catch a ride." "Catch a ride" was code for a request for one inmate to get the other high.

"Sounds like a plan. Later," replied Terri. "Oh, by the way, two new Cowboys are on the tier." "Cowboys" was the nickname the inmates gave to new correctional officers.

"Thanks for the heads up, " replied Martina.

Once in a while, Martina would get lucky and get her hands on a colored pencil or two. They were perfect for creating an eye shadow effect, or lip liner. In prison, if you are the proud owner of colored pencils, you are "In like Flynn" and can get practically anything you desire. Martina was fortunate enough to be able to steal the repurposed graphite pencils from the art therapy class she was encouraged to attend. Her civilian counselor had hoped the art therapy would "help deal with the symptoms of Martina's chronic depression."

Terri made a point of befriending Martina within the first week of her arrival, and kept her well stocked with whatever art paraphernalia she could safely procure. Terri made it her business to make sure Martina, also a former pill popper, would be treated for depression—one of the lucky ones. Terri knew firsthand that most inmates in federal or state prison who suffer from various mood disorders and mental illness never received the help they needed. Not to say the courts don't mandate treatment, but in reality, it usually means only inmates who are severely mentally ill get help, especially inmates afflicted with schizophrenia.

The amount of inmates suffering from anxiety, mania, and post-traumatic stress disorder was mind-boggling. Since suffering from depression wasn't considered a security risk, the institution rarely went out of its way to identify and treat it.

Martina, however, after much haggling and a few well-rehearsed "episodes" had been prescribed daily happy pills to keep her feeling more "balanced." In reality though, it was more like keeping her high since Martina's so-called "depression" and subsequent symptoms were all a bi-product of Terri's extensive research and cleverly detailed coaching.

In exchange for saving Terri whatever pills Martina could smuggle back under the nurses' deficiently unobservant eyes, were magazines Terri would purchase with her sporadic commissary money. With those, Martina was able to apply her jailhouse trade by vigorously scratching off the ink from the magazine's many pictures, and mixing the scrapings with Vaseline to make a vast array of colors—all in the effort to keep the clientele happy. In exchange, Martina's clients would pay her handsomely in the form of commissary treats and select sexual favors.

Although the focus on outward appearance while in prison might seem a bit over the top and superficial in the eyes of outsiders, monotony among the female inmate population remains a significant issue. Forget how these beauty practices were potentially harmful and could cause a host of health hazards, including blindness; women in prison tend to have little else to do to keep from going stir-crazy. Boredom and vanity, even behind bars, is big business, yet the ingenuity of the inmate population is pretty impressive if you don't mind the potential for contracting lead poisoning, or even cancer. This, and a few other semi-harmless distractions, tended to keep the population calmer and make time tick by faster. However, for Terri, who had other plans in the making, remaining under the radar continued to be her *modus operandi* all along. Now, it was finally going to pay off. She hoped.

* * *

Martina was what Terri referred to as a "parasitical survivor," the type of individual who instinctively knows how to live off the backs of others like second nature. Terri despised these personalities, but she understood them and knew how to use them to make them do her bidding. Most of all, Terri accepted the fact that she needed Martina, so she purposely treated her with kid gloves, making sure to stay friendly enough, without drawing her in too close.

Although commonplace, Terri didn't engage in sexual relationships often. As far as Terri was concerned, many of the so-called "consenting" relationships were nothing more than forms of rape, with the victims too intimated to put up much of a fuss, pretending to consent when confronted, and becoming the perceived "property" of the offender. As is common in prison settings, some of the sexual exchanges were to repay debt. Others were purely forms of dominance and control, known by prison officials as "protective paring." The dominant partner uses their power and control over the other inmate, with the promise of protection from more forcible rapes and violence. Very few "real love" relationships occurred or survived.

In truth, Martina was infatuated with Terri, although at the same time, a little afraid of Terri, to be honest. Secrets inside have a way of becoming prison fodder, and it wasn't long before Martina, and practically every other inmate on the pod, knew the supposed gory details surrounding how Terri murdered her folks. Martina, who was inside for armed robbery, had never killed a soul. She didn't have the stomach for it, nor did she understand those who did so with such a cold-blooded mentality. Nevertheless, the two women seemed to appreciate how each one could coexist without issue, as long as neither one transgressed upon the other. On quite a few occasions, working together even turned rather profitable. All the same, each woman knew her place, and so far, neither itched for trouble.

"Martina, come in." Terri was fiercely territorial and private, so she only allowed Martina and one other inmate in her house. "Do you want to sit?"

"Nah, I'm good, thanks. Just cadillacing," she replied, while sneaking a few wrapped pills to Terri. When Terri first got locked up, she had to learn jailhouse lingo quickly. "Cadillacing" was the standard mode of passing from one cell to the other. Inmates could visit one another during certain times, as long as they weren't in the SHU (Special Housing Unit).

"If you take a glance over on the side of the dark-blue book on my desk, you will see your magazine. You'll find a pencil in there, as well, but be careful. The new CO is in her picket, minding your business big time right now." A "picket" is where a Correctional Officer can sit unaccompanied and control doors and locks behind Plexiglass, surrounded by cellblocks. Terri's helpful advice and warning were her way of making Martina think she was watching out for her welfare, but in reality, Terri never said or did anything altruistically where her fellow inmates were concerned.

"Yeah, I can feel her hot, stale breath on the back of my neck from here," Martina joked. "She's just trying to make a point, prove her worth. How many more visits will you need before I call it a wrap?" Martina had saved Terri close to twenty pills so far, under the impression Terri was using them to sleep.

"Not sure yet, just keep them coming. Are you having any issues?"

"No, that dumb-ass Nurse Ratchet is too busy flirting to notice me cupping. Once she puts it in the wicket, she goes back to her pad to write down whatever she writes."

"Cool," confirmed Terri as she handed Martina the magazine, play-acting as if she was showing her an article to read. "I'll check you out again next week. Same time, same place."

Martina laughed and gave Terri the thumbs up. "Always."

CHAPTER 8

THE CABIN

RAVEN DECIDED TO CALL it a night. While she enjoyed reading, she moved through the pages super slow. Feeling exhausted, she hoped her head would clear up with a bit of necessary sleep under her belt then she would seriously attack the stack of papers with a bit more clarity and gusto.

Preparing for bed, she couldn't help but be annoyed, wondering why the Grants never shared with her that they had known her sister. They never seemed to be the secretive types, or so she'd thought. But what would have been the big deal? What could have been the harm in disclosing it?

Raven wasn't sure how to feel about Terri knowing a boatload more about Raven's life than Raven had assumed all along. *Maybe I'm just projecting... Wishing it was so, but Terri never seemed to take this much notice of me when she was alive.*

Raven planned ahead, that within the next few days, weather permitting, she'd take a hike on the land to find the so-called elusive cabin. She distinctly remembered that as a child, she had seen it from the outside several times when her and Pop would take off on one of their hunts for firewood, combing the land for fallen or dead trees to cut up.

"What's that building over there by that stream, Pops?" Raven asked pointing.

"A cabin."

"Who lives there?"

"Nobody now. It's been empty for some time." His face gave the impression of deep sadness, but Raven, being young, blindly plowed on with her questions.

"Can I go see inside?"

"That's not a good idea, Raven."

"*Pleeeeaase*, Pops?"

"It's not in the greatest condition anymore. See how the porch slants? The inside is probably all rotted out by now, too. You could get hurt foolin' around in there. Besides, I've meant to take it down for years."

"Please, Pops? I just want to see—"

"You stay out of there. Hear me, girl?" Pop snapped. The sternness in his eyes left no room for debate. "Don't let me find you going in there. It's too dangerous."

"Okay, Pop... I won't." Raven had never seen him get so irate. She chalked it up to his concern over her safety.

Raven hadn't thought about the old cabin for years, but now with Terri's letter and poem in her possession, she had to wonder if her safety had been all there was to Pop's caution.

* * *

When I awoke, I thought it was still morning, hard to tell by how dark the cabin remained inside. I was stiff and hungry, but the urge to pee something fierce forced me awake. After answering Mother Nature, I traipsed outside to collect more wood for the fire. The logs and twigs from the night before had become nothing but coals, and I needed to get the morning chill out of my bones. The outside air was crisp, but not too cold. A trip into town to get some food and supplies with the few dollars in my possession was going to have to happen soon, but the problem remained which direction to go. I assumed I had travelled past a town, maybe two, over the length of time it took me to arrive here at the cabin.

I liked the idea of being out of my immediate area, where nobody knew my family, or me. If I could have stayed in the woods my whole life, without seeing another living soul, that would have been all right with me, too.

As the fire reignited, much easier now with hot coals to work with, my heart almost dropped when I heard the distinct sounds of heavy footsteps coming up the porch. I didn't know what to do, so I grabbed my travel case and ran to the back room to hide. I know, it didn't make any sense. Evidence of me being there was everywhere, but I didn't know what else to do!

"Who's in there? Come out of there right now!" a strong, older man's voice demanded.

I was too frightened to answer him.

"I mean it," he warned forcefully. "I have a gun and I'm not afraid to use it."

At this point, too scared and freaked out to come out of hiding, I replied something to the effect of, "Sorry, Mister. I got lost and needed a place to stay last night. I'll leave."

"Who else is in there?" he asked.

"Just me."

The door to the cabin creaked open…the footsteps were now inside. "Come on out of hiding. I won't hurt you," the now gentler voice pled, much softer than before.

I don't know why, Ladybug, but I believed the voice… He sounded so polite. Does that make sense? What choice did I have, right? I was trespassing, and he supposedly had a gun. So I cautiously stepped out of hiding and came face-to-face with an older gentleman. He was probably in his late fifties, tall and sturdy, holding a rifle, just like he warned he was. He stared at me… Or to be more accurate, at my belly.

"What's your name, child?" he asked me.

"Terri-Ann Stone,"

He nodded while gnawing on the inside of his lip. "Okay, Miss Terri-Ann Stone, why exactly are you in my cabin?"

"I-I got lost, and I was cold. I needed a place to stay for the night. I did call out to see if anyone was home, but it looked abandoned. I honestly didn't know anyone lived in here. I'm sorry… I didn't mean to break into your house…err, cabin… I'll get my stuff and leave." I turned to gather up my things, hoping he wouldn't come any closer.

"Why are you in these woods at all?" he asked me.

"I had to leave home." I shrugged, thrusting my few belongings back into my case.

"Are you in trouble?" he asked.

I glared down at my belly. "Long story, but I have no place else to go."

"I see. Well, have you eaten?" he asked.

"No, sir."

"Follow me back to my house. My wife is getting breakfast ready. She always makes too much, no matter how much I tell her it's only the two of us."

"Wait, what's your name?" I yelled, but before giving me an answer, he spun around and took off in the opposite direction, heading, I assumed at the time, back to his house. I was so hungry. I grabbed my travel case and followed him without giving it a second thought. A few minutes later, without stopping, he replied sternly, "My name is Robert Grant."

So Terri wasn't lying, she did know the Grants. Raven felt less betrayed but still confused. Knowing her parents, they were probably just being kind to her. Then Terri probably remembered them when she found out I was adopted and put two and two together.

Raven kept reading.

For an old man, this guy could sure walk fast. I had a hard time keeping up with him, and it wasn't just my protruding belly giving me a difficult time. From the stress and anxiety, I honestly think I had a combination of dehydration, mental exhaustion, and starvation. Inside, I could feel my baby kicking at me, reminding me to eat. At that point, I hadn't had a real meal for over a day.

I'm not a religious person at all, but on that day, I was seriously thinking how only through God's intervention could I have been brought the help I desperately needed. By following this complete stranger, I was going against all my innate survival skills, yet I wasn't the least bit scared or hesitant. As I followed behind the tall, strange man, I whispered my first real prayer of my entire life.

"God, if you are listening, please protect my baby and me. Please don't let this old man be some whack job out to lure lost, pathetic females like myself into the woods to keep captive, and then use as some creepy sex slave."

God must have had a slow day because He sure was listening to me whine to him. Walking only a short distance more, I caught a glimpse through the clearing of the most charming white farmhouse I had ever seen up close. It was picturesque, with its flat, green, manicured lawn. I recognized what I thought were apple and peach trees lined up on one side of the enormous yard. Located in the far back corner of the open plot were beehives, along with a substantial garden in what must have been considered the backyard. They had smartly fenced in the yard, I guess to keep the deer and other rascals from eating their vegetables. And although it was fall, not a leaf could be found on the grass. This couple was clearly house-proud.

On the wraparound porch sat a welcoming white wicker furniture arrangement with a wooden swing positioned at the end of the deck, bolted from the rafters. Big baskets of glorious, red-orange fall flowers hung everywhere. It was like a dream, an oasis; like one of those photos from a travel brochure.

As we approached, an older woman, presumably the old man's wife, came outside wearing a pair of faded, baggy jeans and a long white shirt with an apron. She had her wispy, white hair pinned up in a loose bun. While she didn't appear to be wearing any makeup, her skin seemed healthy looking, even from a distance. The way the old woman continued to study us as we approached the house made me feel like I was in front of an old schoolmarm. I half expected her to pull out a ruler from her apron pocket and begin whacking my knuckles if I dared thought about getting out of line.

"And who do we have here?" she asked her husband with a sweeter, more inviting voice than I would have assumed.

"Found her in the cabin. What's your name again, girl?

"Terri-Ann Stone."

"Yes, ah-huh, Miss Terri-Ann was in the old cabin," he explained to his wife. "She's cold and hungry. I told her you were making breakfast."

"That's fine," agreed his wife, stepping down the stairs with surprising agility, clearly summing up my situation, including my visibly protruding belly. "My name is Mrs. Grant," she said, extending her hand to shake. "Come inside and wash up. Breakfast will be ready in a minute. I hope you like eggs and pancakes. Nothing fancy, but it will stick to your ribs."

"That would be wonderful. Thank you."

Well, let me tell you, Raven, Mrs. Grant was just being modest. Her not-so-fancy breakfast was mind-blowing and beyond delicious, from the first to the last bite. Along with the homemade pancakes made from scratch, and eggs, she served raw honey and molasses, homemade raisin cinnamon bread sliced up and toasted, hot brewed coffee that smelled as delicious as it tasted—however, she made me drink a large glass of milk first, and on the side, homemade applesauce. I ate until it was hard for me to breathe.

The whole time I chewed, the couple never asked me a single question, although I was half expecting them to interrogate me. Instead, I was fed while they chatted about home chores, the expected weather for the next few days, and what was in the morning news.

And there I was, sitting there stuffing my face. I kept thinking about how people like this don't exist. They were too, I don't know, perfect? Okay, not perfect. Wrong choice of words. But they were ideal, wonderful. Kind. I knew there had to be a hitch. There was always a hitch, and I was waiting for it.

"So, Terri—can I call you that?" asked Mrs. Grant.

"Yes," I replied while nodding my head with a mouthful of toast and honey, preparing myself for the shoe to drop on this temporary and heavenly bliss.

"The cabin in the back, did you find it too rundown, in need of repair?" she asked.

What a strange question to be asked. Almost like I had been an invited guest instead of the interloper I truly was.

"Um, well, the porch sagged a bit on one side, but the steps seemed sturdy enough. The inside was clean, a bit dusty, but nothing a cleaning job couldn't handle. Same with the windows. I lit a fire in the fireplace last night to keep warm…I hope that's okay. I apologize for just barging into it without asking, but I thought it was abandoned."

"How could you have known otherwise?" Mrs. Grant replied, gazing at her husband, their eyes communicating only in the way married people can do when they have been together for over half a century.

Now Mr. Grant chimed in. "The porch needs work, I agree. The chimney needs a thorough cleaning to make sure no animals have left any surprises in there, especially the birds. They like to nest in there."

"Did the water in the sink work? It has well water," inquired Mrs. Grant, glancing at me.

"Yes," I answered, peering back and forth from his to her eyes, unsure of what was going on.

"Good. That's a relief." Then Mrs. Grant stood up and began to clear away the dishes. I stood up to help her, but she waved me back

down. "No, you sit and drink your coffee. You look malnourished. We're going to have to do something about that. We wouldn't want you to have a tiny, sickly baby."

Mr. Grant peeked at his wife's face. She was beaming. He knew what she had in mind, and he was going to do anything in his power to make it happen, even if it meant only a temporary fix. "I'm going to finish up outside and head back over to the cabin to work on the porch and chimney," he announced. "It's empty in there. Do you want me to take the furniture from the attic and bring it over? I think we still have a bed frame, dresser, and a few other incidentals," he asked of his wife.

No screaming, no brokering of deals or contesting. I remember feeling confused, but desperate for whatever these two people would be willing to share with me.

Mrs. Grant, with her back to her husband, answered, "Thank you. And while you're out, Terri and I will get a few things done around here; but first, I think this young lady needs to rest. Come with me upstairs, hon. We have a guest room you can relax in while Mr. Grant gets the cabin ready for you."

And without further ado, I was accepted into their lives. No judgments, no lectures, and not even any questions. Absolutely nothing was asked of me until I was ready to share. I fell into their life, and they opened up their hearts to me. People like this, I found out first hand, do exist; but I wouldn't have believed it had I not lived it. For the first time in my life, without any strings attached, I felt wanted.

* * *

Raven wanted to be angry all over again, but this time she couldn't. For whatever reason, they had all decided to keep her in the dark about their relationship, and although she was upset, there had to be a perfectly good explanation.

Raven felt tears welling up in her eyes again. *What a crybaby I've become.* Losing the Grants had been painful. Hearing about their life together with Terri before Raven had come along, seemed disconcerting. Her sister's recollections resonated deep within Raven, dredging up old, fractured memories and rekindling the indescribable sense of loss she had fought hard to control. The childhood bestowed upon her, along with the endless blessing of being loved by two of the most unselfish people Raven had ever known, made the feelings all the more tender. Opening up their hearts to a total stranger had been exactly what they would have done. For the Grants to make a homeless stranger feel welcomed and cared for, was who they both were. Giving Terri a place to stay unconditionally sounded precisely like something they would do. Hadn't they done the same for her?

Terri's detailed description of Raven's adoptive parents accurately described the way in which they'd lived. Not religious, but faithful to the core of their being. Living God's word, but never preaching or cramming it down anyone's throat, nor did they ever proclaim sweeping, self-righteous assertions for salvation. These two people truly put into action what they held sacred every single day, in the way they chose to live, and in the manner by which they took care of others.

CHAPTER 9

LIFE BEHIND BARS

Terri

AT NIGHT, THE CELLS on the tier were purposely kept dark. However, the light continued to filter in from the open and centralized, well-lit pod area, which was more than sufficient for Terri to continue to see and write.

Eventually, the deafening noise from the tier leveled off. Once in a while, the echoing swish of flushing institutional metal toilets could be heard, along with the clang of keys opening or closing a cell. Terri knew by now when the guards were changing shifts, or searching the tier with their flashlights, peering into each cell, and conducting their mandatory head count.

Head counts took place all throughout the day at regular intervals. The inmates knew when to line up in front of their cells. When a guard called for a count, they were checking to make sure no one had gone missing, or a prisoner wasn't where they weren't supposed to be.

Head counts during the middle of the night were less demanding. For those, Terri could usually remain in bed unless someone went missing or was in the midst of causing a major crisis. Then all kinds of crazy hell broke loose. If an inmate should decide, for whatever reason, not to line up on time, they could be quite sure that swift disciplinary action would be in their immediate future.

Minor infractions were usually nothing more than "shots" or a mark in the prison file of the inmate. Eventually though, these marks could add up and become an issue, returning to haunt a prisoner if they tried to seek parole, or request permission for additional privileges. The amount of shots on an inmate's record could be the difference between getting out early or not. So far, Terri had no shots on her record, although her chances of ever getting out were zero.

Guards are people, too—some mellower than others. The majority were there to do their job, mind their own business, collect their paycheck, and go home to their families—and as long as you didn't bust their chops, for the most part, they didn't bust yours.

Others, with something to prove, were just plain old ball breakers out to establish a position of power at the expense of inmates and other guards, as well. Terri considered these characters to be the most hostile types, and the sort the inmates took aim for when they wanted to cause trouble or put a hurting on someone.

Certain guards were known to hand out discipline by arbitrarily ransacking a so-called offending prisoner's cell under the guise of legitimately searching for contraband. Should anything come up, no matter how minor or major, the inmate would face a more severe punishment—allotted time in solitary confinement, also know as The Hole. The first year Terri was inside, she had spent an inordinate amount of time in solitary, all as a result of making a name for herself, ensuring she wasn't seen as a pushover or someone who could be easily manipulated.

Another punishment involved removing any accumulated "good time"—time taken off an inmate's sentence for good behavior—with more days tacked on to the prison stay. While not necessarily a concern for a lifer, if an inmate pushed a guard far enough, the institution could have the offender transferred to an even less desirable prison, possibly farther away from family and friends.

Due to the issue of prison overcrowding, many prisons keep two prisoners in each cell, sometimes even more. But so far, this particular woman's prison had held off, at least on this cellblock. For Terri, the solitude of the cell made living in a cage more bearable.

Danger was always lurking, so the guards needed to stay alert and one step ahead of the inmates. These guards normally did not carry firearms on them; however, if an inmate disobeyed a direct order or became confrontational, correctional officers were then permitted to use necessary physical force, or even pepper spray, to subdue an inmate.

Guards toured the floor more during the day. At night, they kept an eye on the prisoners from the comfort of their security booth, or the "guard house" as Terri liked to refer to it; a sort of kiosk protected by thick glass and solid metal meshing, located in the center of the block with cells arranged all around it. If the prisoners were in the yard to get fresh air, socialize, or exercise, they were kept under constant surveillance by armed guards from the towers above the yard. Should any conflict arise, it wasn't uncommon for a guard in the tower to fire warning shots at prisoners—kill shots, if necessary.

Along with everyone else's cell, Terri's had been ransacked on many occasions, thus she disciplined herself not to keep anything of actual value inside. Several guards thought nothing of damaging or confiscating some of an inmate's property as retaliation in response to a perceived slight or open disrespect. Therefore, anything worth keeping, Terri skillfully hid. So far, despite a few close calls, she had been relatively lucky.

With the other inmates, Terri mingled sporadically, just enough not to be marked off as a recluse, but not enough to be considered one of the crew. She preferred it this way, finding isolation helped keep her under the radar where the correctional officers were concerned. Young Bloods and career criminals out to prove themselves instinctively knew better than to mess with a lifer like Terri, and focused their unprovoked attention more on the weaker and vulnerable inmates.

For Terri, the process of writing out her thoughts and feelings had become a welcomed release. Capturing her thoughts down on paper made her feel animated again, allowing her to briefly relive the time in her life when no bars existed. A time and place where she could manage to lose herself, and pull away from the suffocating confines of the walls that now bounded her. The culmination of pent-up recollections was carefully safeguarded, finding a proper home on paper as Terri poured herself into past accounts with total and willful abandonment.

As opposed to standard-sized writing paper, the length of the legal papers worked out surprisingly well. Terri found she was able to fit more on the back than first assumed, as long as she kept her printing small. Writing at night when the rest of the world slept lent her mind a much-needed reprieve. Terri's only concern was if Raven would fully understand everything shared, or if in anger, she would shut Terri's words out before declaring her unbridled hatred. Terri wasn't entirely sure writing this letter would amount to more than an exercise in futility or a desperate attempt at revisionism. Nevertheless, Terri continued to pen her memories the best she knew how.

* * *

Life with the Grants turned out to be a mini-miracle of sorts. Under the close tutelage and authority of his wife, Mr. Grant had the cabin fixed up by the end of my first week. Stored furniture from their attic adorned the inside, along with a few sets of curtains I made with Mrs. Grant's help. These welcoming additions hung above the newly cleaned and replaced glass windows. The once threadbare kitchen now showcased a full set of cookware, plates, utensils, and a host of other necessities. Outside, my stack of cut wood began to grow. I was left in charge of collecting twigs used for fire starters. Lucky for me, the forest floor never failed to disappoint.

The small room in the back turned out to be larger than I had originally assumed, certainly big enough for a full-size bed. The dresser from their attic was placed into the large room to hold linens, but after two months, Mr. Grant surprised me with a handmade tall and narrow armoire for the bedroom.

Food was plentiful. The garden, which I now helped tend, was bountiful with some of the ripest, most mouth-watering vegetables you could ever imagine. Fall came to a close, and in a little while, the apples from the trees would need harvesting, along with the turnips, beets, carrots, and radishes. Mrs. Grant taught me how to properly can the peaches and other gleaned vegetables, as well as how to make bread from scratch. Although the Grants kept a few beehives, no other animals lived on the land as pets. However, a visiting cat I dubbed "Cleopatra" and her adorable growing brood, were a common sight under the front porch.

The farm took care of most of our needs, but the Grants still had to go into town for certain staples once a month. They offered to take me, but I wanted to stay clear out of sight, panicked I would mistakenly run into someone who would know or remember me, despite being two towns over from where I grew up.

A day in town would be an almost routine all-day affair. The first stop was inevitably the post office, followed by a few minutes in the drugstore, and then a solid hour in the fabric department of one of those warehouse kind of places. Despite their monthly outings, for the most part, life for all of us revolved around the land.

The cabin became my home. I loved fixing it up, gathering wild flowers for vases made from discarded cans, and getting it ready for my baby's arrival. I never felt alone, scared, or vulnerable. I had never felt so safe.

As my due date—only a guess on my part—loomed closer, the Grants became almost as excited as I was, maybe even a little bit more. Mr. Grant built a small bassinet while Mrs. Grant's nimble fingers worked tirelessly on booties, caps, blankets, and other baby items. Whatever we didn't have already or couldn't make, which wasn't a whole lot, we would shop for in town when I went to see my obstetrician. Yes, that's correct, your adoptive mother forced me to go see a doctor in town a few times, so the baby I carried would come out complication free—God willing.

In the few months I had begun living on the land, the Grants cared more about me and my baby than my own mother ever did. Whenever I would get moody or sulky, ready to host my own pity-party, they would sense my mood swing and I'd be put to work peeling, cutting, or cooking something. There was never time to be self-indulgent or ungrateful around these two, so I learned early on that all my self-deprecating thoughts had to wait until I was back at the cabin for the night. Eventually, even the haunting memories of my past began to be nurtured right out of me. I guess you could say I was healing, or becoming whole again, perhaps for the first time.

The cabin had been an excellent idea. The Grants intuitively knew how much I needed my space, but I now had "my family" to rely on for direction and help. Please don't think I took advantage of their kind nature or that I hadn't tried to bring up the subject of rent, but neither of them would have it. Informing me that my rent was waived, I was now an honorary member of the family for as long as I liked, and Ladybug, I liked that big time. They also told me that the cabin was my home for as long as I wanted or needed it to be. That alone took a heavy weight off my shoulders.

Eventually, the more I became acquainted with the Grants, the more trustful I became. I started to open up about how it was I came to run away from home. I have to hand it to them, they never directly asked me, never pried. They gave me the time and space I needed to express myself and share. Honestly, I'm not entirely sure I could have been as respectful and patient to some waif like myself, who showed up on the stoop pregnant without demanding some reason, but they were.

As I shared, they listened. Once in a while, they'd interject for clarity only, and then intently listen again. Over time, I poured out all my skeletons to Mrs. Grant. I didn't mean to, but she had become a sort of surrogate mother figure in my life. Yes, me, too. Your adoptive mother was like a mother to me, as well. But before you get your panties in a twist for our not telling you about all of this, just trust me when I say, keep reading. You'll understand soon enough. I promise you. Then, if you don't like what you've read, you can burn everything I wrote. Scream at the top of your lungs declaring your unbridled hatred for me, and go on living as if I never existed. But until then, all I ask is that you just keep on reading. Give me a chance to explain.

While living with the Grants, I came to find out more about them as well—probably nothing you don't already know yourself. They were a childless couple, always wishing they would have a large family of their own. After a while, they contemplated adopting but never had the kind of funds to make it happen, which is sad. They would have made amazing parents to a large bunch of needy kids. They acquired the land and built the house, hoping to one day fill all the bedrooms with children, but after a few years of trying without any success and not being able to afford to adopt, they reluctantly decided it wasn't in the cards. "God had another plan for us," they told me. You know, I really have to say, something is seriously wrong and unscrupulous with a system that makes it financially impossible for two loving, selfless people to give needy children a loving home and family. I don't get it, but I'll get off my soapbox now.

By the way, as far as I know, my mother never tried to find me during this time, not that it would have mattered. I was never going back to live with her or her idiotic, sadistic husband again. Anyway…

Mrs. Grant, who I affectionately called "G-ma," came from a small farming family out in Oregon. She met Pop while attending college in the New York state area. They fell instantly in love at first sight, and married a week after she graduated.

Mr. Grant, who I dubbed "Pops," was retired, a former Correctional Officer at the local men's maximum security prison close to where they lived. Prisons are big business in upstate New York, and most folks were either working in or for corrections in some capacity, or were permanent guests of.

Correctional guards make decent enough money, but G-ma decided it was her job to become as self-sufficient as possible, minus cultivating animals. She wasn't comfortable working with or around animals, but no doubt made up for it in the way she grew her fabulous fruits and vegetables. The woman was a regular super-human, green thumb. A vegetable whisperer! She had a real instinctive knack for it, but her talents didn't stop there, as you probably already know. G-ma knew how to sew, knit, and crochet, and she made most of my baby's garments and quilts. At first, she attempted to teach me a few easy, basic stitches, but it didn't take long before she realized how unskilled I was. I did enjoy cross-stitching, but never completed a project.

Pops spent most of his time working the land. Once retired, he had the time to devote to tending all its aspects, including chopping firewood, building much of their furniture, and keeping the house in tip-top shape.

Years before, Pops had been motivated to build the cabin for hunting season. It seemed that when the hunting season came around, he wouldn't wash for days so his body scent wouldn't alert the deer or bear. Apparently animals can pick up a human scent and get spooked rather quickly. G-ma hated it with a passion when Pops pulled his going-back-to-caveman-times act. In fact, she hated it so much that she told him he should live in the barn like an animal since he certainly smelled like one. Not one to be so easily deterred, Pops replied, "Good idea," and did just that! Did they ever tell you this story?

No, Terri, they did not. Seems to me all three of you left out telling me a whole lot of stories!

CHAPTER 10

A GUY NAMED PADDY

RAVEN CONSIDERED PADDY to be a good-natured, dependable, and trust-worthy sort of guy. He was the type of person who was more than content to stay put where he'd been raised, make a decent living in the family business, and work hard toward settling down and starting a family of his own. In Paddy's case, his affection remained with Raven—if she'd ever let him get close enough to her. She was hard to read—one minute she could be warm and inviting while the very next cold and distant. His patience with the emotional seesaw teetered on the verge of waning. However, with all the recent upheaval in Raven's life, Paddy decided to back off, give her some space, and try to be as patient as possible. Maybe if he did all these things, she'd soon realize he was the right guy for her.

Raven valued her alone time, whereas Paddy had a tendency to crowd her. This had been a constant bone of contention between the two, coupled by the fact Raven was not ready to officially commit. This made Paddy wonder if her ambivalence and tension were a temporary issue, or something more permanent and unfixable. Raven shared the same concern. Lately, the two were continuously annoyed at each other, with Raven anxiously refusing to allow Paddy close enough to observe her imperfections and vulnerability.

When the doorbell rang, Raven practically jumped out of her skin. Unexpected company happened near to never. Even UPS and FedEx, rather than driving the back roads to her home, left all packages at the post office for pick up.

"Raven, it's me, Paddy. Geez, open up. It's freezing out here."

Paddy? What was he doing here? Raven thought, both pleasantly surprised and irritated all at the same time. "Coming! Hold on," she screamed through the door. "Give me a second," Raven yelled back over her shoulder, rushing to throw on actual clothes instead of the ugly bathrobe she'd been living in.

"I don't care what the heck you're wearing, just open up. It's seriously Arctic temperatures out here."

Feeling rushed and flustered, Raven muttered a litany of less than kind sentiments under her breath before unlocking the front door to half-heartedly welcome Paddy inside.

"About time!" Paddy hurriedly stepped inside, teeth chattering and chilled to the bone. "What took you so long?" he asked, stomping his snow-covered boots on the mat.

Paddy wasn't necessarily cute in the face, but he did have an appealing, rugged type of handsomeness coupled with a delicious, manly demeanor. The gravitational pull of his clear, hazel eyes and long lashes had the power to make Raven swoon; but it was his sandy brown hair, which he wore on the long side, that clinched the deal and completed the overall effect. Raven enjoyed joking with him about his "California beach-bum look," but secretly she hoped he'd never be swayed to cut his wild locks.

"What are you doing here?" Raven asked accusingly, sounding ruder than intended.

"Hello to you, too."

"I'm sorry, hi... I didn't mean to—"

"Of course you did," taunted Paddy. As he took off his coat, scarf, and hat, he casually leaned in to give Raven a peck on her cheek. "Here, grab this. It's food, something you rarely feel inclined to purchase or consume."

Catching a quick glance at herself in the hall mirror made her wish she had spent a little more time and energy on her daily appearance instead of happily rollicking in what could only be described as "homeless chic attire." Paddy, bless his soul, didn't seem to take notice, and she added another plus to his long column of attributes.

"Oh, stop exaggerating." Raven raised an eyebrow. "You'll use any excuse to come visit," she teased him back. "Did you have any trouble getting here? I haven't had a chance, or desire, to clear a path yet."

"Oh, really? I couldn't tell," he kidded. "I had no problem. I took Dad's truck." It was a four-wheel drive monster with a plow. Paddy often helped his dad in the winter with the plowing. Not a horrible way to earn some extra cash. "Your road is cleared, My Lady."

"Aw, you're the best Sir Padraic, but what's really in the bags?"

"I'm not kidding—food. Healthy food. Real food. Don't recognize it?"

"Oh. Super. Thank you."

"I fight the snow, ice, and blizzard to make this delivery and that's all I get? 'Oh-super-thank you?' Why don't you entertain me? Tell me what you've been eating recently, or rather what imitation food you've been eating? Your body will probably go into cataclysmic shock if you introduce it to real food rather than the instant, or comes-out-of-a-box, or metal-can variety—or even better, the crap that has had all of its nutrients nullified by being nuked in the microwave."

"Would you please stop mothering me, Paddy," Raven playfully muttered back, taking both bags of groceries into the kitchen. She peered inside: yogurt, spinach wraps, kale, bananas, pears, popcorn chips, and mango salsa. "Gluten-free, frozen, organic pizza?" Raven yelled from the kitchen.

Paddy laughed, "Hey, don't knock it till you try it. Plus, it was on sale." She thought she heard Paddy snicker.

"So how are you doing? I mean with all the, you know, burial and sister stuff you've been dealing with?"

"I don't know, honestly," Raven replied back, plopping back down on the sofa next to him. "It's all so confusing. First the Grants, and now Terri's dead. I'm not sure how I'm supposed to feel."

"There's no right way you're supposed to feel, Rave. Just take it one day at a time. Eventually, it will all work out. It always does."

"I guess," she mumbled softly. "But here's the thing, I'm so mad at myself. After my parents died, I told you how lost I felt? At first I thought I could cope by ignoring the gnawing in my stomach, the anxiety of not knowing what to do next or how, and the loneliness… And then I started to feel like I was regaining my footing, beginning to put some of the pieces of my life back together. But as soon as I did, Terri goes and takes her life, and in an instant—" Raven snapped her fingers for emphasis, grabbing the legal folder off the sofa table and waving it frantically in the air toward Paddy's face. "Every freaking thing I thought I had under control comes bubbling back up to the surface again, and I'm back where I fuckin' started!"

Upset and losing control, Raven bolted off the couch and began to pace back and forth, wearing the floor out, yelling, "Then on top of all the insanity, Terri decides to write me her life story on the back of her legal papers, before offing herself. For years, she mailed me cards and letters, and not once, *not once*, did she deem it necessary or important enough, for whatever reason, to fill me in on all of the stuff she's now dumping all over me. While stone dead! *And*, this is the *best part*! To add insult to injury, I signed away her body to the state. I wrongly assumed when they told me 'they would take care of everything' that they meant they would bury her, but after *actually reading the paperwork* they gave me to sign, I find out they will probably sell off or give away her body parts to science or some human chop shop. And there's not a damn stinking thing I can do about it!"

Paddy made an expression that all but said he wasn't sure how to respond, or if it was even safe to do so. "I'm sorry, Rave, I didn't mean to get you upset…you don't need to explain to me."

"Yes, I do! Which is why you're here, right? To hear all the gory details? Watch the next installment of how 'Raven the fuck-up' strikes again!"

Paddy knew how Raven could become cold, brutally blunt, even downright cruel at times, but this was becoming routine. Fed up, Raven watched Paddy shake his head, slap both his knees and stand up.

Enough. Better to leave than go head to head with her when she got like this, Paddy thought angrily to himself.

Paddy marched across the room to the closet to grab his stuff without saying a single word or glancing over in Raven's direction, and readied himself to leave.

"No, no! Don't go! I'm sorry. I shouldn't have said that. You didn't deserve any of it."

Fuming and hurt, Paddy bent over to put his wet boots back on, ignoring Raven's pleas. "The best thing I can do right now is leave you to your misery. You obviously resent me being here," he shot back.

"No, I don't. I'm just…frustrated. I'm—I shouldn't have taken it out on you," she pleaded. "I said I was sorry."

"Sometimes, being sorry isn't enough, Rave. I know you've been through hell and back recently, but don't attack me. I've never, *ever* spoken to you like that."

"You're right. I don't know why I'm such an ass; I'm just…"

"You are always trying to push me out of your life and it's getting old. I was just trying to help—to support you, be here for you, a shoulder to lean on. But you obviously want to be alone, so stay alone. I'm beginning not to care anymore."

Raven felt like a fool. She'd done it again—made Paddy feel rejected and hurt. She knew she had been unnecessarily spiteful, but this was why she always kept Paddy at arm's length. Not because she didn't love him; she did love him. She just didn't know how.

"Call me when you're done being… you, Rave." And the door slammed shut behind him.

"*Shit*!" Raven screamed as she buried her face in the couch pillow. *What is wrong with me?*

Paddy climbed back into the truck and slammed the door. A few moments later, Raven glanced out the window and saw his truck peel out of the icy, gravel driveway.

CHAPTER 11

MEMORIES COLLIDE

Terri...

I KNOW THE DRUGS *and alcohol messed with her head, but after running away, I continued to hold onto the ridiculous hope my mother would eventually come looking for me, but she never did. As sick as that sounds, I thought I needed her approval and her love. That somehow, if the drugs and alcohol left her system, she'd wake up and realize that she loved and cared about me, too. I now know I displayed the typical mindset of a neglected and abused child.*

Winnie was a narcissist with a skewed sense of what a healthy mother and daughter relationship entailed. Being raised by this damaged, cruel woman in a state of emotional captivity left me wounded and unstable. I can see some of my destructive behavior in the ways I keep my relationships at a distance, feeding off the same destructive pattern my mother used so skillfully against me. I should have been able to rely on my mother for protection and emotional support; but instead, I never knew what would trigger one of her violent outbursts, a slap, or a punch. Her erratic responses tormented me, and as a result, I grew emotionally distant, never fully understanding at the time the actual depth of damage she caused me through her abuse and chronic neglect.

Part of me wants to believe my mother knew all along where I was staying. I think I told that to myself to block out the truth, that she didn't give a shit where I was staying as long as I wasn't underneath her man. Her only concern centered on her next fix. Being strapped down with a daughter who she suspected was impregnated by her worthless husband didn't fit into Winnie's convoluted world. High or not, she never gave a damn about what happened to me.

Terri slammed her pen down. *What the hell am I doing writing this to Raven? I can't tell her about this part of my life, especially these kinds of gruesome details. Raven doesn't need to know this crap*. But Terri couldn't stop herself. The time for keeping secrets and editing out the pain of the past was over. For years, she'd kept everything bottled up, protected from discovery. Now, as her time drew to a close, everything—every single recollection and hurt—had to get written down. Documented. Recognized. Acknowledged. Grabbing another piece of legal paper, she was determined to continue writing.

The first time Carl raped me, my mother was passed out drunk on the couch. I could hear her snoring all the way from my bedroom. Whenever she laid on her back, she'd sounded like she was cutting down a rainforest. Between the heavy snores and intake of breath, she'd grumble or cough. The years of drugs, cigarettes, and alcohol abuse were catching up to her.

Carl was also a drunk, but his tolerance for hard liquor surpassed my mother's tenfold. Somehow, he was able to knock back copious amounts while remaining standing, although his liver was probably scarred, fatty, and diseased. The tiny membranes around his eyes sported a hue of yellow, resembling jaundice. The flaccid, over-aged skin on his face looked waxy, his nose home to a host of red spider veins. Although short in stature, he had a brute strength about him, which only increased when intoxicated. On the rare occasion when Carl wasn't totally smashed, his demeanor was somewhat easygoing. However, once he began drinking, which was almost always, all bets were off and his natural inclination toward meanness came pouring out of every rancid pore in his alcohol-soaked body. Instead of food, he drank most of his meals.

Around his bulky waist, no matter the pants Carl selected, he'd have on a worn black leather belt with a thick brass buckle in the shape of a horseshoe. He once told me the belt "brought him good luck." I remember a few times, hearing him use the strap to smack the table to either make a point, or scare the living crap out of my mother. As soon as the fear generated from slamming the table with the buckle became obsolete, he'd aim for my mom's back, arms, or legs instead, leaving a trail of swollen welts along the length of her body. If the belt, for whatever reason, wasn't readily unavailable, he'd use his stubby hands to slap her senseless, or his feet to kick her in the back. Carl was a brute.

Carl was also a bully, taking pleasure in making fun of me, calling me names like, 'fat ass','ugly', and 'slut'," and his all-time favorite, 'Heifer'. If Carl got thirsty, he'd yell, "Hey, fat ass, get me a bottle of beer."

I mistakenly failed to chalk up his beady stares to anything more than him being his usual smutty self. As I got older and began curving up in all the right places, Carl began taking note. Glaring at me in a whole different depraved manner, stripping me bare with his eyes. Pretending to "accidentally" bump into my chest or rub up on my ass. Bottom line, Carl was a mean, vile little man, and I did whatever I could to stay out of his way; but regrettably, evasion wasn't enough to spare me from his attacks.

The memory of the first time Carl cornered and raped me has remained fixed in my memory as if the assault happened only yesterday. He frightened me to the point where I became too afraid to fight him off, knowing that to resist would cause him to become even more violent and depraved. With no one I could trust to turn to for help, I remained powerless, vulnerable, and a target. Unable to get away and with nowhere to hide, I knew I was trapped. There are times even now when I lay on my cot, I swear I can still feel Carl's stumpy fingers probing my body.

A few months after the assaults began, I experienced difficulty falling to sleep. I was severely traumatized to the point where I was constantly on edge, anxiously listening for footsteps or the insipid noise of my door being slid open. Concentrating on any single task became problematic. Particular smells and places would trigger in me a detached feeling, like being in a thick fog, while silence made me feel jumpy and irritable. It's ironic how a damaged mind can repeatedly summon up this sort of detail. I'd rather forget actions in my life that fall out of the range of what is considered "normal." I beg to forget, but instead it has left me debilitated, wallowing in belated or intrusive responses, a constant unwelcomed companion.

The day of the first attack took place in the bathroom, of all places. The lock, like most everything else in the damn house, never worked. So for privacy, I would try to time my showers for when the dynamic duo were either sleeping off their hangovers or out of the house altogether, but of course, that wasn't always feasible.

While undressing and getting ready to take a shower, all of a sudden the bathroom door opened, Carl barged in, and he slammed me against the sink's edge. I never even heard the old reprobate climbing the steps, but he was on a mission and came prepared, holding a kitchen knife in his hand. With no room to move or turn, he pressed his considerable body weight against mine, holding the blade to my throat. The wretched fumes from his stank breath wafted in my face, demanding I keep quiet—or else.

His good luck belt already unbuckled and pants unzipped, Carl used his body strength to again ram me against the sink as he forcibly pried my naked thighs apart with his one knee. I tried as hard as I could to wiggle out of his clutches and shove him away. I twisted and turned my body, stretching my face away from his, but the more I fought, the harder he'd jam his knee between my legs. The pain forced me to double over, gasping for air while the knife's serrated blade pressed harder against my neck.

Through guttural growls and pushes, Carl taunted me. "You know you want me," he said.

"You can trust me," he said.

"Don't be frightened. You know me, I won't hurt you," he said.

"But if you dare tell anybody—anybody—I. Will. Kill. You," he said.

And then he proceeded to rape me.

Carl ignored my whimpering for him to stop and just laughed at me. He told me to shut my sniveling, ugly face up. Told me I made him sick to his stomach, and that he'd never fucked such an ugly whore before. I felt cold, cheap, and bare.

It was excruciating. Sickening. Completely humiliating, but thank the Lord it was also quick. Carl popped his cork before I had a chance to realize all of what he was planning to do to me. All I was certain of was just how much it hurt, and boy did it hurt. Badly. Exposed, I began to shake uncontrollably.

He reminded me again with threats to kill me if I decided to defy him or tell anyone about what happened. Shaking nonstop, I eagerly told him whatever he wanted to hear, anything to make it all stop. I tried to grab a towel to wrap around my body, but before I could pull away entirely,

Carl reached out and grabbed me by my hair. Yanking me down, forcing me onto my knees, and pinning my wet, tear-stained face into his fetid groin. "Next time, I'll teach you how to please me this way. I promise you'll enjoy it," he cackled sinisterly.

The bile in my throat rose, building up, ready to explode. Carl shoved me back, causing me to lose my balance, and I landed flat on my ass. Then, just as casually, he zipped up his pants, tightened his black leather belt, and patted his horseshoe buckle. "Yep, brings me good luck every time."

From this point on, Carl used any opportunity he could to get me alone and corner me into submission. It became the vilest game of cat and mouse. I tried to hide, stay out in the open, stay out of the house at all hours, even making noise to alert my drunken mother, anything; but nothing ever worked. He'd find me and force himself on me, and each time it happened, I died a little more inside. Eventually, as repulsive as he was, a part of me became numb and gave in to my fate until I could figure out a way to permanently disappear.

* * *

Heart racing, Terri hadn't realized the toll the litany of protected, horrid memories took. Racked in a cold chill, her undershirt clung to her body in a malodorous sweat. With each written syllable, her body excreted the culmination of all the pent up, toxic emotions in her system. The nightmares she held inside came rushing out, draining her in a cathartic release. Word by horrendous word, each pain-filled memory fouled the same paper used to justify her incarceration, saturated and now memorialized.

Never before had Terri shared the particulars of her battle with anyone except Mrs. Grant. It seemed pointless and uncomfortable. For years, Terri carried with her a deep-seeded guilt for not killing Carl when she had the chance, but at the time, she had been a frightened little girl, utterly defenseless and just trying to survive.

Terri picked up the two pain-filled sheets of paper and began to viciously rip them up into the tiniest of tiny pieces, small enough to flush down the toilet. The description of the rape was not something Raven needed to be burdened with. Yes, the unbridled truths of her life needed to come out, but now that they had had their chance of disclosure, even if it was only words written on paper, the power behind the hurtful memories were now stripped of their control over her. Terri's survival had been validated and honored. Carl couldn't take this from her, nor could the prison; but Raven would not be soiled by every last facet of her past, at least not in this way. Raven had enough to contend with.

Terri scooped up the papers and flushed the small pieces of her life's nightmares down the toilet. *How fitting,* she thought bleakly.

Sitting back down at the small desk, Terri yet again picked up pen and paper and began to write Raven, but this time, all she could muster to share with her about the rape was this:

> *Carl was an evil, sick man, Raven. He used his brute strength to force himself on me repeatedly, and I had nobody to call on for help and no way to escape. Then to keep me in line, he would say awful things to scare me into submission, and it worked. To this day, I can still remember his words…*
>
> *"You know you want me," he said.*
>
> *"You can trust me," he said.*
>
> *"Don't be frightened, you know me, I won't hurt you," he said.*
>
> *"But if you dare tell anybody—anybody—I. Will. Kill. You."*
>
> *And then he proceeded to rape me.*
>
> *The abuse didn't stop until I turned up obviously pregnant. Then Carl had the nerve to act as if he had nothing to do with it, and I was just some loser whore, turning tricks with every guy I met. "Terri's a regular bitch, isn't she?" he told my mother. Then directing himself at me, "Well, this is what you get, girl, for lying down with dogs—baby fleas." This cracked him up to no end.*
>
> *My narcissistic mother never bought his cockamamie story. Winnie knew all along Carl was a pig; but instead of protecting me, siding with me, turning the piece of scum into the police, she turned against me. With no concern for my safety, she recklessly exposed me to repeated, traumatic, psychological suffering, forever imprinted on my memories, and daggered into my heart.*
>
> *You can't imagine what an oasis it was landing a place in the cabin, under the love and protection of the Grants. I finally felt human. I even*

began to think I could carve out a future for myself, and for my baby. But life doesn't always work that way. Not for me at least.

"Lights out, Stone," barked the new CO. "Time to close up shop for the night."

Terri carefully put all the papers back into the legal folder. Toward the back were other legal papers, the most important documents of all. Those she would never write on. She made a mental note to put them in a sealed envelope with the instructions clearly labeled on it:

"Do not open until after you finish reading the entire letter, Raven!"

CHAPTER 12

TO READ OR NOT TO READ

RAVEN WORKED AROUND the house, but couldn't get the argument with Paddy out of her head. He was right—she knew she'd gone too far this time, but right now was a difficult period for her. Focusing on his feelings and needs while simultaneously trying to sort through her sister's emotional mind field of a legacy left Raven's emotions in a jumble. Although frustrated, she could only handle so much, which for Raven meant putting their spat on the back burner until she had a chance to sort through the entirety of Terri's eccentric letter. Somehow, Raven had to figure out how she became inextricably entwined in Terri's life. *Paddy will understand, hopefully. I'll make it up to him somehow,* she thought, trying to convince herself.

Back to the drawing board. Picking the folder up, Raven slid only the top few sheets out this time, attempting to keep the pile somewhat organized. Using a potato chip bag clip to secure the parts of the letter already read seemed to do the trick, giving her a sense of accomplishment, even if it was nothing more than an illusion.

There was nothing unbroken about Terri's life. Each word in her letter had been vigilantly assembled with the last to create an anguishing post-mortem, laden with suffering, yet reeling with intrigue.

Reading the part about the rape had been terrible and awkward. Her poor sister… Raven always believed there had to have been a clear rationale as to why Terri all of a sudden lost it. Raven wasn't necessarily justifying cold-blooded murder, but Terri's narrative shed light on her sister's personality and limited choices.

Terri could have just stayed with the Grants on that fateful day. What happened that made her go back to the same home that brought her so much pain? What drove her to murder Mom and Carl?

Raven knew more to this unfolding account was on its way. Terri had claimed repeatedly how wonderful her life had become living in the cabin, learning all kinds of survival stuff, cooking, and whatnot. She repeatedly mentioned in her letter about how the Grants had become as close to parents as she could have ever wished for. So why blow it all by going back? Why throw your entire life away by doing what you did, Terri?

The draw of her sister's story beckoned her to keep reading.

I don't want to dwell too long on Carl, our mother, or the rape. What's done is done, and it can't be undone. Plus, I don't want you to think I'm over here making up excuses for what I felt I had to do, because I'm not. I swear, just tolerate me a little bit longer. Read this letter in the order I wrote it; don't jump ahead if you want it to make sense. Eventually, most, if not all, of your questions will finally be answered.

So, let's resume…

It didn't take a genius to recognize way before I began to show, the heap of trouble I was in. The odds of not getting thrown out of the house as soon as I started looking pregnant were not in my favor. My resources were limited, and I was at a loss as to where to go and what to do. At one point, I even came up with a stupid, lamebrain scheme to blame the pregnancy on Diarmuid, a boy I had been seeing pretty steadily. Thankfully, what was left of my conscience kicked in and made that pathetic plan fizzle out almost as quickly as I'd thought it up. It seemed cruel and selfish to put him through all that. Diarmuid had been one of the kindest people I had known up to that point.

He never did me wrong, and I wasn't about to ruin his life along with mine. Had things been different, I don't know, I would like to have believed Diarmuid and I would have had a shot at a real life together, but crap happens, right?

The fact is, I'm the one who did the hurting. I broke Diarmuid's heart.

Diarmuid was such a romantic. Although technically still a teenage boy, he was an old soul. Blessed with charm and chatter, he'd tell me the most incredible stories. He claimed he came by "the gift of gab" genetically, as a true descendant from Ireland and all. One story was my favorite, though, the one involving his name. I kept mispronouncing Diarmuid until he explained, "It's not difficult, Ter, just pronounce it like 'deer' plus 'mid.'" Then I asked him what it meant, and he told me, "Without enemy." How cool, right, Raven? Can you imagine being without an enemy in the world?

Then he told me how back in the days of kings and queens, Diarmuid was the handsome lover of a beautiful woman named Grainne. She was part of some warrior band and the daughter of a high king. Her father betrothed her to some older guy named Fionn. When Grainne saw Fionn at her wedding, she knew she couldn't go through with the betrothal, so instead, she put some spell on the guy's nephew, who was Diarmuid. For sixteen years, the two lovers had to hide from the angry Fionn, who was tirelessly hunting them both down. Each night, the two lovers slept somewhere different, and legend has it the beds they made together can still be seen along the countryside.

Isn't this story romantic? I'm not sure if any bit of it was real, but I honestly never cared.

Anyway, getting back to my story. At the time, I was preoccupied with my deteriorating situation at home. It was getting harder and harder to hide the pregnancy, and the symptoms were even more difficult. I had the so-called "flu" more times that year than any person known to mankind. I never heaved so much in my life. I thought for sure that if it didn't stop soon, I was going to throw up my baby along with my meal. It was a wretched time.

My feelings for Diarmuid were increasing, and I was falling in love with him. Hiding what was happening to me at home with Carl was more out of embarrassment and fear than exposure. Carl threatened me repeatedly that if I dared open my mouth, nobody would believe me, and that he'd tell everyone what a lying slut I was. I couldn't bear having Diarmuid see me this way. I was in some deep shit without a paddle, and I knew it.

I got into the practice of keeping my most important things packed in an old travel suitcase, one a friend had given me, just in case I had to leave quickly. I was determined that when I left, it would be forever. I had no intentions of leaving all of my meager belongings behind and then having to beg to get them back. Forget that shit.

The case wasn't large at all, but it was big enough to hold my more treasured items, most of all, the necklace Diarmuid gifted me. I wish I knew where it was now, but I think I lost it in the cabin. I never had the chance to go back and search for it after that infamous last day…

You know, I've always wondered what happened to Diarmuid. All I know is that he married and had a family. I assume he still works with or for his dad, although by now, he's probably the owner. When I knew him, he was a genius at working with his hands—he could fix anything.

Diarmuid deserved the best in life. He truly did. I only wish I could have been a part of it.

Raven sat back, taking it all in. Terri had been in love. With all the hurt she wasn't spared, she still managed to find someone special in her life. Someone who saw more in her than she probably saw in herself. Diarmuid sounded like he would have made her happy, had they been given half a chance. Poor Terri; every time she had a shot at happiness, something or someone swiped it all away, almost as if she was destined to self-destruct. And poor Diarmuid! His young, romantic heart must have shattered into a million pieces when Terri turned up pregnant. If only she would have told him the truth... I wondered if he would have married Terri had he known the truth? Too bad Terri couldn't have been his Grainne.

* * *

Terri

Typical jailhouse relationships tend to be based on need and greed. Martina was under no delusion—she assumed Terri was using her, but so far, the arrangement equally benefited them both. As long as the two kept the agreement on track, Martina would make sure to keep her end of the bargain. However, she also knew she was taking a big risk sneaking out the pills. If the nurse caught her, or a strip search slid south, Martina might as well have bet she'd be sent to solitary confinement—or possibly moved to a new tier entirely. Martina didn't fancy testing those precarious rocky waters.

"Next!"

Martina sauntered up to the sliding glass window. The nurse glanced up with the same exact monotone, bored expression plastered across her dull face as she did every day. Martina wished she could slap it off her.

"Number!" bellowed the nurse challengingly.

"99-C-0012." Martina rattled off her number without a second thought.

Martina's number, also known as her Department Identification Number, indicated she had been locked up since 1999. Her reception center where she had been initially admitted represented the *C*, and the 0012 meant she had been the twelfth inmate admitted into the center that particular year. All prisoners were assigned an identifier once placed in the custody of the Department of Corrections, and were expected to have it memorized.

The nurse jotted down the number and asked Martina a few basic routine questions. Then she checked off a few boxes and slipped the two pills on a paper napkin under the Plexiglass window panel before instructing Martina to, "Swallow."

Martina popped one of the pills. The nurse glanced up, hardly registering what was happening. but Martina cupped the other.

"Stick out your tongue."

Martina did as directed, sticking out her tongue to prove she had swallowed the pills. Then the nurse slid the clipboard into the slot and ordered Martina to sign by the *X*, indicating she had received the medication. Without glancing up, the nurse hollered, "Next."

"Yes, ma'am."

Back in the day, Martina wouldn't have hesitated to wipe the floor with a fool like this nurse. Nobody on the street was stupid enough to mistakenly speak to Martina in a dismissive tone, but here in prison, one wrong move would undoubtedly be met with immediate punishment and retaliation. Martina, almost at the end of her long sentence, hoped to be up for parole soon. She couldn't afford to slip up now. If keeping her nose relatively clean meant sucking it up, even with creepy nurse face, then that's exactly what she would do...

* * *

Raven stretched out her cramped legs and arms. It had been days since she last exercised, although calling what she did exercise was probably a bit of an exaggeration. For Raven, who hated sweating, exercise consisted of a few half-assed attempts at sit-ups, crunches, the occasional running in place, but mostly walking. Walking was the key to keeping her weight under control, but winter storms mixed with unbridled anxiety and her constant snacking and grazing, weighed her down. But clearly not enough to make her zip her lips shut.

Without missing a beat, Raven leaped off the couch and headed for the refrigerator. Rummaging around for something to quench her hunger and sweet tooth, she grabbed one of the yogurts Paddy had so generously brought over, along with a handful of her stashed chocolates—a perfectly winning combination.

Each bite tasted delicious, until a mild sense of remorse crept in as she continued taking sumptuous mouthfuls. Raven reflected on what had happened with Paddy. She had treated Paddy unfairly, lashing out at him, and it wasn't the first time either, although this time, she'd soared way over the top.

Paddy's reaction had been a shocker, a first actually. Raven tried to convince herself that he simply overreacted—as if what she accused him of hadn't been enough for him to split on her. Then again, this wasn't exactly the first time she had lashed out at him recently. One of these days Raven was going to push him too far. It would serve her right if Paddy called it quits.

Before she had a chance to change her mind, Raven grabbed her phone and dialed Paddy's number. Apologizing never came easy, but by the fourth ring it was apparent Paddy, who usually picked up, wasn't in the mood to hear her spiel. By the fifth ring, his voice mail automatically sounded. Either Paddy was busy, or he was purposely screening her calls. Either way, Raven took a deep breath and began rambling at warp speed, trying to get in as much as possible before the *beep* cut her off.

"Hey, you. I'm calling to apologize for talking to you the way I did today. I'm stressed to the breaking point, and all of this stuff is just getting to me. Not an excuse, I know, just the truth." Raven felt stupid leaving a message but she wanted to get it over with. "I'd like to also thank you for bringing me real food and coming to check up on me. Please don't stay mad at me for too long. Well, okay then. Call me back. I promise not to be a shithead."

* * *

Paddy had felt his cell phone vibrate and took a quick peek—Raven. But he continued driving. Raven's behavior had begun to border on hostile. He was seriously growing weary of her constant verbal attacks and condescending attitude. He wasn't willing to be her lap dog, no matter how much he cared about her, nor was he quite ready to make nice. *'Let her stew in it,'* he thought to himself.

The frigid air outside fogged up his truck's windows, making it a feat to see the road. He was glad to be only a few minutes from the shop. Due to the inclement weather, the trip had taken him double the amount of time. He shoved his phone back into his coat pocket and leaned over to adjust the heat and the defroster. Moments later, he arrived back at work, irritated and edgy.

Before getting out, Paddy reached over and popped open the glove compartment where the felt jewelry box remained eerily undisturbed. He struggled to stay realistic about his relationship with Raven, but recently, the transformation in her personality had gone from mildly insecure to virtually unstable. The rift between the two of them seemed to be widening the more she stayed secluded in her world—a world nobody, it seemed, was allowed to penetrate. Including him.

Paddy kept trying to convince himself how the fracturing of their relationship was nothing more than temporary, but a larger part of him had begun to consider the possibility that he was deceiving himself. It was probably nothing more than wishful thinking on his part, but time would tell. Until Raven gave Paddy a clear indication he was a viable part of her life, and not someone she was willing to throw away, the fancy felt box with the white-gold engagement ring inside would remain hidden away.

* * *

The storm finally subsided, replaced by the glorious full moon, which lit the night sky with a sea of stars that could be seen twinkling like tiny ice crystals. Nights like these caused the loneliness within Raven to swell, more than she cared to admit. Without her parents in the home or Paddy lying next to her, the abrupt lack of closeness left her feeling exceptionally vulnerable and unsettled.

The sounds from outside seemed to resonate in the quiet of the night. The occasional echoes of twigs snapping as deer plodded through her yard could be clearly heard. After an unusually heavy snow, and as the sun's warmer rays of the day shone, large chunks of melted ice from the roof would fall on the porch. Upon impact, the thud would scare Raven half to death.

Tossing and turning and unable to find a comfortable position without straining one part of the body over the other, Raven finally gave up, turning to lie flat on her back. In the still of the cold night, periodic gusts of wind rattled the old windows, forcing air through the small cracks of worn-away insulation. The room felt nippy, but not at all uncomfortable under the thick quilt comforter made for her years ago.

Raven's mind was exhausted, but her body continued to fight back—and tonight, her body won the argument. Swinging both legs over the side of the bed, Raven let her feet blindly grope around for her slippers. She squinted at her phone's screen, fruitlessly checking to see if she had somehow missed a call or text message from Paddy. Nothing. No surprise.

All the skies of her days were crashing, as the mountains were crumbling. The trees, too, had bent in sorrow the day Raven laid the final clumps of dirt on the graves of Earth's two most loving caretakers. Many of Raven's recent outbursts came from the dark, foreboding hole building in the pit of her stomach and soul. Coming to terms with loss and death had released in her fury and devastation so potent, she didn't know quite how to manage them yet. Paddy, her only outlet and connection left in her heart, bore the brunt of these attacks, turning him mercilessly into her emotional punching bag.

Raven knew what she was doing was wrong, and how her erratic behavior was destructive, not only to their relationship, but to herself. She knew she could be terribly cruel, abrasive, and unfair. But with the constant upheaval to her life, she hadn't yet figured out a healthy way to manage the building resentment. Everyone she loved was being ripped away from her.

Raven scrolled for Paddy's home number and pushed call. *Pick up! Pick up the damn phone*! Again, the answering machine—but this time, she began to sing her message. "I just called, to say, I love you…"

Just as Raven took in a deep breath, ready to belt out the second stanza, Paddy called on the other line from his cell phone. Raven's heart skipped a beat as she immediately pushed accept. Before she could say hello, Paddy chimed in.

"Please, for the love of God and all that is pure in this world and in the heavens, whatever you do, don't sing. Stevie Wonder has done nothing to you to warrant such maltreatment," Paddy teased.

"Hi…" Raven almost whispered.

"Hey."

A few seconds of silence lingered uncomfortably between them.

"I'm so sorry," Raven began just as Paddy was saying something. They had the habit of long-time couples who talked over one another or at the same time.

"You go first," he voiced, almost whispering into the phone.

"I know I've been a jerk lately. A big, fat jerk…and I'm sorry. I never meant to go off on you like that. You have to know I would never intentionally try to hurt you, not after all we've been through… I'm just, I don't know… Everything is so hard right now… Forgive me?"

"I don't know about fat, but you have been a jerk," he teased.

"Shut up, you!" Raven joked back. "But you forgive me, right?"

"I don't know, Rave—"

"Tell me what I want to hear or I'm going to start singing again."

"No, no, not the singing, anything but the singing! Okay, Rave, I forgive you. Of course, I forgive you, but we need to get on the same page again, you and me. You can't keep locking me out of your life, despite the stress and shit you're going through. I'm not your enemy."

"You're right. You're not." Raven loved the sound of his voice, even when pissed at her. "Can I make it up to you?" she asked.

"What do you have in mind?" he asked mischievously.

"Well, if you are inclined to brave the cold, wind, and snow one more time, I just might be able to show you."

Raven, of course, couldn't see the smile smeared across Paddy's face from ear to ear, but in her mind, she suspected it was there.

"Leaving now."

* * *

Hours later, comfortably resting in Paddy's warm, strong embrace, Raven felt more content and happier than she had been for a long time.

Paddy kissed her forehead gently. "Cold?" he asked.

"Not in the slightest, but you, my friend, need to get some sleep. Don't you have work today?"

"I know." He yawned while pulling slowly away from the shared, warm embrace, turning over to his side to face her. "I'm so comfortable. I wish I could call in sick, spend the entire day in bed with you, but Dad's short staffed right now."

Raven smiled, lightly kissing Paddy on his soft lips. "I wish you could, too, but like you, I have to get up. I have given myself the next week to get everything settled with Terri's stuff. That's it, so bear with me for just a little bit longer."

"And then what?" he asked.

"And then it's going to be time for me to find a job. Or maybe sign up for school. I seriously need to do something for my future."

This was news to him. Raven was never a big fan of school, although certainly smart enough to make going back happen if she decided it was what she wanted to accomplish. So far, she hadn't been motivated; not after losing her parents, and now with this Terri situation.

"I don't know… I haven't gotten that far in my thought process yet. Bottom line, I just don't want to feel stuck at a no-future job, making minimum wage for the rest of my life."

"Well, I think you should go back to school and earn a degree, if that's really what you want to do, but find something you can be happy doing. My dad says, 'Find a career in life which makes you feel like work's more of a hobby. Then you will always be happy while you earn your keep.'"

Raven laughed, "Well, personally, I think your father is right, but it's kind of hard when you don't have a clue about what you want to do."

"You have the money now to go to school, or start a business, anything you want really, Rave. Your parents made sure of it. The only thing stopping you now, frankly, is you."

Paddy was right, which lately seemed to have become a trend. "I know. I'll figure it out," she replied.

While both admittedly were young, she and Paddy had discussed marriage on quite a few occasions, but recently, the topic had been shelved for obvious reasons. Raven wasn't necessarily against the idea of marriage, but she just wasn't sure she would make Paddy, or anybody, a suitable wife. He seemed so traditional, sentimental, giving, and too easy to please. Raven considered herself more of a selfish type personality, leaning toward self-centered and moody, but also loyal to a fault. Maybe her loyalty was the characteristic that attracted him most to her. She'd have to ask him…

Paddy's parents had married young, and from what he told her, they were still very much in love. They seemed to have a steady marriage.

Raven enjoyed their company, and they had been nothing but kind to her whenever she had been invited over.

And her parents? Well, their relationship remained a mystery; but the Grants, who Raven considered her real parents, had married in their early twenties and were a prime example of two people making their marriage work to the end. If she and Paddy could have a love that endured like theirs, then marriage wasn't so farfetched. For now, Raven didn't plan on giving that level of commitment another thought. It wasn't like Paddy had officially proposed or anything.

For now, both young lovers remained content to simply exist, tangled up together under the warm blankets, drifting off into a deep, welcoming sleep.

CHAPTER 13

THE EXIT PLAN

Terri

WEEKS HAD GONE BY since the conception of the letter-writing campaign started. Unexpectedly, Terri's concentration began to wane, quite possibly due to her feelings about reliving the past. The more she revealed about her past life through her writing, the more exposed and vulnerable she felt.

As Terri's letter writing remained somewhat stilted, her mounting collection of pills had been, so far, successfully hoarded and securely concealed. Thanks to Martina's diligence and insatiable hunger for the acquisition of things, the quantity of pills needed to do the deed had almost been satisfied.

Unlike her writing, Terri's obsessive determination and maniacal fixation with controlling her death never wavered or faltered. Admittedly, the pill stash was her secret weapon and the last mark of authority over her miserable existence. Terri wasn't about to sell herself short. The only thing holding her back now, taunting her to remain breathing, was the fact she hadn't finished her letter to Raven.

Mentally preparing for a final exit plan meant getting back down to business, regardless of how uncomfortable writing made her feel. Raven had the right to know everything.

* * *

Word flew around on the pod—there was going to be a surprise cell search going down soon. Tensions grew as the smell of desperation and con inundated the air. Guards read the signs, assuming something was up as the noise on the tier suddenly leveled off. Random card games ended, and inmates started heading back to their cells voluntarily. The prison grapevine remained one of life's great mysteries. How prisoners got wind ahead of time that a tiered search was on its way baffled staff to no end, but until the official word from the captain filtered down for the searches to commence, there was little to do but wait.

For Martina, this could mean the end of her side business if her stash of "cosmetics" were discovered, at least for a short period. Quickly and as efficiently as possible, she began tearing up and getting rid of what she could easily replace. Cleverly hiding whatever else, Martina hoped her stuff would not be confiscated or, even worse—confiscated with her receiving a write-up for being in the possession of contraband. The symphony of continuous flushing toilets on the tier became almost comical.

Terri wasn't as concerned as Martina. Besides the pills, her cell was exceptionally clean. Her shrewd hiding places were as secure as possible, and so far, hadn't let her down, but there was always a first time for everything. It all depended on which guards did the searching, and how detailed they decided to get with it. Nothing in prison was a guarantee, so like all the other inmates, Terri found herself playing the waiting game, anxious to see how it would play itself out. The proverbial catch-me-if-you-can match between guard and prisoner never failed to entertain or stretch the limits of the human imagination to conceal and survive.

To keep her mind off the search and the obvious stench of panic in the air, Terri parked herself back down at her desk to write. But this time, instead of focusing on the actual letter to Raven, she embarked on the task of designing a card with a drawing. Something this innocuous might entice the guards to inspect and read, and perhaps confiscate; that would hopefully keep them occupied and off the trail of what she was really hiding.

The game was to keep them concentrating in one direction, as opposed to searching where Terri didn't want them in her business at all. That was the trick—making the guards think they were close to catching her doing one thing while she kept them away from where the action was actually taking place. Nevertheless, Terri was well aware that if the guards found her stash, she was in deep trouble. They'd demand to know how the pills came into her possession, and from whom, but Terri would never be a snitch. She knew better. "Snitches get stitches…"

It had to have been close to midnight when the cacophony of banging lids, yelling, whacking on doors with batons, and the heavy booted stomping could be heard consuming the pod. A team of heavily suited guards, boasting full facemasks and shields, started shouting out instructions, pushing doors open to startle the occupants into compliance.

"All inmates are ordered to step outside of their cells and take a seat on the floor!" yelled the officers, over and over again.

Terri, who hadn't fallen asleep, calmly left her cell, wrapped in her blanket, feet in flip-flops, doing as she was told.

Martina looked exhausted as she exited her cell. Too uptight and anxious, she hadn't been able to sleep when the guards came bum-rushing in. Nevertheless, she, too, plodded her way out of her cell, checking the corridor, discreetly smirking at Terri, who was making her way to the floor.

A few of the younger, dumber inmates decided to put up a fight, refusing orders to come out of their cells, and, of course, this only caused more tension, threats, and screaming.

Show time.

One younger woman, a new inmate, put up the loudest and most bizarre protest. She barricaded herself in the cell, stuffed up her toilet and refused to leave. Her ear-splitting yelling, cursing, and aggressive behavior drew most of the negative attention and adrenaline her way.

Suited up with facemasks and cans of pepper spray handy, a horde of guards barreled in, spraying the screaming woman in the eyes. With face burning and eyes now stinging, she was quickly subdued. The guards wrestled her to the ground as she wildly lashed out in every direction. Once safely restrained, the woman was placed in handcuffs and seated in the "Crazy Chair"—a wheelchair for prisoners who might hurt themselves, or others—and wheeled off to her new digs in solitary confinement.

For Martina and Terri, who sat on the floor watching this well-played-out performance, this was magnificent. It meant that most of the energy and angst would be spent in the crazy girl's direction as opposed to them, which had been the plan all along. Terri had suggested the idea in passing. Martina, as one of the more influential inmates, was more than happy to encourage the scared newbie that it would "behoove her to comply, if she wanted future protection." Being new and deathly frightened, the newbie grudgingly accepted her assignment.

A bit less than two hours later, all inmates were sent back to their cells except the few who had caused the most fracas and put up the loudest fights. Another inmate, a real trouble hound and sociopath, had had her homemade shank found during the cell raid. She, too, got hauled off, kicking and screaming at the top of her lungs about how "unfair" the guards were, always hassling her for "no reason," planting shit in her cell just to get her in trouble, and how she didn't do anything. She was also thrown into a holding cell to await her reprimand. But for now, the immediate threat of detection had passed, and the coast was clear. Terri and Martina were back in business.

* * *

Tossing and turning, too wired to fall back asleep after all the hullabaloo, Terri finally gave up, deciding to stay awake to write. Most of the time, Terri earnestly focused on exposing her past story; but sometimes, like tonight, she felt the need to vent about what life was really like for her in this hellhole. Normally not one to complain, writing felt right, a release. Being able to put down all the crap on paper had become cathartic and she hoped Raven wouldn't detest her for it. Then again, there was so much more Raven could hate her for; this minor deviance probably wouldn't matter in the long run.

Tonight the guards came on the floor, suited up to the hilt, ready to tear this joint to pieces. They do this routinely, and for the most part, we know when it's going to happen. The guards think they are so smart and tricky, but they fail to understand how the walls in this place are thin. It's almost impossible to keep anything secret. Despite the bars and locks, there are ears and eyes everywhere. Don't be fooled by the uniform, Raven; everyone has a price. In a place like this, you have to learn the dos and don'ts quickly, because your life literally can depend on it, and I am not exaggerating.

Most of the time, I try to keep my cell "clean," since I don't normally stash much. I frankly don't need the headache. I'm a lifer. Why should I rock the boat when I don't have to? I'm comfortable in this cell and on this tier, if one can call it that. I sure as shit don't need guards riding me or getting myself thrown in the hole, and I seriously don't want to have my stuff—the little I do own—arbitrarily taken away from me. I have a life sentence, Ladybug, and shit in here is real enough without compounding my predicament, you know what I'm saying?

I have my books, which I treasure, but they are all legit, right from the prison library or bought. And my commissary extras—they are state approved. I have no weapons hidden. No real use for them. I can only guess my so-called reputation as a "loner-psychopathic murderer," and the fact I methodically keep to myself, is enough to hinder the usual nonsense from knocking.

I purposely make a point out of not socializing or befriending many of the head cases around here—it's less cause for drama, which the women's prison is full of. I won't gross you out with the gory details, but let me just say this... Between the sexual hook-ups and entanglements, as well as the underground drug-contraband market, tensions remain high. Everyone has a scheme up their sleeve. Nobody here does anything altruistically. There's always a hitch, a catch, a scam, and a fee.

The limited few in my inner circle know better than to cross me, or I them, so those kinds of nuisance dalliances tend not to trickle to my doorstep. Guards leave me alone since I leave them alone for the most part, and I don't bust their balls. At the same time, I always have to watch my back and be willing to put a hurting on someone if they are crazy enough to try to come at me. It's predatorily stacked against you in here, and to survive, you can never let down your "guard" —no pun intended.

Don't think for a second any of this has been easy for me in here, locked away with a bunch of social misfits. Not surprisingly, a large portion of the inmate population is educationally ignorant, unable to write even the simplest of coherent sentences, and these morons are proud of it. They sit around yapping, harping on and on about how their life on the outside sucked, and who screwed them over the most, and how school "wasn't their thing." All of a sudden, every one of them becomes a super mom, bemoaning on and on about "missing their babies" and what they will do with them when they eventually get out. Such bullshit. I'd say less than 1% ever follows through on those promises or declarations.

So of course, the majority of inmates in here don't or can't read for pleasure either, even though books are readily available. I find this mentality utterly idiotic. My books, and the time to read them, are the only redeeming qualities left in my life. You better trust and believe me; without them I would have killed myself a lot earlier.

Sorry, I probably shouldn't be so flippant about killing myself. It's just that I don't care about existing anymore. This place does that to you—no hope of ever being free again. No hope of having a regular, normal life on the outside. Crimps a gal, ya know?

I'm pretty pleased with my ability to write well now. It's "well," not "good." I used to say, "I wrote good," but one of the books I read said that wasn't proper grammar. Learning to write took time, years of practice, and came from reading anything I could get my hands on. Then, whenever I came across a word or phrase I didn't know, I'd look it up, write down the definition, or ask someone how to pronounce it. Then I'd try to use it in an actual sentence, just like how I was taught in grade school. It works. Believe me.

Another survival tactic we employ here at Camp Insanity is that we inmates never discuss our crimes. You never know who's a snitch and who wants to use your information to buy a ticket out, or who wishes to hurt you, because somehow, your crime offends their delicate criminal sensibilities. I never say a word, so it doesn't trickle down, because if somehow it does, I could be putting myself in danger with the other inmates.

Openly discussing any crime is frowned upon, especially if you are some type of child molester or pedophile. Most of those are placed in protective custody, and for good reason. These types of inmates are housed in a special unit, but the few who slip by onto the regular tier are taking a big risk. For the most part, the majority of women on my pod are here for drugs, prostitution, forgery, theft, and the occasional murder, like me. We're a real batch of special, huh?

Food, drugs, cigarettes, and sex are all hard currency in here. Doing favors also pulls some strings. Learning to mind your own business is paramount, and keeping your mouth shut is mandatory. Anybody who can't get it straight usually finds herself wishing she had, and most so-called "accidents" here are anything but.

In a strange way, Raven, this place is my home. Don't get me wrong. It's not at all where I wish I could have spent the rest of my life if given the choice, but my reality is, I'm here. All my options are gone, and I have had to make the most of it… Until I don't. You know what I mean.

The way I see it, we are all inhabitants of our own prisons, whether in a prison cell or not. We are a nation that likes to boast to the world of our inherent freedom, while we all live in a world of perpetual locks—locks on our homes, on our sheds, cars, even on our bedroom and bathroom doors.

Schools have locks everywhere, including on lockers. Even drawers in our homes get locked up. People put money in banks, locked up in safes with even better, stronger locks and combinations. Select ID is now used to unlock doors, encrypted information, and files. Credit cards and computers have locks on them. Passwords used to keep others supposedly out, is wishful thinking. I read once in the newspaper about a family who kept locks on their refrigerator to help them control shoving food down their throats. Crazy right? Maybe not. Who am I to say?

People write songs and sing about closing their hearts, locking away dreams and thoughts, keeping a lock on their feelings. As a society, we glamorize and hard sell the concept of being unattainable and closed off as something normal—something to be achieved, celebrated and protected. Then we mix it up with the propaganda of individualism. As a society, we boast an admiration for those who are exceptional, until we are threatened, or the exceptional have the nerve to question the lack of individualism or the accepted status quo. Then, all the keepers of the flock busy themselves tearing the rebel, freethinker in half, shredding them out of existence until their beliefs are unrecognizable and mere fodder for comedic vultures to mock. Yes, hail to the sanitized individual! Be yourself, as long as you remain steadfastly nestled between the lines. Don't dare make waves or have a genuine thought outside the herd.

Locks, locks, and even more locks. Some locks keep folks inside, while others are meant to keep people out. But instead of a pot of gold at the end of the rainbow, there's still nothing at all but a bunch of damn locks—a touch of lunacy if you ask me.

I'm babbling…sorry. I just have so much I want to tell you, Ladybug, to share and finally get off my chest. Everything up until now has been bottled up tightly inside my head with no way of getting out. Now, as I mark down my minutes, crossing out days on the calendar with purpose, the need to impart has become all-consuming. Does this make sense to you?

So where does all this bring us, you and me? Back to the past, I'm afraid. Back to where my demons were born, and permitted to play unsupervised.

CHAPTER 14

WHEN LOVE IS NOT ENOUGH

RAVEN LEANED BACK in an attempt to let Terri's words soak in. Emotionally drained, she laid the paper softly on her lap, tightly squeezing back tears of disappointment. Reading Terri's missive hadn't been like reading an ordinary letter. First off, it was posthumous, which already lent to the macabre. Secondly, her words were fiercely cutting, venomous, and toxic.

Terri wouldn't have known how Raven's eyes leaped from one word to the next with a burning and numbing intensity. Or how Terri's words tore away at the inner core of Raven's stilted inner being until only raw, exposed nerves were left, or how every statement was deliberately used to reveal another clue in the web of confusion Raven now felt ensnared by. Terri had been correct.

She sure did know how to write, and her story was making Raven physically ill.

Compassion wasn't Raven's strong suit, but as she read, she tried to comprehend her sister's pain, despite coming from an outsider's point of view. She empathized with Terri's frustration and loneliness, but certainly not from the same concentrated, dark place or experience.

Terri had been angry. Her letters did nothing to hide that fact, but she'd been surprisingly reflective as well. It was as if by sharing her reality, even through writing, that she could somehow empty her damaged soul and lift the weight she had been forced to assume.

Raven tried to keep Terri's story in perspective, but she couldn't help feeling resentful. *Why couldn't Terri have communicated all of this with me before taking her life? What's the point of dropping all of this on me now? What can I do about any of it?*

Raven also didn't share Terri's opinion about the world being concerned only with locks. These were not her experiences, nor had life offered Raven the same plate of poison to swallow and choke on.

* * *

Paddy left early for work, forfeiting a shower so as not to disturb Raven, who slept comfortably and finally stress-free. Ever since Raven told him about her sister's suicide, Paddy had worried about what it was doing to Raven's mindset. She'd barely begun to face up to how she felt about her past. Raven glossed flippantly over details when asked, and Paddy assumed this letter fiasco was opening up a whole new can of ugly worms. The entire fallout was yet to be revealed.

Paddy loved Raven, believing she felt the same way about him most of the time. However, recently it had become glaringly apparent that Raven, harboring a valid dread of being vulnerable, continued to struggle with commitment—not necessarily of being in a committed relationship, per se, but publically declaring it. In the company of strangers, she still introduced Paddy as her friend, leaving a carefully constructed psychological barrier firmly positioned between them.

Lately, Raven had just begun on her own accord, to describe them to others as a couple. However, with the currently magnified and profound sense of loss she was experiencing, Paddy suspected Raven would understandably fold back up into her defensive cocoon. She would be unwilling to expose herself to a life reliant on, or connected to, anyone she cared about and could lose.

"You're early," Paddy's father observed, smirking disapprovingly at his son's rumpled appearance. "Weren't you wearing the same clothes yesterday?"

The upper rim of Paddy's ears warmed, no doubt turning a light shade of embarrassed pink. "I overslept. Didn't want to be late."

"Ah, huh, well, grab yourself a cup of coffee and meet me in the office. I want to go over yesterday's invoices with you. Plus, we have a busy day ahead of us. I need everyone working together. No screwing around."

"Who's screwing around?" Paddy replied, annoyed. Typically a laid back kind of guy, Paddy's father had been on edge recently. Short on patience, moody, and highly critical about nothing. Something was irritating him. He just wasn't his normal self.

Pointing his stubby finger, Dermot shot Paddy a steely stare and sucked his teeth. "Five minutes in my office," he growled. "Let the rest of your brothers know to get their butts in there, as well. I'm tired of all the goofin' around."

McMahon & Sons faired well monetarily, with a constant stream of loyal local customers consisting of mostly neighbors, friends, and family. The shop was situated conveniently in town, with easy access right off the highway. It drew in a nice amount of commuter traffic, but their success depended mostly on word of mouth.

Paddy and his father had a healthy working relationship; the two of them had established the pecking order early on. At his father's insistence, Paddy had taken on more than his fair share of the workload, and his younger brothers continued to defer all business decisions to Paddy. At the end of the day, it changed nothing. Until retired, if ever, Dad would interminably be known as "the boss."

The hours were long but steady, affording Paddy ample opportunity to squirrel away funds toward his future. It was no secret amongst the McMahon family and friends that Paddy eventually planned to ask Raven to marry him, but the jury was still out on exactly when. Paddy knew rushing Raven into anything would prove disastrous. Raven was struggling, feeling pressured to figure out what she wanted to do with her life. Now with her sister's death consuming her, the subject got tabled for the foreseeable future. Paddy didn't necessarily care what she decided, as long as he was in the final equation.

* * *

Dermot was fond of Paddy's girl, Raven. What wasn't there to like? She was awfully well mannered, obviously intelligent, and sweet on his son. Over the last three years, she'd become a welcomed fixture around the McMahon dinner table, and she fit in like a glove. He enjoyed Raven's quick wit, and willingness to banter and stand up for herself. Telling a good tale was a family requirement, and while Raven never shared much about herself, she had little difficulty shooting from the hip when pressed.

Without the slightest pretense, she'd belly laugh like the rest of them, and it was clear to all that his son's soul paid rent in that girl's heart.

But Dermot was also a realist. Life had taught him early on not to blindly trust anyone ever again, regardless of how they may appear. Only over time would Dermot entirely concede and drop his caution…maybe. When he'd met his wife, Kendal, he was young, genuinely thoughtful, but also sometimes unnecessarily abrasive. He'd noticeably nursed a raw and wounded heart. Kendal Riley had been the complete opposite. Heart unscathed, she had been ready to nest, falling hard for the handsome, brooding young man. She hadn't wasted any time making her intentions known that she was going to nail the young Dermot McMahon; and frankly, there hadn't been a darn thing he could do to stop it, nor had he wanted to. Kendal's steadfast stubbornness had paid off, and soon the two were a couple.

The rest was, well, history. They'd married, a traditional wedding held at the local church, filled to the rafters with family and friends. Very soon after, Paddy was born, and like a stepladder, the rest of the McMahon boys soon followed.

The shop could get noisy at times. Nevertheless, it was the practice to keep a radio playing for background noise. For years, the boys and their father relentlessly bickered back and forth about the kind of music they'd prefer to listen to. Dermot insisted soft rock was the way to go, declaring most of his clientele would appreciate "real music," while the boys wanted current pop, the stuff their generation favored. When dad wasn't at the shop, the boys had their music blaring, usually louder than necessary. As soon as dad arrived back on the scene, he'd yell for them to "Shut that shit off!" and demanded his tunes immediately turned back on.

"You call that noise, music? You boys wouldn't know good music if it bit you in the ass." Finally, a truce was called, and a benign local station was chosen. Now, all they heard was a safe permutation of mainly talk shows, along with news and weather updates.

Two days ago, news of Terri's suicide flooded the airways. At the time, Dermot was under a car, working on some guy's brake pads when the news broke. Thankfully, out of view of a few waiting customers and his sons, Dermot had to stop what he was doing, too stunned to believe what he'd heard. A host of old haunts and buried hurts came rushing back, as if they had just occurred. After all these years, he fought to forget Terri. Now, with one solitary, two-minute newscast, he was right back emotionally to where he had started. Never in his wildest imagination would he ever have thought she'd take her life. *Then again, what do I know? I never thought that she would have cheated on me and gotten pregnant by some other guy, either. And I sure as shit never thought she'd murder her parents, even though, from what she had told me, the pair were nothing less than worthless dregs. But still—to kill yourself?*

A lone tear escaped Dermot's eye and trickled down his stubbled, middle-aged chin. Stinging memories now came pouring back. He was no longer Dermot McMahon, successful business owner, husband, and father, working under a car in his shop, but the young, vulnerable Diarmuid McMahon, back under the bleachers behind the football field, the iniquitous day he found out that Terri was pregnant by some other guy.

"We can't see each other anymore," Terri shouted at him, unwilling to meet his eyes, which frantically searched hers for answers. Diarmuid tried to reach for Terri's hand, but she jerked it away.

"What are you talking about, Terri? What did I do?" he pleaded.

"You didn't do anything… I just, we can't… It's over. That's all." Terri's fingers subconsciously toyed with the necklace Diarmuid had given her as a birthday gift.

"That's not good enough. You just can't dump me without telling me why. I love you, Terr. I want to be with you for the rest of my life."

Terri loved him, too, but all the love she felt for him wouldn't change what she needed to do now, this very minute. *I might as well tell him and get it over with. He'll hate me for sure, but it's better this way. He deserves so much better.*

"I'm pregnant, Diarmuid." There. Said.

Diarmuid took a step back, his face registering nothing but confusion. They'd always used a condom. How could this have happened? Finally, he asked, "I'm the father, right?"

"No."

"No—wait, what? That's it?" he yelled "No explanation? Nothing?"

Terri just stared at him blank faced, offering no justification or excuse.

Furious and deeply hurt, Diarmuid began pacing back and forth, running his fingers violently through his hair, unable to put into words the wide range of emotions exploding in his chest. "Who then? Who's the father? Tell me, Terri! I have the right to know!" Diarmuid glared square in Terri's eyes, wishing he could force her to speak, but instead, Terri shook her head no and merely turned away.

Diarmuid's first reaction was to reach out and grab her. Shake her, and force her to tell him why she did this to him, *to them,* but something held him back. Now, all he could do was watch the back of her head as she veered further away, his shoulders sloped in defeat.

"Don't walk away from me, Terri!" he yelled, but Terri never turned around.

An all-consuming rage took hold. Diarmuid began running with no set direction in mind. He just had to get away. The choking hurt seared his throat as tears fell uncontrollably down his face. Diarmuid wanted to punch something, break anything, as a million crazy thoughts bounced around in his head, ready to explode. Eventually, he found a secluded place away from prying eyes and wagging tongues. A private place to stop, sit, and sob.

How could she have just walked away, offering no explanation? Diarmuid was incredulous. No matter how many times or ways he tried to reach out to Terri, pleading for answers, a reason, even an argument, she adamantly refused to speak with him or see him again.

The saddest part was, had Terri given me a shot and trusted in my love for her, I would have forgiven all and still married her.

But Terri never gave his love that chance, choosing to believe the worst as they drifted apart permanently.

Dermot never disclosed to Paddy, or any of his other sons, anything about his past relationship with Terri-Ann Stone. Kendal knew, of course, but not in any detail. All he shared with Kendal was that he used to know a girl named Terri. They went steady until she did him wrong. So wrong, that Dermot could never bring himself to forgive her. Kendal willingly accepted his explanation without hesitation, if a bit too naively, and Terri was barely spoken of again.

Of course, Paddy and the rest of the family had no clue as to why all of a sudden Dermot had become irritable, losing his temper over insignificant issues, even yelling in front of the customers. His foul mood rubbed off on everyone around him. Even Kendal couldn't figure out what his problem was. And then he got worse.

News of Terri's death on the radio had been awful enough, causing his memories to start playing havoc with his heartstrings. Then an hour or so later, Paddy came back from Raven's place, sporting his fetid mood. When it rains, it pours...

Dermot suspected the two lovebirds had had an argument. Thinking about it now, maybe he should have just left Paddy alone, seeing how upset he already was, but hindsight is, of course, twenty- twenty.

"What's eating you?" he asked his son whom he found brooding in the office with the door closed tightly.

"Nothing."

"Doesn't look like nothing. What gives?"

"I don't feel like talking about it."

"Ah, come on, son, what's a dad for, huh? You and your girl have a fight?"

"I said I don't want to talk about it," snapped Paddy.

"One of these days, your mouth is going to write a check your ass can't cash!"

Browbeaten, Paddy apologized. "Raven's mad at me. She hasn't been herself lately. She's still pretty upset about losing her parents and all. That's understandable, and I've tried to be supportive."

"Of course she's upset—what ya expect? It's hard enough to lose both your parents, but that poor kid lost hers only weeks apart. She's gotta be hurtin' something fierce. No wonder she's feeling moody, son."

"I know that, Dad, but now that her sister just died on top of all that, she's inconsolable, lashing out at me, and I'm the one trying to be there for her."

"What are ya talking about? A sister? I thought she was the Grants' only kid?" Dermot naturally assumed like most folks in the town, that Raven had been the Grants' change-of-life baby. Now news of a sister stopped him dead in his tracks.

"She was the Grants' only kid. Raven told me the Grants' adopted her when she was a baby," replied Paddy. "Her older sister is her half sister from their biological mother."

"Ah, I see." Dermot sat down across from his son still somewhat perplexed. He'd been feeling unexplained waves of nausea and dizziness all day. He assumed he was coming down with the flu or an ear infection. "Why didn't you ever tell me she was adopted? Does your mother know?"

"What difference does it make whether she was adopted or not?" Paddy answered accusingly. "I haven't told anybody."

"Whoa, I'm not saying it makes a difference, and watch yer mouth when you speak to me… I'm just sayin' it would have been nice to know all the same…especially because you claim to wanna marry this girl and all. Don't you think your mother and I have a right to know anything about her?"

Nobody would have ever suspected Raven had been adopted, and if she was, nobody would have cared. The town wasn't large, but the couple had stayed to themselves. The rumor mill, for whatever reason, had left them blissfully alone.

Dermot had always liked the Grants. Kind people, salt-of-the-earth types who never had an unkind word for anybody. He respected the husband, who on rare occasions would stop by the shop with his pickup truck—only when stumped, and that wasn't often. They'd shoot the breeze, tinker under the hood for a bit, discuss and agree on a price, never any issues. When the older couple passed away so close to each other, his heart broke for the girl. It couldn't have been easy losing the only parents you ever knew, adopted or not, and only a brief time between. He wondered if people could die of a broken heart.

"I didn't think it was a big deal. Sorry," responded Paddy. "I thought you knew."

"Yeah, well, all right… Gosh, your Raven is sure getting the short end of the stick lately. Poor kid. So now tell me what's going on between the two of you."

Paddy shrugged. "I don't think she cares about me as much as I care about her. It's like she has this wall up all the time. Doesn't want anybody getting close to her. Then at other times, she's the complete opposite. I can't get a read on her. She's driving me crazy, if you want to know the truth."

Dermot snickered. "Yeah, well, welcome to the world of women, son. I still can't figure your mother out half the time."

At that, Paddy chuckled.

"How did her sister die?" asked Dermot.

"She committed suicide."

Dermot's stomach lurched. *Another suicide? What the hell's going on?* "Suicide? Geez. No wonder she's upset!"

"Yeah… I know, Dad, but she's not taking it well."

"Tell me, genius, how does anyone take suicide well? I mean, come on, already? Think."

"Yeah, I guess…"

"You guess?" Dermot shook his head. Kids. "When's the funeral?"

"Ah, yeah, well, that's the thing. Raven doesn't know."

"She doesn't know, or she hasn't made the plans yet? Which one is it?" Getting information out of this guy was like pulling teeth.

"Neither. The prison had her sign some paperwork for the burial when she collected her sister's stuff. Being upset, Raven naturally never took the time to read the fine print and, well, now she's not even sure if her sister is getting buried, cremated, or sold off for medical parts. It's freakin' her out."

"Prison?" Dermot's face turned pale. The room started to spin. *It can't be. It just can't be.*

"Yeah, that's where her sister's been at all this time. She was a lifer, and get this, Dad… Her sister was the one who killed Raven's real mother and her mother's boyfriend. I'm not even sure I understand why Raven had any relationship with her to begin with."

Dermot had to ask, but he already knew the answer. "What was her sister's name?"

"Terri Stone."

A tsunami of past hurts and unresolved anger came storming to the forefront. The shock of realizing his Paddy's Raven was his own heartbreaker's sister, was just too much to process. Dermot abruptly stood up. The chair clattered and almost tipped over. "Let's get back to work," he grumbled to his son.

CHAPTER 15

A BABY IS BORN

THE BED FELT DELICIOUS. Raven twisted her body to glance over at her alarm clock. Time to get up and start the day. The side of the bed where Paddy had slept still held his inviting scent. Pushing her face into his pillow, she drew in a deep breath, already missing him.

Padding her way to the bathroom, Raven stopped a moment to take a listen. The winds outside had finally begun to calm down. Sliding her bedroom curtain to the side, she realized a new coat of snow had fallen as she'd slept. Even now, large snowflakes continued to cascade down to earth, joining the already established growing mound. *Perfect. More shoveling.*

After washing and then donning another old pair of running pants, Raven needed a cup of coffee and something to eat. She wasn't in the mood for yogurt, so she rummaged through the cabinets and disappointedly settled on a bowl of dry cereal. The need to chew and crunch always dictated her food selections much more than any of her cravings.

Raven turned on the television and flipped through the stations, eventually settling on the local news. This station was the one with the goofy looking weatherman who changed hats every broadcast. Today he wore thermal underwear and a wool hat with goggles, waving his hands all over the weather map, blathering on and on about snow.

"Across our coverage area, some snow showers are expected this morning—mainly for our southern viewing sections—then gradual clearing is expected throughout the evening. This afternoon, stronger winds are expected to return, with wind gusts up to fifty miles per hour and the cold front boundary moving southeast. Unfortunately, there will be a continued drop in temperatures after the expected front moves through the area. We'll then return to below normal temperatures. We are keeping an eye on the next system, which is set to arrive early Thursday morning, and for some, that's right, folks—means more snow. We'll keep you posted throughout the day, although we anticipate a tough call in narrowing down actual accumulations expected. Stay warm, stay safe, and if you can, stay home."

More snow. Raven groaned. *I'm so sick of it. Why can't I live someplace warm all year long? Balmy nights, palm trees, the sound of waves crashing into the pier, sandals, the footwear of choice? Why do I have to deal with this crazy, unpredictable weather, freezing temperatures, and Wizard-of-Oz winds?*

She snorted and glared at the table with the still substantial pile of Terri's papers. *Might as well.*

Back to the drawing board she went.

* * *

For over a year and a half, life became wonderfully predictable. The Grants generously invited me to stay on. I didn't know them, they didn't know me, and despite their apparent kindness, I didn't want that awkward feeling of being a mooch, or worse, outstaying my welcome. But then they offered me a rent-free stay in their cabin, even promising to help me fix it up. Mr. Grant decided he'd secure the porch, patch up the loose bricks in the fireplace, and build me a proper bathroom so I wouldn't have to use an outhouse. Mrs. Grant told me there was extra stored furniture doing nothing but collecting dust, up in the attic. I was more than welcomed to it. She also volunteered to sew up some inviting curtains for the windows along with a "suitable tablecloth."

Honestly, I would have been a fool to decline the offer, although at the time, being the untrusting soul I am, I wasn't sure why they were acting so kind to me. I was nobody—a stranger, a pregnant wayfarer who trespassed on their land and into their lives uninvited. At first I kept thinking, what's the hitch? Nothing this wonderful has ever happened to me before. It had to be a scam, right? I couldn't believe anyone would open up their home, whether it was a cabin on their land or not, for a complete stranger. Rent-free? What did they want from me? What would they get out of it?

Putting all my trepidation to the side out of desperation, making the decision to stay wasn't brain surgery. It took me all of fifteen seconds to agree. I was anxious to call somewhere my home. The combination of being both pregnant and broke certainly limited my choices. Secondly, it wasn't like I had anyplace else to go. Nobody was beating down doors to find me; nobody missed me, and nobody certainly wanted to house me. Well, except these two elderly people. Third, and probably the biggest reason I accepted their offer, I was scared. Frightened to death. I had no idea what I was doing and how to make it on my own, and I was at least smart enough to know it. Having somewhere I could call home, even for a short while, felt heaven sent. And if things didn't work out, well, no big deal, right? I could always disappear. I was good at leaving, running away. In this case, though, leaving was the last thing that crossed my mind. While I'm not the biggest fan of God, that day, he did me a solid.

And so, I moved in permanently. I stayed in the big house only until the cabin modifications were complete. At that time, Mr. Grant, already retired, worked all day not only to secure the porch, but to build me a bathroom with a small walk-in shower, as well. While he worked inside the cabin, I began clearing a pathway, nothing fancy, just something to lead back to the big house, plucking up rocks and stones so I wouldn't trip over them. Then I started collecting twigs as fire starters for the fireplace. The days were warm, but the nights sometimes became cooler. The fireplace would be my only source of pure heat come the winter. Mr. Grant told me never to mind about the larger pieces of wood, he'd take care of those.

I can still remember how much I enjoyed working side by side with Mrs. Grant, our hands filled with earth, feeling the cool, fresh soil trickle through my fingers, watching for signs of planted vegetables coming to fruition, and knowing I played an integral part in it. Biting into a sun-ripened tomato or cucumber was mind-blowing. The juices dribbled down my chin. I never knew how outstanding fresh vegetables and fruit tasted. Nothing like the canned swill they serve in this place.

She was not like anyone I had ever met, Raven. Never yelled or called me names. She barely instructed. I was merely told to watch and learn, and that was what I did. Surprisingly, I turned out to be a quick learner, and soon the chores around the farm became rote and a source of comfort.

Without formality, sharing meals together at the house became customary and assumed. Three solid, delicious meals were served every single day without fail. I had never eaten so well. After we ate, we'd divide up the chores. After working together for a while, we established a set routine, knowing individually what needed to get done and by whom. The arrangement was peaceful—no hidden surprises, no lurking threats or emotional baggage chucked my way.

Before meeting the Grants, I resentfully accepted being pregnant, but now I began to get excited to see the little person forming inside me. I'm not saying that I still didn't have to block out the father's existence from my mind, because that goes without saying, but after awhile, that no longer mattered either. I was too content, too at peace to care about anything from my life before the Grants—except for Diarmuid. I missed him. I've never stopped missing him.

Days turned into months, and my belly continued to get bigger. Mrs. Grant stated I "carried well." I didn't know what that meant exactly, but I was pleased to hear it.

Of course, the baby actively kicked and turned the most whenever I wanted to sleep. What a weird sensation knowing a real-life person grew inside me. My child.

Time continued ticking away and eventually my due date arrived. I had begun making my baby a quilt with some of the fabric swatches Mrs. Grant gave me months before. I worked with small, deliberate, and sometimes too-tight stitching that left much to be desired, but in the end, the quilt didn't turn out half bad. And for that matter, neither did the cabin. The newly reconstructed porch with its clean, welcoming planks sported potted flowers, two wooden Adirondack chairs, and a bench. Each window was covered with handmade white curtains, and the wood table displayed the promised suitable tablecloth from Mrs. Grant. In the center of the table, I kept a vase filled with fresh-cut flowers. It was really just a collection of gathered weeds, but was pretty all the same. They made the place feel homey.

Mrs. Grant fixed me up with a small dresser for my clothes, and a thick, soft quilt of my own for my bed. She hadn't been exaggerating when she declared her attic was filled to the brim with stuff, all organized, labeled, and ready for the taking. I teased her that she could have opened a small consignment shop with all the stuff hoarded up there.

Thinking back, I kind of think Mrs. Grant enjoyed decorating the cabin almost as much as I did. She was undoubtedly better at it than I was. Even the way she meticulously stacked the dishes on the open shelving her husband built, or the way she organized the utensils. By her example, I learned that everything had its proper place and was perfectly ordered.

My cautiousness and my natural affinity to immediately distrust were soon put to rest, but only where the two of them were concerned. I'd say within the first week, I felt like I was more a friend than a guest. After a few months, I felt more like their daughter. I guess you, of all people, can understand how special that felt…

As the day crept closer to my due date, the Grants had a surprise for me. We were eating dinner together as usual when Mrs. Grant, looking like she swallowed a canary, was ready to burst.

"Are you feeling okay?" I asked her.

"Oh, I'm all right. We just… Well, your due date is getting closer, and well—"

"Just tell her already," Mr. Grant supportively chimed in, enjoying his wife's enthusiasm, appearing almost as eager.

Glancing from one face to the other, I tentatively asked, "Tell me what?"

"Come with me," she instructed and grabbed my hand, pulling me along. Their excitement was contagious. Together, all three of us strolled outside toward Mr. Grant's workshop, converted from their old barn. In reality, they strolled as I waddled.

I had only been inside once, maybe twice before, but not recently. I knew he preferred to work in there undisturbed. Usually after dinner, Mr. Grant would head off to his workshop, closing the door behind him while we stayed inside to clean up. Once the dishes were washed and put away, Mrs. Grant and I would sit together in the parlor stitching and chatting. A few hours later, Mr. Grant would emerge from his workshop and head up to bed.

Mr. Grant flipped on the light. In the middle of the room, tied with a homemade red ribbon, sat the most precious handmade wooden cradle you have ever seen in your entire life. Next to the cradle stood a matching rocking chair, equally as beautiful, and a small, six-drawer dresser. Attached to the dresser was a small, antique, oval mirror with the loveliest scrollwork adorning its edges.

"Well, Miss Terri, what do you think?" Mrs. Grant asked me.

"They're so beautiful..."

"It's all yours!" Mrs. Grant exclaimed, smiling from ear to ear, clapping her hands together.

"What? All of this? Is for me?" I couldn't believe I hadn't known what they had been up to all this time. "You both made these for the baby?"

"Yes, well, the baby is coming soon," reasoned Mrs. Grant, "and you're going to need a few items to make mothering a bit easier...we just thought that, well..."

Mr. Grant wrapped his arm around his beaming wife's shoulder, lovingly pulling her into his embrace.

"We hope you like them, Miss Terri," he muttered, "and we hope you know you're welcome to stay in the cabin for as long as you like. You're a part of our family now, and well, we'd be honored if you'd call the cabin your home."

Had I not known better, I would say Mr. Grant was blushing. Mrs. Grant, all smiles herself, nodded in agreement, eyes piercing mine, anticipating an immediate answer.

I was flabbergasted. If I had wings, I would have soared. Never in my life had I felt so loved and wanted. "Thank you both so much." I couldn't stop blubbering as I hugged the crap out of both of them. "I wouldn't want to be anywhere else."

Nobody had ever made me anything before.

Living on the Grants' land turned out to be the best decision I ever made. To me, the cabin felt like I was living in the Taj Mahal. No stress, nobody sneaking into my bedroom at night, climbing on top of me, demanding I do...heinous things. But more than that, I loved being loved and cared for, with no strings attached.

* * *

The weather had been fickle the night I went into labor—snowing pretty treacherously one minute, cold and windy the next. The muddy path to the cabin became slippery when wet or icy. At first, I began having a crazy amount of Braxton Hicks. It was decided that the best thing for me to do was stay in the guest room in the big house until the storm passed and the ground dried up a bit.

Smart too, because in the middle of the night, my water broke on my way to the bathroom—all over my nightgown, leaving a nice-sized puddle around my feet. I must have let out a louder yelp than I thought because seconds later, Mrs. Grant came bustling out of her room in her bathrobe to inquire if I was all right. One peek at my face and then down at the floor, and she let out an enthusiastic laugh of her own. "Well then, the dam has burst. I think the baby has decided it's time. Are you having any contractions?"

"A few," I admitted, but after my water broke, they started coming on stronger.

"Why don't you go get yourself cleaned up and ready to go to the hospital? I'll wake up Pop and tell him to get the truck warmed up."

"But my baby bag and stuff are back at the cabin."

"Not to worry. We'll take care of all that. You just get yourself ready to leave."

Thank God they were there to help me. In hindsight, I wouldn't have had a clue what to do next, and I didn't know how I was going to pay for any of this.

Less than a half hour later, we were all crammed together in the truck heading to the hospital with me deep breathing and Mrs. Grant timing contractions. By the time we reached the hospital's main entrance, my contractions were about five minutes apart. They say that with a first baby, it can still take quite a while before the birth, so naïvely, I wasn't worried. At that point, the reality that at any minute my baby was coming still hadn't seemed real. The pain sure was, though. After being checked and asked a slew of intake questions, the nurse settled me in my birthing room.

"This baby sure wants out," she announced.

My contractions were coming hard and fast. "I. Have. No. Money," I grunted through gritted teeth.

The nurse checked my chart. "Hmm, well, says here your parents are taking financial responsibility."

My parents? Just then the on-call OBGYN doctor entered my room.

"Hello!" he bellowed good-naturedly. "My name is Dr. Travis." He grabbed my chart, perused it quickly, and stuck it back in the wall slot. "Terri-Ann Stone," he murmured. "Okay, Miss Stone, I'm going to see how close you are to giving birth. Can you please sit back and try not to move for a second."

My next contraction was a whopper. The doctor picked that moment to initiate his internal examination. "Stay still, please," he barked. "I know it hurts."

I found that hilarious. "Yeah, I bet you do," I sarcastically added.

The nurse in the room held my hand. "You're doing great, doll. Stay still. Breathe. Breathe …"

"You're eight centimeters," declared Dr. Travis, ignoring my quip.

"What does that mean?" I asked through gritted teeth. Another painful contraction was on its way, building up and ready to drive me into the bed writhing.

The doctor blinked, taken back by the question, but he answered, nonetheless. "You're getting close to delivery, only two more centimeters to go. Do you plan on having anyone in the delivery room with you?" he inquired.

Without a second thought, I blurted out, "My parents are in the waiting room. Can you ask my mother, Mrs. Grant, to come inside?"

I know, Ladybug, the nerve of me.

The nurse nodded and left to fetch Mrs. Grant, who thankfully didn't hesitate to join me, sleeves rolled up, and ready to rock and roll. I had to laugh. She was adorable.

"Ready, baby cakes?" she asked me.

"Ready," I grunted back between clenched teeth and audible moans. Those contractions were no joke.

Two hours later, my perfect baby girl was born. You were so beautiful, Raven.

CHAPTER 16

PAINFUL REPERCUSSIONS

PADDY WORRIED ABOUT his father. He had never seen him quite so agitated before. Ever since they had that chat in the office, his dad's face appeared waxy and pale. He had begun snapping at everyone—curt with customers, and tight-lipped with him and his brothers. Paddy peered down at his watch, *almost quitting time*. He intended to spend the night at Raven's again, safely away from his father's glare. Paddy had repeatedly caught his father staring at him from across the shop as if he wanted to tell him something, and then thought better of it.

Last night had been beautiful. The quietness of the shared warmth competed with the onslaught of winds blowing outside their window, while Raven melted into his embrace, protectively nuzzled in his arms. Paddy hoped Raven would leave Terri's letters alone for a few days. She needed a break from the constant misery. Besides, he didn't want her mood to plunge again, not after last night.

Most everyone had left for the day. Only Paddy, his Dad, one of the other mechanics, and a customer waiting for his vehicle, remained. Collecting and storing away his tools for the day, Paddy glanced across the shop just in time to see his father grasping at his chest. "Holy crap, Dad!"

Paddy jumped to his feet, hauling ass across the room, but it was too late. His father, gasping for breath, had already fallen to his knees, still gripping his chest, unable to speak. Just before falling forward with terrified eyes locked onto his son, he made one last failed attempt at speaking before finally collapsing.

"Call 911!" Paddy yelled to the mechanic, the only one left, watching confused from the door. "Dad! Dad, don't try to speak. Just stay with me. Oh, my God, Dad. Please, Dad, just stay with me."

Paddy held his groggy father in his arms, rocking back and forth, gently wiping his brow and begging him not to die. The ambulance arrived quickly, but it felt like ages. Before fastening the oxygen mask onto Dermot's face, one of the medics placed an aspirin in Dermot's mouth, and commanded him to chew as best he could, in the hopes of thinning his blood. Then a glyceryl trinitrate tablet was placed under Dermot's tongue to dissolve while the other medic administered morphine intravenously to help with pain management. Unable to ride in the back with his dad, Paddy stuck close behind the ambulance, gripping the steering wheel. As Paddy's father lay on the gurney being whisked off to the hospital, his son's own young heart raced along with him. Back at the shop, calls were made. The McMahon clan was on their way to the hospital.

* * *

Paddy hadn't meant to ignore Raven's calls, but the whole situation was moving too fast. Questions from medical staff needed answering. His dad demanded his attention, and the pressing circumstances in general were making it impossible to step away, even for a second, to fill her in.

Not much later, Paddy saw through the glass when his frantic mother and brothers arrived. He stepped from the room as quietly as possible and into the hall, greeted them, and promptly filled them in, explaining in muted tones what had transpired up to that point.

"The doctor confirmed Dad had a mild heart attack. The doctor said help arrived quickly, so they were able to start treatment at the shop, which made all the difference."

"Is he awake?" asked his brother.

"He's conscious, but resting."

"Is he in any pain?" asked his frightened mother in a shaky voice.

"They plan on running some more tests, but they are keeping him comfortable," answered Paddy.

Kendal lovingly squeezed her son's trembling hand. He had done his father proud. She glided into the ICU room alone, quietly pulled up a chair, and sat at her husband's bedside. For Paddy and his brothers, this situation was particularly difficult—they had never seen their dad so frail and vulnerable before. Everyone in the family, including Paddy, depended on him. Now, who knew what was going to happen? The whole situation felt bewildering. The entire ride over, trailing behind the ambulance, Paddy couldn't imagine losing his father the way Raven had lost both her parents. He now thought he understood her a little bit better. A tinge of what she had been feeling, the sense of helplessness being the most unbearable of all the emotions swirling around in his head.

Raven! Paddy stole a glance at his watch. Hours had gone by. *Damn, she must be so worried.* "Look, I have to go make a quick call. You guys stay here. I'll be right back." Paddy left his brothers sitting in the waiting room while he made his way into the designated area for phone calls.

With a modulated voice, he called Raven, who picked up before the second ring.

"Hey, I'm sorry—"

"Paddy! Where are you?" They were both talking at the same time. "You first," urged Raven.

"I'm at the hospital. My dad had a mild heart attack. My mom's in the room with him right now."

"Oh, my God. Is he going to be okay?"

"The doctors think so. We'll know more after they run some tests. Right now he's pretty doped up. They have him sleeping."

"I'm so sorry, Paddy… When you didn't answer I thought… I knew something had to have happened."

"Yeah… I knew you'd be worried, but I couldn't phone. I didn't want to leave my dad's side."

"Of course. Do what you need to do. Do you want me to come down to the hospital?"

"Thanks, but not right now. I'll keep you posted. I gotta go back… My imbecilic brothers are here. They're pretty upset."

"I understand. Go back to your family. Let me know if anything changes or you need anything, even if you have to text me, night or day."

"I will… Raven?"

"I'm okay, Paddy." And then, not meaning to she mumbled something under her breath about "how nothing was ever going to be okay again."

"Wait, what did you just say?"

"It was nothing."

"No, I know I just heard you say something else."

"I said it was nothing. I'm just tired. Go."

Raven hung up the phone. She'd lied. He knew she wasn't okay, but she ended the call before he could clarify what she meant.

CHAPTER 17

MARTINA

Terri

SO FAR, MARTINA HAD BEEN coming through, slow but steady. Terri's well-hidden collection of pills was almost complete. Eventually, she'd grind them into a powder and either drink the concoction in one long, nasty gulp, or somehow hide the foul taste in a strong-tasting food. She'd have a way to mask the taste a bit. Her natural gag reflex would mess her up otherwise, but the thought of swallowing forty to sixty pills was even less appealing.

Terri's biggest concern revolved around not ingesting or keeping down enough medication and waking back up in this place, or being discovered too early. Then she'd have to have her stomach pumped and still find her ass back in this hellhole. Even worse was the possibility of being left with brain damage and becoming a vegetable. Her goal of sixty pills was overkill, no pun intended, but she had to collect enough of a supply to guarantee death.

The daily twaddle on the tier mimicked the waves of the ocean. Like the tide, with its ebbs and flows, in came the torrent of arguments and disagreements, and out trailed the infernal retribution and retaliation. Right now, the dingbats were quiet, or what Terri called "low tide." The current batches of troublemakers were safely locked up in segregation for the next thirty or so days from the last search or fight, licking their wounds and swearing life was unfair. A few had been shipped off somewhere else. Terri didn't give a shit which. As long as the pod stayed quiet and the guards kept off her back, life plowed on.

Some women on Terri's tier lived for the drama. She swore these kinds of females wouldn't know what else to do with themselves without their lover spats, name-calling, scheming, and storytelling. Others just wanted to do their time and go home. Unlike male prisons, where homosexual relationships were not sanctioned and inmates were often separated into different tiers based on sexual orientation, the same could not be said for women's prisons, where lesbian relationships were tolerated, or flat-out ignored. The issue wasn't so much the relationship, but the complexity of managing the behavioral problems that those types of hook-ups in a concentrated, contained area inevitably could cause. Issues like petty jealousies, sex-for-drug exchanges, and, of course, prostitution.

Some female inmates were inarguably predators. They had used and hurt people on the outside, and nothing changed once inside. The guards kept an extra eye out for those particular types. Others inmates were just "gate gays," which merely meant their sexual orientation was straight outside prison walls, but would willingly indulge in gay relationships', while inside to satisfy their urges. What boggled Terri's mind was the crazy way some of these women would jump in and out of bed with no forethought or common sense about the possibility of catching hepatitis, HIV, or any other STDs, all of which ran rampant behind prison walls.

Open displays of affection were a gray area. A few of the guards would intervene if they caught two women overtly hugging or holding hands, but for the most part, they most simply looked the other way. Not that the guards were necessarily endorsing the lifestyle, but from a management perspective, if these love connections had the ability to keep the tier and its occupants happy and out of trouble while secured, then what the hell, so be it.

Several guards on the tier made it their business to keep an ear to the ground for any brewing upsets in the making by openly engaging prisoners in relationship discussions. Getting the jailhouse soap opera scoop about which prisoners were exclusive couples, and which ones were now backstabbing each other and sleeping around.

For the most part, life on the pod was nothing more than a microcosm of life on the outside, only magnified by contained dysfunction—a collection of social misfits and harbingers of failure.

Terri couldn't be bothered with any of it. A few times over the years she been broached, but she didn't bite, preferring to stay on her own and out of the mix. Terri wasn't known to pry or get involved. The fact that she was a lifer with nothing left to lose, made women on the tier cautious, happy to leave her alone. Many were simply much too occupied consorting with their own exploits and tricks to be overly concerned with hers—and that's just the way Terri preferred it.

At night, when she would lay on her cot, her mind would inevitably drift off to memories of Diarmuid. Theirs had been a romantic love, innocent and pure. In Terri's mind, his face and body remained young and untouched. His strong, set jawline and prominent cheekbones safe from the ravages of time, his sapphire eyes a welcome refuge for her soul. The tone of his voice no longer resonated within her memories, but the gentle intent of his words did, visiting her in her dreams.

Terri fought off any and all impending thoughts of what his life was really like now, not allowing her imagination to grant him a love outside of the one they had once shared. In her mind, Diarmuid had no wife or partner, nor a house filled with children. His memory existed outside of those norms. In her dreams, he was still only hers.

Terri often wondered if Diarmuid ever thought about her. Did he, like everyone else, consider her a monster? Did he curse her very existence? The hurt on his beautiful face and in his eyes tore her heart violently, recalling the day she told him it was over between them. How could she be pregnant by someone else, he kept yelling. How could she destroy their promise to one another like this, he'd accused. From that day on, they never spoke again.

Fate dealt Terri a lousy hand. Diarmuid should have been her lover, her husband. He should have been the man she'd married and built a life with.

Feeling particularly glum, Terri knew now more than ever, she had to finish her letter to Raven before she could let anything else happen. Anything final, that is.

* * *

Raven hung up the phone, relieved to have spoken to Paddy, but heartbroken to know his father was so ill. The last thing Paddy needed was her personal nightmare dumped in his already full lap. He had enough to contend with, without any added stress.

On the table, the pile remained, taunting her to come back again and ride the emotional merry-go-round. Even from the grave, Terri sure gave one hell of a performance. Raven knew there was little else to do but finish the letter. Curiosity killed the cat, she knew, but there was no stepping back, no ignoring the floodgates forced wide open, and the only viable option left was to let the torrent flow.

The compilation of all the lies and deceit hurt Raven the most, and not only from Terri. What about the Grants? The two people in the world she had trusted the most had blatantly lied to her, even just through the omission of the truth. What Raven couldn't figure out was why? Why did they do it, and what transpired that would convince them to go along with all of Terri's deception? Had they loved Terri like a daughter, the way she claimed, or was it something else, something more nefarious and evil? What kind of hold did Terri have looming over them?

The answers she sought most likely transpired within the remaining pages.

Raven assumed she had no tears left. Perhaps that was a blessing in disguise since there was a whole lot more to this story waiting to be discovered. With Raven now wide awake and anxious, sleep became a lost cause. Swiping the largest chocolate bar from her hidden stash, she grabbed the remainder of the stack and sat back down, determined to get through another few pages before calling it a night.

CHAPTER 18

DERMOT

THE PAIN MEDICATION caused both legs to become weighted to the bed, his arms powerless to lift. Unable to do much of anything else, Dermot rested in his hospital bed, eyes closed tight, feigning sleep. Stoically, Kendal sat by his bedside, absentmindedly caressing his arm, but he didn't feel like talking—not to her, or anyone else. He just wanted to be left alone with his thoughts.

The day Terri told me she was pregnant was shocking enough, but the day I heard she had murdered both her parents almost killed me. And now, I find out she committed suicide while my son is in love with her sister.

He needed time to think. After what seemed an eternity, Kendal finally decided to take her leave. Closing his eyes, Dermot's mind began drifting back in time and place.

How did I miss the signs that she was violent? Crazy? Homicidal? What has to snap inside of a person to make them go on a murder rampage? The heat of the moment? Hate? Terri would never open up to me about her home life except to say that her mother was worthless and her father MIA. She did tell me her stepfather was a creep, but no other details. What did they do to her? I should have known something wasn't right with her. I loved her. I loved everything about her.

I would have helped her escape had she let me into her world. No matter how wrong, I would have helped her. Does that mean I'm just as guilty? Are my hands stained with blood, as well? But Terri never came to me. She never trusted or loved me enough to bring me into her world, her real *world, no matter how convoluted.*

Living with that admission, now as a husband and father, made Dermot sick and ashamed. He'd never freely admit to anyone any of this, ever. But his heart had known the truth all along. The second his chest became tight and his breathing labored, he knew for a fact his heart knew he'd been a fake, guilty as charged.

I let Terri touch me, caress me, hold me with the same hands she used to kill, to murder. I allowed her lips to take me away… To places, I never knew existed, but I wanted to remain holed up with her forever. She took hold of my young heart, filled it with expectation, only to shred and destroy it. I've never understood, no matter how many times I have gone over it in my head, all moments that led up to that last day. I could never figure out why she let another man love her, fill her womb, where my children should have grown.

Dermot thought after all these years he had moved past it. Past her, past the shame, but hearing her name dredged up all the old feelings again, and now he was forced to relive that entire fucked-up chapter of his life. So many times he wanted to write her, visit her, force her to explain, but he never did. He'd tell himself that contacting Terri was akin to breaking his marriage vows, and he'd never go there.

But I guess that's cheating, too. It's bad enough I still loved her, despite everything she did.

I look at Kendal, my wife and life partner, mother to my children. She's been more than wonderful. I have no complaints. I love her, and I care for her, but am I in *love with her? I think she suspects my emotional detachment but never complains, so she's got to be either a saint or a masochist. I don't know which.*

I've stayed on course, faithful to my vows, never swaying from my responsibilities to her or the boys, not once—but she knows. She knows in the way I don't reach out for her. The way I don't confide in her. The way I don't seek her out in the dark. Together we have built our family, four upright boys, strong, healthy, and dependable. Year after year we go through the motions as husband and wife. I think we're what they call, "functional." Our marriage has never consisted of any physical fighting, no name calling—Terri taught me that. She told me that words can hurt more than a punch. I asked her how she knew, and she said she just knew. I never forgot she told me that. I should have made her tell me how she knew. I failed her.

Now my Paddy is in love with Raven, Terri's baby sister. What if Raven does to my Paddy, what Terri did to me? What if Raven has the same capacity to hurt, lash out, or even murder? I can't help it. I know Raven's never done anything wrong, but how can I trust her now that I am aware of who her family is? It's so undeserved, but from now on, every time I will look at or think about Raven, I'll think of Terri. How can I live with that? I know it's irrational, unfair, but Terri's blood runs through Raven. It's poison.

The doctor said I had a mild heart attack. I guess a person can die from a broken heart, if there is such a thing. All I know is, Terri broke my heart over and over again, and finally my heart fought back.

CHAPTER 19

THE LETTER CONTINUES

I KNOW YOU'RE MAD*. Furious. Appalled, even. You want to lash out. You don't know whether to love or hate me. You wish I were standing there, right now, in front of you so you could poke my eyes out. You have been lied to, deceived, and you don't know who's left on this planet that you can trust. You're not even sure if you can believe anything I'm telling you in this letter. I understand. I do. I know because I would've felt the same way had I been in your shoes and just been told that someone like me was my birth mother. But I can explain if you allow me to…*

First off, try not to dwell too much on the lying part. I mean, yes, you were lied to. I'm not ignoring that or playing it down, but instead of considering it is lying, per se, let's think of it as being protected, because that was precisely our intent at the time. We were all trying to keep you safe—not only from the truth, but also from the dire consequences.

Are you ready to listen? I know I don't have the right to ask this of you, but I need you to hear me. I need you to put all your hate for me to the side for a little while longer, just until I can finish telling you what you need to know. Then you can burn or toss this letter away forever, and hate my guts and pray that I reign in the pits of hell. But first, just finish.

So, where were we? Ah, yes, you just found out that I am your biological mother. Aren't you excited? NO? Go figure, but I am your mother. The world as you know it, is not over. That I know for sure. It's whatever you want to make of it, if you have the guts. I didn't have the guts. That's why I'm dead, but let me continue anyway.

I fell in love with you the second the doctor placed you in my arms. Until then, you hadn't been real enough to me to love. Don't get me wrong, I cared about you, but how was I supposed to love you? Up to that point, I had been fighting my terror, scared to death about how I would react and treat you, because of how you were conceived. But all that ceased to matter as soon as I laid my eyes on you and held you in my arms… Your pouty little lips and chunky, rosy cheeks were so perfect. No eyelashes, but the doctor assured me that they would grow in. I remember being relieved. You wouldn't believe how strange you could look without eyelashes.

From the day you were born, you had a beautiful head of thick, jet-black hair. I never expected you to look the way you did, expecting something totally different. Beyond ecstatic, I named you Raven. As a matter of fact, I wrote you a poem called Raven. I hope it's still in this pile when they give the file to you. If it's there after you finish this letter, you'll understand the poem and who it connects you to from your past.

You were a nice-sized baby, Ladybug—seven pounds, eleven ounces. Long, delicate fingers, chunky delicious baby thighs, but no butt.

The delivery nurse in charge stamped an impression of your feet into two boxes and gave me a copy. I don't know what happened to that piece of paper. Another part of your life's history I let get lost somehow.

You were so perfect; I was shocked you came out of me. I never "made" anything so beautiful before. After the nurses cleaned you up, they brought you back to me, bundled in a light-pink receiving blanket, sleeping. One nurse kindly asked me to read my name and identification number while she checked yours to make sure they matched. She nodded, smiled, and then laid you securely in my waiting, hungry arms.

I wasn't the only one besotted with you, you know. The Grants were just as happy—like typical grandparents filled with pride and joy. Everything you did thrilled them to no end, and I do mean everything—even your first poop was cause for celebration.

I bet you never knew any of this. I bet you always wondered what your first two years on this earth were like…if anyone loved or cared about you…if you were wanted or cherished. Special.

And this is another one of the reasons why I decided to write you. Not the only reason, but a big part of it. You see, I never knew why I was born to a mother who apparently detested mothering and then tossed me away. I never understood how my life progressed from terrible to worse to amazing, and then smack back into hell. That's not what I wanted for you... These uncertainties floating around, plucking away at your reserves, and creating doubt where only conviction should reside. At the moment, you may feel alone and vulnerable. That's only normal. I'm dropping a lot of shit on you. But by the end of my letter, you will never again have to wonder or doubt if your real mother had loved you, because I did, and I can prove it.

When I took you home from the hospital, I didn't have a clue what to do with you. I hadn't been around babies, so I studied how the nurses handled you, trying to mimic what I saw them do, but there was more to taking care of a baby than that.

Mrs. Grant knew I was lost. I was always lost, and she wouldn't hear of letting me—no, us—back into the cabin until she had time to nurse me back to health. A part of me thinks it gave her the opportunity to bond with you, and she certainly did that. Her and Pops couldn't get enough of you. I never had to worry about your safety or needs with those two guardian angels. I rested. They fed me back to full strength, and before I knew it, I was feeling like my old self again, ready and excited to mother you.

I guess you'd enjoy knowing a few more particulars, so I'll tell you what I remember. Yes, you were an excellent eater. Your favorite fruit was bananas and your favorite vegetable was carrots. Sleeping, well, as long as you were held, you slept. The minute anyone of us tried to lay you down, you'd scream holy hell. Of course, you hardly ever got put down, so that wasn't much of an issue.

You started to walk early, not crawling for long—I think you hated being on your knees and preferred being outside, except when it was too cold or snowy. You never gravitated to that weather, but during the summer you practically lived outside from the moment you woke up until I put you down for a nap.

You had one of the coolest, addictive baby-belly laughs ever. The warm-up gurgle sound you'd make would turn into a deep-throated laugh that would send all of us into stitches. When you started to teethe, you weren't too bothered. You got moody a few times, but nothing like the books warned me about. Pops would wet his pinky finger just a smidgen and run a little alcohol on your gums to soothe you down. Worked like a charm.

You were a lovely little thing... You still are from the photos I've seen of you. Yes, Mrs. Grant sent some from time to time. I plan on destroying all of the pictures before I, you know... I don't want to take the chance of having images of you falling into the wrong hands when they come to collect my stuff. I couldn't bear to think about anyone using your picture to get off. Sorry, but there are some seriously sick fucks in this place, and I'm not just talking about the inmates.

Where was I? Sorry I keep going off on a tangent, but it's hard to stay focused writing when you know it's your last formal letter. I'm trying to make sure I remember to include all the important stuff that I know has been lurking in that mind of yours. I need to fill up that huge space the best I can with the time I have left.

Oh! I know what I wanted to share with you. I bet you never knew why I called you Ladybug all these years, right? Come on, you know I'm right. As mad and furious as you probably are at me at this very minute, you still want to know. Okay, I'm going to tell you. Your favorite toy was a wooden pull toy with a string in the shape of a ladybug. Pops made it for you by hand while I was pregnant, and gave it to you the day you were born. It was the prettiest toy, all painted in a dark primary red color with big black dots on top. As soon as you could crawl, you'd pull that damn thing everywhere you scooted. I can still remember the clunk-clunk sound the wooden wheels made on the cabin floor. It drove me nuts, but I didn't have the heart or desire to take it away.

I'm sure you've seen the cabin, or at least passed by it a dozen times with Pops. You've had to. It's not that far from the house, although I suspect you've never been inside since I left. That was the Grants' decision, and I abided by it. You have to understand, once I was arrested, I wasn't coming back home. I knew, and so did they. From that moment forward, you became their daughter, and, therefore, their responsibility. I've never tried or wanted to usurp or burden them any more than necessary with backseat parental driver opinions. Besides, look where my views and decisions landed me. No argument there.

If the cabin's still standing, and you should want to explore, I would only warn you that I don't know what exactly you'll find. I never planned on killing anyone the day the "event" went down, which I will explain later. Nothing was premeditated, so I left the cabin the same way I always did before heading out with you for the day. I don't know how time ravished the place, or maybe Pops emptied it out. I have no idea. I never asked. It wasn't my place.

In any event, I assume you're going to ignore everything I just wrote and go inside—if it's even still standing. Believe me, I understand you think you need the closure. You want confirmation, to see if I'm telling the truth, to see for yourself the place where I claim we shared a life together, if only to nail shut that chapter of your life once and for all. I know with every ounce of my being you'll go, because I would do exactly the same thing, and you're still my daughter, like it or not. After all, no matter the distance, the time, or the circumstances, you still have my blood running through your veins. That genetic code has a mind of its own. Am I correct? You don't have to agree.

Whatever you find, or don't, I want—no, make that need—you to understand the cabin was a happy place. We, you and I, lived in peace there. Those walls hold our secrets, the benevolent, healthy kind of secrets. Those walls protected us and watched us as we slept, laughed... And they witnessed how much I loved being your mother. I wish they could tell you themselves.

Happy hunting, Ladybug!

* * *

Nothing made sense anymore. Swirling thoughts crept over and around her. More pages of Terri's letter awaited reading, but Raven couldn't swallow any more bombshells tonight. She'd already had her fill. The whole sordid situation was disgusting. As much as she wanted to divorce herself from it, Raven knew she couldn't, and the more she thought about Terri, the angrier she became.

A few days ago I had been none-the-wiser, content in the knowledge that I had been loved and cared for by the Grants. It never bothered me for one second that I was their adopted daughter. As a matter of fact, I was proud to be called their daughter! What the hell is Terri playing at? How dare she try to steal them away from me? Plug into my life after she's dead. What kind of loose screw does this? Wasn't it enough she took my real mother and father? Oh, God, my father...he raped Terri... I'm a product of rape, and the daughter of a murderer. And now, all of a freakin' sudden, out of the blue, all because she wanted to off herself, she decides to write me this...this diatribe, claiming to be my long-lost mother. Who does this?

"I hate you, Terri," she openly sobbed. "You lying bitch." Raven cried out uncontrollably, her body soaked in sweat, shaking. She couldn't stop. She didn't want to stay. All the weeks of silent mourning and pent-up anger could no longer be neatly contained or repressed. Raven's toxic compulsion to rationalize her losses now knew no bounds. The way she had relentlessly downplayed the impact of her mounting hurts, minimizing the intensity of her rage, and her incessant desire to hide behind a self-manufactured and perfectly distorted reality, now came screeching to a halt. Denial, then shame, and finally guilt, tasted like bile burning in her throat. How could she have ever been connected to a lowlife like Terri? And now, not only was she connected through her as family, she now had to swallow being the product of this murderer's womb. Terri might be dead, cold, and stinking six feet deep or in some doctor's petri dish, but the reach of her vile umbilical cord raged on.

Tonight was the night, and Raven let it rip.

"You're a liar, Terri-Ann Stone! A sadistic, sneaky bitch!" she screamed while punching wildly at the couch pillow. Anyone listening would have thought she was being skinned alive by the piercing wails coming out of every aperture of her body.

But Raven's desperate pain-filled cries fell on empty ears. With clenched fists, she pounded every available surface: the couch, the table, or the wall, until her hands were raw and bleeding. But her agony remained her secret. There were no witnesses to garner her fears or soften the blow. Her crying jag continued until her tears ran dry and her body lay spent. Everyone was gone. She was alone.

CHAPTER 20

KENDAL

KENDAL'S MIND RACED in every direction. Angrily, she paced back and forth across the bedroom floor. Feeling out of control, she grabbed the pillow off the perfectly made bed and hurled it across the room, exerting the necessary care in her rage not to knock anything down. Then calmer, with swollen, tear-filled eyes, she staggered over to where it had landed, picked it up, and fluffed it back into shape. She gently placed it on the bed where it belonged. A battle brewed in Kendal's mind.

Dermot didn't know, but Kendal heard the news on the radio, too. She heard how that Terri woman killed herself, *and good riddance,* she muttered. Terri had been the poltergeist in the room for as long as Kendal had been with Dermot.

My Dermot. Not her Dermot. Terri and her tacit presence, hovering in the background like the proverbial third marital wheel, waiting to pull him back in her clenches, for him to join her. And today, even dead, she almost won.

For the life of me, I've never understood my husband's fixation with that devil's spawn. Adamantly refusing to discuss what happened between the two of them, never opening up or talking to me about her, and willing to get snippy and irritated with me the moment I did. He thinks I don't know, but I've always known.

Kendal thought she must have been delusional in thinking that those silly boyish feelings would disappear. How could she have been so blind to believe that Dermot could be restored and repaired with the endless love and years of devotion she provided? No, instead he's stuck, spinning his wheels going nowhere except on a gurney to an emergency room.

When they had first started dating, her friends warned her and dropped hints about how Dermot and Terri had been a serious thing. But really, who hasn't had some bigger-than-life puppy love in their past? They come and they go, and they feel real while they last, but then they stop. They become a memory. She had never in her life expected Dermot and Terri's relationship to be anything more.

Dermot swore up and down he was a virgin when they married. Told her he and Terri never strayed that far, but she always wondered if that was true. She had her doubts. *Dermot was my first. You'd think that would have counted for something.*

Then they married, raised a beautiful family together, side by side. A team. Up to now, he'd never given her any cause to distrust him. *Sure, in the beginning I'd purposely search for signs, anything that would indicate that I had put my trust in the wrong place, but nothing ever panned out, and I was happy. I thought our life together turned out pretty good for us. We built a respectable life together, a beautiful home, and our business continues to do well. We have kind, upright friends, and pleasant enough neighbors. Our boys seem happy, well adjusted, and content.*

I admit, through the years, I've aged. We all have, but I do what I can to keep myself nice for my husband, and he's never complained. My rich chestnut locks are maintained by the hairdresser's bottle, while Dermot's silky, blue-black hair has become grayer. And at night when we're alone, I have never turned him down. I have never turned my back to his needs or his wants, and I have never given him cause to distrust me—more so than Terri, that's for sure! While other marriages have dissolved, ours has continued to be strong—or so I thought.

Yet, this dreg of society, who probably couldn't bear to live the rest of her worthless life in prison, decides one day, without any warning, to commit suicide. Then out of the blue, Dermot just coincidentally has a heart attack.

I know for a fact he heard the news. Dermot keeps that stupid radio in the shop on the same damn station day in and day out. What other possible reason could there have been to cause his heart to snap to this degree? What else could have set him off? Paddy told me his father had been irritable for the last few days, coinciding with the day Terri killed herself. I blame her.

The minute Kendal heard her name and that she was dead, she thanked the Lord. *Was I wrong to wish her dead all these years? I didn't kill that appalling woman, she did it herself, the coward. Dermot will probably accuse me of being irrational, but my gut tells me otherwise. For hours, I sat and watched Dermot sleep in the hospital, groggy, intermittently opening his eyes only to flutter them shut again, and still without a word to me, or for me. He knew I was there, rubbing his arm, wiping his brow. He knew I wouldn't hesitate to be by his side— I'm always by his side. I thought he'd be by my side too, but all along, a portion of his heart has remained attached to hers. Even dead, Terri has still managed to find some godforsaken way to meddle in our marriage, to take up permanent residence and priority in Dermot's heart. Who can compete with that?*

When we first married, Dermot used to say her name in his sleep. I heard him. Oh, he tried to deny it of course, told me I was hearing things and to leave it alone. "Stop dredging up trouble," he would say.

Kendal would accuse him of still seeing her, still being in love with her, but in response he'd just scowl at her like she was pathetic. Would shake his head and leave her standing there, feeling like a fool. *He wouldn't even give me the satisfaction of arguing with me about her!*

Kendal once thought about going to visit Terri in the prison and meet her head-on, woman to woman. If Dermot wouldn't come clean and tell her about what happened between the two of them that had caused such a long-lasting rift, maybe she would. *I needed to know what kind of person earned such lasting devotion, convincing myself to confront her once and for all, and find out if they still stayed in contact.*

Even going as far as calling the prison to find out what I had to do to get a visit so I could face that bitch. What a joke! The Correctional Department informed me, "Inmate Stone refuses all visits." What a system. Apparently, unless Terri herself placed me on her visitor's list, and Corrections approved, I wasn't getting in. At least I then knew Dermot hadn't been lying to me about that much. He hadn't been visiting her.

After that, with the wind blown out of her sails, Terri became a moot discussion. Pointless really. She was serving a life sentence with no chance of parole. For all intents and purposes, she'd live and die in that godforsaken place, so Kendal decided not to bother worrying about her any longer and put her out of her mind. She pretended Terri didn't exist. *What kind of threat could she still be from inside?* So for years she left the subject alone.

Most of the time, I successfully blocked her out of my head completely, and it seemed, so did he. We proceeded to open the shop together. For a long while, I worked reception and helped with the books until Paddy was born, and then like clockwork, our next three beautiful boys came onto the scene. I was on firm ground. No longer just his wife, but the mother of his children, all of his children, and his life partner.

Lying there, hooked up to his heart monitor, Dermot looked so pitiful and helpless. The doctor believed he had some calcium build up around or in his arteries. *That's no surprise. My husband loves his daily portions of red meat along with a host of other not-so-healthy foods, so why am I not entirely shocked? Still, why now, and why today? I still blame her.*

Kendal stayed with Dermot for hours, not wanting him to be alone, just in case, holding his hand as he had the audacity to pretend to be sleeping. That was her husband's tried and true approach to blocking out the world he doesn't wish to face. Then, without realizing it, he'd drift off into a real sleep with his breaths coming in choppy spurts. It had Kendal nervous listening to him labor to catch his breath.

Initially, I planned to stay at the hospital with Dermot through the night… until he mistakenly began chattering in his sleep. The first time sounded like an incoherent mumble, gibberish. Then only a few seconds later, he muttered again, so this time I made it a point of moving closer, wanting to make sure he wasn't crying out in pain.

Kendal stood over him, her face up and close to his for over a minute. Then, just as she was ready to give up and sit back down, Dermot groggily mumbled again. Stretching her neck, she leaned in even closer, not wanting to miss a single syllable. This time she hit pay dirt. No mistaking his ramblings or whimpers for mere unrelated twaddle. She heard him. Clear as day. With the power of one single, suffocating word blurted out subconsciously her life took a turn for the worst and crashed in all around her. She wanted to choke the remaining breath right out of him.

I never told Dermot, but Terri's pathetic correspondence arrived a few months after being incarcerated. The nerve. The sheer audacity to think she could try and lure Dermot back into her life with her tale of "woe-is-me" baloney. What did she expect him to do? Read the letter, realize he made a mistake marrying me, and rush off like some knight in armor? Break down the prison walls to rescue her like she was some damsel in distress? This is real life you stupid, stupid woman.

Kendal zipped open the bag kept safely hidden all these years. Inside, the infamous letter remained folded in the opened envelope, bearing the prison address and time-stamped postage. Handwritten on the front, evoking a sense of intimacy and history, was Dermot's name in flowery, cursive script.

I should have destroyed her letter years ago, burned it to a crisp, but no! I had to convince myself that I needed it as evidence, proof for the day he got the nerve to confront me about her. I needed to show him that Terri was nothing more than a contemptuous manipulator, a first-rate user, only out for herself. Got herself knocked up by some guy, broke my husband's young, impressionable heart, and then embarked on some crazy, homicidal killing spree. As if that wasn't enough, this piece of demented work decides after she's caught, to rewrite history, spinning her deceitful pack of lies and deceptions in a letter. Painting her as a murderer turned victim. Priceless.

Kendal read that ridiculous letter over a hundred times. *Raped? Give me a break. And by her stepfather, was it? Was that the excuse Terri used when she gunned that sorry bastard down in cold blood?* Kendal don't believe a word that woman wrote. *She's nothing more than a two-faced liar, an emotional parasite, and even six feet deep in her grave she'll always be a fraud to me. I only wish Dermot could have seen through her schemes and lies as easily as the jury had.*

Terri's letter was full of begging, seeking absolution and mercy. All of a sudden, Dermot's compassion and forgiveness were life and death for this toxic woman, but I wasn't about to let her manipulate him again. She was nothing but a scavenger, returning to pick away at Dermot's bones until there was nothing except a crushed, unrecognizable spirit in her wake. The exact condition I found him in when we first met.

It was me *who put him back together, gave him a future and a life, offered him a family free of complications!*

I *was the one who restored him, shielded him, and fed him back his self-esteem with a silver spoon!*

I'd be damned if that human waste of a woman would hurt him again. Not on my watch!

Fuming, Kendal stuffed the rumpled-up letter into her handbag. *The mere utterance of that woman's name makes me sick.* Reaching back into the deepest recesses of her mind, she tried to recall any instance where Dermot gave her any reason to distrust him, but nothing jarred her memory. Nothing stood out. Nothing until today, that is. One word. One lousy, measly, revolting word.

* * *

Paddy, as the oldest son, left his mother last night to tend to his father while he drove his brothers back to the house. There was nothing any of them could do at the hospital except get in the way. Plus, the guys were complaining about being hungry. Not only was hospital food expensive, it was less than appealing. Once back home, they worked together quietly assembling a quick meal, jokingly referring to it as "pasta on the plate." Nothing but plain pasta drenched in canned sauce, but nobody had the energy or wherewithal to complain.

Although late, Paddy wanted to hear the sound of Raven's voice, hoping she wasn't already asleep. She picked up in the middle of the second ring.

"Hey you, how's your father doing?" she asked. Her scratchy voice didn't sound sleepy at all. More like she had been crying.

"Are you okay, Rave?" Paddy asked, concerned.

"I'm fine, just tired. How is your dad doing?" Raven repeated.

"He's stable. They want to keep him for observation and run some more tests. My mom is with him now."

"Did they tell you when he's getting sent home?" she asked.

"They haven't said yet."

"How are you doing? You sound exhausted."

"I am. I'm going to stay here tonight, to help out."

"Of course. I understand. Did you eat anything?"

"Yeah, we made something resembling food a little while ago. Listen, I'm gonna hit the sheets. I've got work tomorrow, and with dad laid up, I'll need to run things—just until he's back on his feet."

"Do what you need to do," she insisted.

"Are you going to be okay? I mean, like with this Terri stuff and all? I'm worried about you Rave—"

"Don't worry about me. I'm a big girl. I got this," said Raven. "You take care of things on your end, and I'll do mine. We'll talk more tomorrow."

CHAPTER 21

THE TREK

RAVEN WIPED HER PUFFY EYES and closed the lamp on the side of her bed, finally willing to call it a night. She fell into a deep sleep and awoke feeling less energetic. The meltdown from the day before left her somewhat lethargic and grumpy. Parts of her body, especially her neck, were stiff, and the headache from the day before teetered on the verge of becoming a full-blown migraine again. At the rate she was going, if she didn't finish this letter business and bury the stress once and for all, she'd most certainly make herself physically sick and wind up in the bed next to Mr. McMahon, hooked up to a plethora of machines, pleading with her heart to forgive her.

Before delving any further into Terri's memories, Raven needed to clear her head. She craved actual hard, tangible evidence to corroborate Terri's side of the story. Concrete proof that confirmed they, as mother and daughter, spent two shared years of so-called peaceful bliss together filled with nurturing memories, and presumably hopes and dreams.

Compelled by curiosity to check out the cabin and see what lurked behind the old, dilapidated façade, Raven had to agree with Terri. If only the walls could talk. If they could, would they, in fact, confirm she was telling the absolute truth?

Did Terri have a true expectation for a future with them together, or was this just her mother's propitious hindsight, or culpability talking? A little exploration might do the body and spirit good.

Outside, the sun shined brightly. Although the wind had died down hours ago, the frigid temperatures caused the top layer of newly fallen snow to appear as sparkly ice crystals, twinkling and giving off a fairytale-like appearance. Raven would need to bundle up. She made a mental note to charge up her cellphone just in case, reminding herself that the empty house no longer contained the two people who would have missed her, should anything happen.

The cabin, if her memory served her correctly, was in close proximity to the house. The trail Terri spoke of making was long gone though. Mother Nature had made sure of that.

Although it was blindingly bright outside, the cabin most likely no longer had electricity running through it anymore. Knowing Pop's thriftiness, Raven suspected he would have disconnected that years ago. She also assumed the inside might be dark and gloomy, so she brought a flashlight and a few extra batteries, not wanting to count solely on filtered light to do the trick. She decided to bring along a few provisions and packed nourishment in the form of her favorite snacks—chocolate, a granola bar, and a thermos of coffee to be exact, along with an extra tote she could fold up and store in her backpack. Who knew what kind of keepsakes she'd find.

After making the bed, sweeping, washing the few dishes left in the sink, wiping down the kitchen counters, and tidying up the living room, Raven was almost ready to get moving. She knew she was stalling, struggling with the apprehension and anticipation of what she could discover, or not. There were no guarantees anything at all would be left inside. It could have been emptied years ago. Weathering and animals would have most likely destroyed what Terri claimed to have left. The last time Raven had seen the cabin, the doors and windows had been boarded up, and that was about a year before Pop had passed away. She decided to bring along a few tools as well, to help pry off the boards.

Raven questioned the wisdom of making this excursion alone. Maybe waiting for Paddy was a smarter option, but there was no telling how long it would be before he could break away from everything he was dealing with right now. Besides, she had already told him she was a "big girl," so time to back it up with action. *It's only a cabin, for goodness sakes.*

Her pep talk did little to abate her mounting anxious feelings, but Raven plowed through and gathered up her supplies, convincing herself that she was ready to tackle anything she found.

Hold up, one more thing. Under Pop's bed, in a small wooden lockbox, was a very small handgun. Pop had taught Raven all about the proper handling of guns growing up, and while she didn't care for them for sport, as a tool for protection they warranted respect.

Raven readied the pistol. She checked the chamber and made sure the safety lock was properly positioned before placing the gun in her belt holder. After locking up the house, she headed out.

Bundled up like the Nanook of the North, Raven trudged outside. After being cooped up in the house for the past few days, she involuntarily shuddered as soon as she stepped out into the wintry freeze, but the bright sun made the cold temperatures feel warmer.

Raven grabbed a shovel, deciding first to clear off the front porch and then the walkway, making a sizeable pathway leading to her Jeep. Her vehicle currently remained buried underneath a nice blanket of snow. Still stalling, she cleared a path for Paddy to park his truck should he be able to swing by later.

Finally, even Raven knew when enough was enough. If she was serious about heading to the cabin, daylight wasn't going to stick around forever. The days were still winter short. She hoisted her backpack and tools, and headed off in the direction of the cabin. As Terri said, it wasn't that the cabin was all that far, but trudging through the snow caused the actual trek to feel more ominous than necessary under the circumstances.

The snow crunched noisily under her boots with each deliberate step. Once far enough from the house, just to the entrance point of the usually dense woods, Raven turned around, intentionally peering over at the farmhouse. She tried to visualize its presence through her mother's eyes when Terri had seen it for the very first time years ago.

Raven was intuitively sure that if this excursion into the past held any answers, she would have to force herself to set her anger aside and wear an entirely different set of eyes. She needed to cast off any and all preconceived notions of what should have happened, and accept with open arms the truths as they presented themselves, unbridled and unfiltered. Raven considered all that her mother had experienced as a pregnant runaway, barely out of her teens, thrown out into the world completely unprepared. Terri had been pregnant against her will, repeatedly violated, and then forced to cope with the uncertainty of every decision.

Much of her anger and resentment from the day before dissipated, back into the ravines of her heart, and was replaced with a resolve guided by empathy. Raven sought an approach that would allow her to identify with the woman who bore her, under a cloud of circumstances still painfully unfolding. When the last tear was spent, Raven pledged to face the authenticity of revelation, no matter what was ultimately discovered. Stepping back metaphorically into time and place, and donning her mother's shoes instead of her own comfortable pair, Raven ventured back into an approximate and encapsulated world that she knew almost nothing about. What about this time had fostered in her mother a feeling of fatalism?

Within a few minutes, she stood facing the abandoned and dilapidated cabin, the porch consumed in ubiquitous decay and rot. According to Terri's writings, on the day she had fled to this place, the cabin had appeared to her as an oasis, precious and inviting. Grabbing the tools from her backpack, Raven warily climbed the three steps up to the front door, cautiously wondering if collapse was imminent under the strain of her weight. Mercifully, the well-built steps stood sturdy, despite their appearance to indicate the contrary.

The boards nailed to the door came apart too easily. Raven barely had to pry, as if they had been placed there to deter more than to keep anyone out. Once off, Raven was able to lift the latch and enter. With flashlight firmly in hand, she pushed the door open slowly, stomping her feet a few times in the hope of scaring away any resident vermin. Placing her hands firmly in front of her, Raven stood still. She needed time to allow her eyes to acclimate for a minute, adjusting to the surrounding darkness, which after a few seconds, wasn't dark at all.

Stepping farther inside, Raven stood dumbfounded, immediately struck by the rustic attention to detail evidenced in the quaint, open space. Everything, from the floors to the walls, remained intact, an inviting blend of stone and wood, all impeccably maintained despite the accumulated layers of dust. On one wall, nothing but rich brick housed the fireplace Terri told of, initially warming herself by that very first night alone. To the back was the open kitchen area with a long-standing wood table and four ladder-back chairs. The middle of the table hosted one large, handmade ceramic jar that had probably held her mother's collected wildflowers.

Thick, dusty white dishes remained neatly stacked on the open wood shelving over the sink and stove. A college-dorm-sized fridge was positioned under the counter. On top of the stove remained a cast-iron teapot—her mother's kettle. Hooks beneath one of the shelves held an array of mismatched teacups. A large can displayed Terri's collection of wooden spoons and spatulas. Raven softly opened one of the cabinets and found an extensive range of cast-iron pots and pans.

From the ceiling hung a light fixture in the shape of a lantern. One small cut-out window overlooked the back of the cabin. She peeked through a space in the slats. Despite all the snow, she could see a narrow creek off in the distance, snaking through the ice and snow in the backyard.

In the middle of the room, an oval accent rug and sofa faced the stone fireplace. A trunk took the place of a coffee table, probably used for added storage. Off in the corner sat a wooden rocking chair. Most likely, it was the same chair her mother had mentioned, and just as magnificent as she had described. What craftsmanship!

When Raven's eyes scanned down, she immediately noticed a large cradle next to the rocker. *Oh my, this must have been my cradle, the one Pop made.* It gleamed with the same warm wood and attention to detail as the rocking chair. Raven stepped closer, fighting back the building wave of tears. She'd mistakenly thought she'd spent all her tears, but she'd been wrong.

Raven carefully lowered herself down on the sofa, still draped in a protective bed sheet. She opened the unlocked trunk. Inside was a clear, plastic, airtight bag containing a beautiful, handmade quilt. Carefully lifting the bag, Raven was taken aback by how heavy it felt. She slid open the seal, air escaped, and the quilt expanded. A clunking sound emerged.

No way! It can't be—but it was. Like an excited little girl, Raven hastily unwrapped the protected gem from inside the folds of the quilt—her ladybug pull toy! Raven let out a giggle, rubbing and feeling the toy with both hands, unraveling the string—still amazingly intact. *I can't believe this…* Something incredibly familiar resonated from the handling of the toy, perhaps buried memories, or maybe just the description from Terri's letter, Raven wasn't sure. All smiles and choked with joy, she set the toy down and pulled it across the wood floor. *Clunk…clunk…clunk…* It was delightfully annoying!

The back bedroom was tiny yet it somehow comfortably fit a full-sized bed, a dresser, a trunk at the foot of the bed, and a braided oval rug. Over the dresser hung a skillfully framed mirror. A petite wooden jewelry box remained on the dresser undisturbed but empty. It sat next to an antique clock and a single-framed photo of a newborn baby—Raven being held lovingly in a young Terri's arms. Raven picked up the picture, held it tightly to her chest, fell to her knees, and wept.

Terri had been telling the truth after all.

The cabin had been a perfect place to live, to hibernate during the cold, bitter winter months. During the spring, when the woods surrounding the cabin filled in, the trees displayed with the lushness of fully draped canopies, the foliage must have lent an air of majestic serenity and calmness.

Raven rewrapped the toy back in the quilt, along with the framed photo, placing them both next to her tote. Outside, the winds were picking up and soon the sun would set. Chilled, Raven gathered up her belongings to head back to the house. She would return another day, but for now, a significant piece of the mystery surrounding Terri's claims had been satisfied. Raven felt ready to face the rest of her mother's letter.

CHAPTER 22

MORE QUESTIONS THAN ANSWERS

BILL, ONE OF THE OLDER, more experienced mechanics, readily agreed to cover for Paddy so he could visit his dad during his lunch hour. Since Paddy was knowingly pressed for time and faced a heavy workload, the visit would have to be short, a quick in and out, but once Paddy saw his dad face to face, he'd feel better.

When speaking with the doctor, the prognosis had become clear. A serious lifestyle change, certainly a dietary change, was going to have to be implemented. Gone were the days of the fatty, fried foods his dad enjoyed far too much. Exercise would be the other nemesis, but Paddy planned to have that conversation a bit further down the road, once everything calmed down and a normal routine could resume.

Last night had been strange. Just as Paddy hung up with Raven, his mother marched through the front door, catching him completely off guard. Naturally, he had assumed she'd be staying at the hospital through the night. This wasn't at all like Mom, to leave Dad's side above all else in a situation of this magnitude. Obviously something serious had happened, but what?

Perhaps the nursing staff had sent her home, wanting her to rest, knowing the hard work would be in the days to come. Anxious to inquire, but smart enough to keep his mouth shut, Paddy remained silent, keeping those thoughts to himself. Besides, it was apparent by the expression on his mother's face that the last thing she needed or wanted was a drawn-out conversation.

"Is Dad okay?" was all Paddy could think of asking.

"He's fine. Resting."

After kissing his forehead and curtly inquiring if the boys had eaten and were already asleep, Kendal made her way upstairs to her bedroom and pushed the door firmly shut behind her. Paddy left her alone. Everyone coped with stress and handled fear in their own way, he guessed.

Non-confrontational had rapidly become Paddy's go-to strategy these days. He found it quite useful under strained circumstances, and for most people, generally underutilized. His new stance of calmness suited him fine, keeping him above the fray, which was where he preferred to remain.

The doctor had also firmly indicated to Paddy that his dad was to avoid all unnecessary stress. Something had been eating at his dad before the attack came on, but knowing his father, he'd never open up to talk about it, tending to play everything ridiculously close to the vest. Dad rarely unloaded his problems on anyone, except perhaps Mom, and those conversations were also probably far and few between. Nope, whatever was bothering him would need to get shelved some way. Paddy intended to skirt around the topic at the visit and see if there was anything he could take off his dad's shoulders.

* * *

Dermot fell in and out of his drug-induced slumber. Incessantly thirsty and confused, he found himself constantly reminding himself that he was, in fact, lying in a hospital bed rather than at home. The strange noises of the machines kept a steady synchronized beat—low whistles and beeps that refused to end. Combining these with a hectic pace outside his hospital door made it challenging to rest comfortably. The tirade of thoughts and emotions running through his mind made his dreams feel more like nightmares.

All night long, Dermot grappled with whether or not he should approach Paddy about his concerns. Part of him wanted to order his son to walk away and leave Raven and her convoluted and consuming past alone. Perhaps he should force Paddy to go far away where Raven couldn't hurt or damage him like Terri had done to him.

Dermot knew blaming Raven for her sister's actions was wrong. He usually didn't abide by the notion of guilt by association, but in this case, he was willing to make an exception. Here, the apple probably didn't fall far from the tree, and his objective, no matter how unfair, was foremost to protect his son. Then again, it could just as easily backfire.

Paddy believed he was in love with the girl. Dermot knew from experience that there was nothing more perilous or obstinate than a young man with his nose wide open. Lovestruck young men became the proverbial bulls in the china shop, knocking down everything and anyone in their way, even at the expense of personal risk. Trying to convince his son to leave Raven would, in all likelihood, have the direct opposite effect, pushing his son straight into her arms. Sir Paddy Lancelot, son of Diarmuid.

Where is that damn nurse with my lunch? I'm starving.

Dermot fixed his pillows, pushing down on the side lever so he could sit up straighter. He was ready to ring the nurse to give her an earful when the door to his room slowly opened.

"Hey, Dad."

"Paddy."

* * *

Today was a new day. Kendal reached over to her phone to check the time, knowing full well she should have left for the hospital hours ago, but she was still too pissed off to show her face. Knowing her mood, she'd confront Dermot and probably send him off into a full-blown heart attack. Still, Kendal was furious. She needed to figure out her plan of action, how to move forward in this life with a man who apparently preferred to live in his past, even if it meant living there all alone. A hard, uncomfortable pill to swallow, and Kendal wasn't sure she had it in her any longer to bite her tongue and look the other way. She no longer existed as a co-partner in Dermot's heart. Terri had made sure of it.

Hearing him utter that name yesterday, that one single, stinging declaration, had brought all the years of hurt scurrying back up to the surface. The humiliation of loving a man who had only settled for you, took its toll. Kendal was tired of being the devoted proxy wife—Kendal, the good wife, the loyal wife. Kendal, the fool.

For years, she had held back, never saying a word, keeping every verbal onslaught contained within, playing conversations and arguments in her head, as well as practiced verses of condemnation laced with accusation. In her mind, she had pretended that once confronted, her husband would come clean and clear the air, beg for her forgiveness and implore her for continued love and devotion. Then, and only then, would she study his face for signs of sincerity and honesty. Then, they could have a real chance of starting a new chapter in their life, but something always had stopped her, prevented her from having the conversation, the nasty, dirty fight. Kendal starkly realized that unleashing the dubious and deeply painful truth would be harder to wish away and ignore than the supposition she had accepted and lived with.

From upstairs, Kendal could hear the ruckus the boys were making, darting into and out of rooms, tauntingly yelling back and forth as they got themselves ready to start the day. Their routine was as simple as it was predictable. First off to school, then over to the shop to put in a few hours, and, in this case, none-the-wiser.

On any ordinary morning, these loud, familiar sounds ironically soothed and thoroughly entertained Kendal. Not this morning. Kendal impatiently waited for the return of silence as the boys and their combined energy only served to jar her fractured, frayed nerves. Wishing they would head out to school already, she lingered in her bedroom keenly listening for the front door to slam shut, easing the demands of parenthood for the next few hours.

Misgivings and doubts swirled around in her head and made a mess of her gut. Was the family she and Dermot had built together all a lie, too? Was she just his baby incubator as opposed to his lover and wife? Was she merely his housekeeper and cook? His maid? The second-place booby prize? How could one little word have such power and stealth to cut through her like a knife?

Over and over, Dermot's murmurings resonated in her head, the noises becoming louder, stronger, and more wounding. One single word held the unadulterated influence to change the course of her life if she allowed it to. That was a big *if*, because if Kendal wanted the moral authority to steer away from her life and marriage, just pack her bags and call it quits, that one single word would be her ticket out. One biting, cutting word seemed to carry enough of a punch to push Kendal into throwing in the towel and turning her back on all the years of marriage and family.

"Terri," Dermot had moaned in his slumber.

The bile in Kendal's throat rose and burned as her heart raced.

And then he'd whispered it again. She'd heard him. No gaffe, no blooper, no mistake about it. Dermot said it. During sleep, in his subconscious, the very place where Dermot held all his protected secrets and wounds, the memories of yesteryear became today—transparent as glass. At that very moment, Kendal knew that had she been holding a knife, she would have had the vile propensity to thrust the blade deep into her husband's chest. Plunging down hard into his heart the way he had just done to hers. *You want Terri, you bastard? Go join her.*

The hate and jealousy were all consuming, and someone was going to get hurt. When Kendal had glanced over at the machines monitoring her husband's every heartbeat and helping him heal, it had taken all her reserve to fight back the reckless urge to unplug him and let him suffer. That sterile, vile, hospital room ignited every evil desire she had ever felt.

That's when Kendal knew, *I have to get out of here.* She needed to run out of that hospital, clear away from the temptation where her irrational state could cause irreparable damage.

I have to leave before I kill him.

Before I turn into a murderer.

Before I turn into Terri.

Blinded by rage and cascading tears, Kendal made the drive home last night only by rote. In hindsight, Kendal couldn't quite remember exactly how she had made it back home, but for her as a mother, the worst feeling came when she opened the front door and saw Paddy standing there. His pale, over-drawn face registered panic, concern, confusion, and then dismay. Kendal saw the merry-go-round of emotions circling her son's face, knowing full well what Paddy wanted to ask her. She was eternally grateful he hadn't bothered.

Kendal loved her sons more than life itself—but at that moment, with anger fueled by resentment boiling up uncontrollably inside her, she had to quarantine herself for everyone's safety. She had to remain behind a locked door where she could restrain her fury and urge to lash out. Burying her face into her pillow, Kendal had cried angry, lonely, heartbroken tears, mourning for a life that only must have existed in her imagination.

* * *

Paddy dragged a chair close to the side of his father's bed, trying not to stare at the assortment of machines and purposely blocking out their combined noises. The stale hospital air and sickly smell made him feel lightheaded. The cushioned, well-worn chair, which must have witnessed many a hardship, felt surprisingly comfortable, welcoming.

"How're you feeling, Dad? Any better today?

"Can't complain. What's the point?"

Paddy forced a smile. "Did the doctors see you yet today?"

"Yup, unforgivably early. They don't believe in letting the ill sleep in this place. I swear, I can't wait to be home already, be in my own bed."

"I bet…any idea when that will be?"

"Doc said as soon as they regulate me, get my medications together, make sure everything is back on track. They want me to speak to some nutritionist. Put me on some new kinda healthy, fangled eating plan. One more thing for your mother to drive me nuts about." Dermot snickered, trying to lighten the mood. "Who's covering for you?"

"Bill, but I told him I'd be back as soon as I could, so I won't be staying all that long, okay? We don't want to get backed up now that you're…"

"Yeah, well…let the customers know I'll be back soon, but only if they ask. Otherwise, say nothing."

"Of course, Dad, I know. No worries, I got this. Just concentrate on getting better."

Dermot stared at his son. He's a good boy. Better than good. "Listen, Paddy, I wanna ask you something."

"Yeah, sure, okay…"

"How are you and Raven doing? I mean, is this a serious relationship between you two, or are you just buying time?"

"What?"

"You and Raven, as a couple. How are you doing?"

"Where is this coming from, Dad?"

"I'm just worried. You're my son. I can't worry?"

"Worried about what? Don't you have enough on your plate without worrying about my love life?"

"Is it love? I mean, or…?" Dermot wiggled his shoulders and head, making that silly face he often did when trying to lure information out of his sons.

Paddy had to laugh. "Yeah, I guess it is—I know it is. I love her, Dad. Not always sure if she feels the same way about me. Still figuring all that out, but I'm serious about her. Why? Why are you asking me this stuff now?"

"Again with all the questions. Can't a father be concerned about his son?" Dermot was hoping the answer had been different, but had assumed it wouldn't be. His son loved Raven.

"I guess."

"Listen, Paddy... Raven's a beautiful girl and all, but you don't know squat about where she came from. Her history...family, important stuff like that."

"What are you talking about now? I know what I need to know. What's with the inquisition? Why all of a sudden are you worried about Raven and me? I thought you liked her."

"No, no, I do like her, but after you told me she was adopted, it got me to thinking. Then you told me her sister was in jail, and I was like, whoa, this is some serious stuff. I'm not sure I want my son involved with all that, you know?"

"I'm not involved with 'all that,' Dad. Neither is Raven. She hardly knew her sister."

"How is that possible?" asked Dermot.

"Easily. They never even met face-to-face. Now, all of a sudden her sister kills herself, but before she does, she writes Raven some long, freakin' letter supposedly explaining all her life shit."

"A letter? What do you mean a letter?"

"I mean just what I said, a mega-long, freakin' letter. Raven's at home reading it and losing her mind, all upset and in tears. It's a mess, I totally agree, but her sister is dead. Has nothing to do with her, me or us. So... Leave it alone already."

Dermot heard what Paddy had to say. He hadn't expected anything different except for the letter part. He prayed Terri never mentioned him in it. "Yeah, well, okay. But if something does come up, you'd tell me, right? You wouldn't keep your old man in the dark?"

Paddy smirked. "You're becoming such an old lady, you know that?" Paddy chuckled. "Of course I'd tell you, Dad, but for now, can we change the subject please?"

CHAPTER 23

AND SO IT GOES

Terri

One month ago

MAYBE BECAUSE OF THE finality of her decision, or the way time deliberately moved slowly behind bars, Terri was losing control. Hyper, moody, and glum; she'd given up writing for a while now, unable to continue. Writing had originally started out as something cathartic, but now as she moved closer to disclosing the details of the murder, too many dredged-up, painful moments of her life collided once again. Each day was relentlessly the same as the last, each minute consumed with mind-numbing nothingness.

The same moroseness washed over Terri whenever photos of Raven growing up arrived in the mail, causing her outlook about her dire circumstances to become magnified and uncomfortably glaring. On the one hand, Terri was grateful for the images, the microscopic slice of her daughter's life that she could easily absorb. They reminded her that with sacrifice, came ease. As wonderful as it was to catch a capsulated glimmer of her daughter, only mere seconds later Terri would emotionally crash, wanting nothing more than to lash out at anyone or anything to make the pain dissipate, make them all pay for the torment she could no longer manage.

Sorrow became magnified with just a simple school photo, just one more emblematic marker of one more year missed. The innocent expression of hope and anticipation plastered on the impish grin of her baby girl's face tugged at Terri's heartstrings. Instead of throwing the photo away, Terri chose to memorize every aspect of her daughter's face, the long, slender, capable young hands; the delicate curve of her ears, lips, and nose. Terri absorbed the way Raven's thick eyebrow arched when she forced herself to smirk. The high-etched cheekbones they genetically shared, along with their oval faces, were evidence enough that she would become a stunning young woman.

Photos of tiny teeth in, then more photos of small teeth out. The precious, toothless smiles of third and fourth grade made Terri chuckle, while the photos of Raven's teen years inundated with captivating expressions left her worrisome, helpless, and nostalgic.

Please, dear God, don't let anyone hurt my baby girl.

Refusing to re-read whatever she had written thus far, Terri wasn't sure where she had left off. All the memories forced to the forefront of her mind caused her migraines to ensue, leaving her in disabling pain, unable to function. Recently, the headaches had become more frequent. A few times, the pain was so unbearable that she had to seek medical attention, which resulted in being knocked out with shots of Demerol.

Besides the headaches, Martina had recently become an added issue of concern. No longer satisfied with magazines and other paraphernalia, she started dropping hints, intimate clues, suggesting that the terms of their former agreement no longer applied in exchange for her continued pill supply.

"You busy later?" asked Martina on the chow line.

"Elaborate," replied Terri in less than a whisper, not wishing to have this conversation overheard.

"Things are getting tougher. I need motivation," replied Martina, smirking coyly.

Terri squinted and backed up a step, expressing amusement. She didn't take Martina seriously until she saw Martina was not laughing along with her.

"Seriously?" mocked Terri.

"Like a heart attack."

Terri was surprised at first. Martina's time was short, drawing to a close, so why all the sudden urgency to demand anything? It didn't make sense.

At the same time, Terri was street smart enough to know not to brashly brush off a person like Martina, anticipating how the repercussions of such a rash response could backfire if Martina worked herself into a snit. The petty way women handled their manufactured broken hearts in jail was epic, and Terri certainly didn't want to draw unwanted attention. So far, she'd been able to placate her, but that wasn't going to work for much longer. She only needed a few more weeks.

Lips pursed, trying to come up with a way to placate Martina without insulting her and sending her off into a tirade, Terri filled her food tray and whispered against the nape of Martina's neck , "I have some stuff to wrap up. We'll talk."

Martina nodded knowingly and strode away, triumphant.

Terri's mind raced. She counted up the pills in her head, questioning if she had enough to do the deed. Or did she still need Martina's supply to keep coming? Terri wished she had someone to confirm about the lethal dosage. From all that she had read, Terri knew the answer was *probably* yes, but she still wasn't absolutely convinced. Not yet. She still needed Martina's help.

* * *

Terri suspected that once Raven read the part about her being her daughter and not her sister, all hell would break loose. *If she's anything like me, she'll become reactionary, a real spitfire; but hopefully nothing to get her into any long-lasting trouble.* That was the last thing Terri wanted for her daughter.

The time to explain to Raven exactly what transpired that final day had arrived, the day of the murders. The day her life, in effect, had really ended.

A large part of Terri wanted the whole story swept under the carpet, let dead dogs lie, but the need to be vindicated felt all consuming. If nothing else, she just wanted her daughter to know the truth. Nothing else mattered now. At the same time, it wasn't as if Terri was ever going to leave this place excepting in a pine box, and she knew and accepted her lot, but still.

Nevertheless, Terri understood her time was drawing to a close. She needed to finish this letter to Raven and end the nightmare life she had procured. Fighting off the creeping shadow of depression and anxiety, Terri sat back down at her makeshift desk and began to once again put thought to paper.

And so, the story continued.

Dearest Ladybug,

My time is quickly drawing to a close. Life behind this concrete cement wall has destroyed my ability to function. I no longer have it in me to fight to survive, merely to continue to exist without little else to look forward to. All the daily nonsense I have endured has finally gotten to me. It won. But before I do anything permanent, more than I already have, I need to wind this whole letter thing up with you. Fast track my writing, gather my thoughts, release my deepest held recollections, and stamp away my trepidation. Finally flush away all that has kept me from finishing.

I took off a few weeks from writing, and that wasn't too bright, but I just couldn't face my truths without becoming immobilized. It's hard to explain, but writing to you like this has stripped me bare of my deepest, most private thoughts, the one part of me that nobody could lay claim to. Yet here I am, willingly exposing myself to you. The weirdest part is that even as I write, I have to remind myself that by the time you read all this through, I'll be long gone, along with all my troubles. The choice to die and the finality of my decision is what has kept me motivated to finish—that and my overpowering desire to tell you the truth before I die.

This letter is my legacy to you. It is my living will. It is my atonement and my apology. It is my history and my future, and now, it is your truth. Everything I write to you is as accurate as I can fathom from my own, highly damaged and skewed memory. My hurt does not cancel or sway the absolute truth and validity of all I have experienced, but it will most certainly explain the added drops of lethal venom.

So, here I go, back into the den of horrors, and regrettably, I am taking you with me.

You know how I've already explained how living with the Grants had been storybook perfect? And how I told you how the Grants were more like parents to me than landlords? Well, over time, our relationship seamlessly grew stronger until, despite the missing DNA, we were what could only be described as a legitimate family. We lived in familial peace, each one enjoying the others' company, all of us madly in love with you.

You were a wonderful baby. You were easy to please, with a pleasant disposition, healthy appetite, and strong constitution. I think your personality was rounded out by the combination of fresh air and the undivided attention you had from three doting adults, all of whom never tired of showering you with love. Your birth gave us all a purpose. For the Grants, you filled a dark, empty void. For me, you were an oasis, the culmination of all that was unblemished in me. Almost two years flew by, and I can honestly say they were delightfully drama-free. Until the call from my real mother came…

I had assumed all along the old hag knew where I was staying, but up to that point, she hadn't made any effort to contact me, nor I her. There was nothing left to say. When she had the chance to defend me, stick up for me, and show an inkling of mothering, Winnie didn't give one rat's ass that her slimy, degenerate boyfriend had raped and impregnated me. She never so much as intervened, so honestly, what else was there left to discuss?

How she eventually found me, God only knows, but my narcissistic mother circumvented me by calling Mrs. Grant, carping on and on about needing help. Claimed she had some form of unpronounceable cancer, and her last dying wish was to speak to me and make amends before it was too late. That diabolical psychopath laid it on thick, and Mrs. Grant, being the kind-hearted, naïve soul that she was, readily agreed to take me over to see her one last time.

Personally, I wanted to back out. I truly did, but I couldn't stand seeing Mrs. Grant looking so disappointed in me when I told her I'd rather get a lobotomy. She told me making peace with my mother was my duty, and that only through forgiveness would my healing start. Knowing this was a losing battle, I reluctantly agreed—something I should never have done. However, the deal was that Carl wasn't allowed to be present; but since when did my mother keep her word, right?

I should have ignored all of Mrs. Grant's pleadings and disapproving looks and trusted my sixth sense about staying away from that vapid, self-serving mother of mine. I guess I had gone soft over the two years being away from her and all the crap that came with her, more forgiving, secure, and at peace with myself—or maybe I was just so happy and content finally that I didn't think that there was anything left for the old crow to do to me. I may have thought that by agreeing to see her this one last time, that somehow that chapter of my life would be forever shut, and I could finally be afforded the closure I craved. Big mega-mistake.

Pop wasn't a happy camper. He didn't like the idea of any of us making the visit, not one bit, and he and Mrs. Grant exchanged hushed heated words. It was the first time I ever saw him on the verge of losing his temper.

"I'm telling you, I can feel it. This isn't a good idea," he snapped.

"I understand that, but she's still her mother, and Terri needs to decide for herself how she wants to handle the situation," explained Mrs. Grant.

"Who knows what the two of you could be walking into? The woman is pure evil. Terri told us she ran away, but you and I both know that woman threw her own blood out into the cold. What kind of mother does that, and then waits two years before calling to see her again?"

"Again, I understand all that, but maybe this will finally give Terri the closure she needs."

"Closure? The girl doesn't need closure; she needs to be left alone!" hissed Mr. Grant. "Terri's been doing fine without supposed closure." Pop's face was pained, but he knew it was a losing battle. "I'm going with you."

"That's not necessary. I'll be there to make sure nothing happens. I promise. If anything goes wrong, I'll grab the girls up and head for home."

Mr. Grant didn't like what he was hearing, but he reluctantly agreed. "I want you two back as soon as possible, and if anything pops off, you know what I keep in the glove compartment in the truck. As a matter of fact, keep it on you—just in case."

"I do, and we will... Stop worrying so much. I doubt this reunion will even take very long."

Take my word for it, Ladybug, if anyone should ever try to harm you, don't ever be as naïve as I have been. Don't believe that time can produce some kind of miracle and make a person change, because they don't. They never do. People remain the same shitheads they always were, and there's not a damn worth of anything that you can do to change that. Just go on with your life and leave them to the mess they created.

The next day, we headed over. I dressed you extra cute. I wanted my mother to see how beautiful you were, and what a great mother I was, despite being spawned by her. I also wanted this woman to feel in the pit of her alcohol-infested stomach, a trouncing for not being allowed by fate, or me, to be your grandmother. Show the old slush just how little I wanted her in our life, cancer or no cancer. I know, not very charitable of me.

In the car ride over, you had fallen asleep. Gosh, you loved to nap any time you got in the car or truck. I think movement made you feel peaceful because as soon as we were five minutes down the road, you'd inevitably fallen deep asleep.

I remember the weather being unseasonably warm that day. We had the windows rolled down. The sun was out in full force, and the smell of cut grass permeated my senses. I'm not sure why I'm telling you about this ancient weather report now, but whenever I think back on that fateful day, the weather and temperature always play a big part in my memory. For me, warm sunny days with the smell of fresh-cut grass now burns my nostrils with the recollection of the stench of blood and feces. I digress.

When we pulled into the driveway, my adrenaline was at an all-time high. My anxiety was kicking in, causing me to feel lightheaded. I almost told Mrs. Grant to forget the whole thing, but I didn't, more out of not wanting to disappoint her rather than fulfilling any so-called deathbed wish scam my mother had devised.

Carl and my mother lived way back off the main road, farther into the woods. They didn't have the amount of land the Grants did, but the closest neighbor to them was a lengthy hike away. The next town over was a shorter trip in the opposite direction if you cut through the woods. We decided to purposely park the truck on the gravel road, facing the direction of leaving, rather than in the driveway. I mentally needed to know we could leave at any time, unimpeded.

Mrs. Grant waited in the truck, explaining to me how she didn't want to impose on the mother-daughter reunion. Ha! I wouldn't have described it that way, but whatever.

I unstrapped you from your car seat, still fast asleep, grabbed the thin car blanket, threw it over my shoulder, and trudged my way to the front door.

The front door had seen better days. Paint scraped away in high-usage areas, and the walkway leading up to the three cement steps betrayed a trail of old, used cigarette butts strewn about.

I knocked. No answer.

I knocked again, but louder. No answer. Winnie knew I was coming. The visit had been her idea.

I glanced back at Mrs. Grant, who was making some cockamamie hand signal to knock one more time, but louder this time. I did.

From inside, I heard a stirring and a dull, thumping stagger coming closer to the door. Why I didn't take this as a signal from the heavens above to turn around and go home remains for me the million-dollar question.

"Who is it?" Winnie demanded.

"Me."

A latch on the door lifted and the door opened just a bit, only wide enough for a sliver of my mother's old, worn-out face to appear through the crack.

Winnie had aged poorly from years of drug and alcohol abuse. Her eyes were permanently bloodshot, and wasted. She took one long, fixed stare at me, then a disgusted gape at you sleeping in my arms. With pursed lips, ridged tight with wrinkles of a lifetime smoker, she flippantly lifted her shoulders as if to say "what the heck," and opened the door the rest of the way.

"You might as well come in," she garbled, struggling to sound coherent. That was my mother—already sloshed by noon.

The living room was dark, so it took my eyes a few seconds to adjust and for me to get my bearings.

"Where can I lay the baby down?" I asked her, already wishing I had left you in the truck with Mrs. Grant.

"I don't care, put her wherever you want."

So I strode my way over to the sofa, but it took only one glance to see how filthy and grimy the cushions were. In all good consciousness, I couldn't lay you down on that nasty couch, blanket or not, so I headed to my old bedroom instead. There, I laid you down on my bed, which surprisingly appeared unused and unsoiled. Using whatever pillows I could find to box you in, crunching up the bed blanket to make a retaining wall around your peaceful, sleeping body. You tended to roll when you slept, and I didn't want you to fall.

Once I had you set up safe and sound, I returned to the living room, wanting to get this absurd meet and greet over with as rapidly as possible, but Winnie was gone. Sounds of clanking glass and ice were coming from the kitchen. I found her pouring herself something to drink.

"You asked me to come. I'm here," I declared, already past pissed off.

"So you are."

"You told Mrs. Grant that you were ill with cancer. Is that even true?"

"It will be eventually with the way I drink and smoke," she guffawed, finding herself highly amusing.

"So you lied. Big surprise. Just one of your pathetic ruses to get me here. So what do you really want?"

"Get down from your holier-than-thou pedestal, Terri-Ann. Don't come in here, in my house, trying to sermonize me."

"What do you want?" I demanded between gritted teeth. I was in no mood for her shit.

"I need money."

I laughed. "Of course you do. Well, sorry to disappoint you, but I don't have any. Guess this visit was a bust."

"You owe me!" she yelled, slamming her fist on the kitchen counter.

"I owe you?" I yelled back even louder. She no longer frightened me. "How do you figure that?"

"After what you did with Carl, throwing yourself at him, tricking him, getting pregnant and all. It's disgusting."

"Oh, for fuck's sake, you've got to be kidding me." I was heated, and the tensions were quickly escalating. "You think I owe you for what that degenerate rapist boyfriend of yours did to me? You're out of your mind. NEVER GONNA HAPPEN!"

"Ha—rape? That's a laugh." Then she staggered closer to me with hot, stank breath, pointing her gnarled-up bony finger in my face and spewed, "Oh, you'll give me the money all right."

"Oh, yeah, fat chance."

"You won't be singing that stuck-up tune of yours for long. You'll give me some money or I'll have Carl sue you for visitation! He has rights, ya know."

At that second, Ladybug, a burning, hate-filled fervor shook me to the very core of my being. The thought of letting Carl anywhere near you drove me momentarily insane. I shoved her back with all the force I had and she lost her balance, almost toppling over. "CARL WILL NEVER SEE OR COME CLOSE TO MY DAUGHTER," I screamed. "Do you understand me? NEVER!"

I tried to leave the kitchen, but somehow, despite being drunk, Winnie moved fast enough to reach out and grab hold of my arm, forcibly yanking me back. "Yeah, you think so Miss Know-Nothin'? He's got father rights, and the courts will agree with me. He'll take one of those fancy DNA tests, prove he's the daddy, and there won't be a damn thing you can do about it!"

I pulled, trying to snatch my arm away from her clammy grip, as she kept cackling and goading me. "You can run away," Winnie sadistically taunted, "but if you don't give me my money, and I mean monthly payments, that baby of yours will be mine and Carl's. You can count on it!"

That was it. I snapped. Just as I lifted my free arm to smack the smirk right off that witch's face, a loud, ear splitting gunshot blasted off down the hall, coming from the direction where you were sleeping. Then just as rapidly, another shot fired right after. I pulled away and took off running with the lush at my heels.

"Oh, my God, Raven! Raven!" I kept screaming your name as I bolted to the bedroom door, but just as I tried to run in the room, I found Mrs. Grant blocking the doorway, still holding her gun. Lying sprawled out on the floor in a pool of his escaping blood, was Carl.

"Oh, my God!" I screamed as I pushed past her. "Is he dead?" I already knew the answer.

You were so frightened, Raven. Hysterically crying, reaching out your chunky arms to me for safety. Your little eyes like half dollars, wide open. I swooped you up, wrapped you in your car blanket, and nuzzled you close to my chest. The bib of your sundress was marked with Carl's blood splattering. I checked your tiny body for any wounds while holding you tightly in my embrace, still not sure as to what the hell was going on.

Mrs. Grant stood, dazed. "I heard a bunch of yelling and screaming from the truck," she stammered, her voice dead and hollow. "I thought somebody was going to get hurt, so I came inside to get you and the baby. Then I heard you and your mother arguing. I just wanted to get the baby and put her back in the truck…when I found HIM over her—with his fingers..."

Just then, my mother started screaming. "YOU FUCKING OLD CRAZY BITCH! YOU KILLED HIM! YOU KILLED MY CARL!"

"Shut up!" I yelled back at her. "SHUT THE FUCK UP!"

Mrs. Grant stood shaking, but still unable or unwilling to let go of the gun. "When I got to the room, he was standing over the baby, his fingers diddling in her diaper, his belt buckle undone."

My eyes immediately darted down and sure enough, Carl's good luck belt was unfastened. That sick, low-down dirty bastard.

"I had to stop him; I had to…"

"I'm calling the police!" my mother shrieked. Winnie turned to make a run for the phone, but Mrs. Grant spun around first, and without the slightest hesitation, she fired off two more shots point blank. Right through my mother's back, either piercing the heart or hitting a major artery. Either way, she collapsed, falling forward, immobilized; I assumed she was dead. Blood splattered everywhere, and on everything. It was a horrendous scene.

You were still in my arms, crying hysterically. I was shaking. Mrs. Grant remained fixed in the doorway, but finally lowered her gun. I couldn't believe what had just happened.

"I heard what your mother was threatening you with, Terri," Mrs. Grant told me matter-of-factly. "What she was promising to do. I couldn't let her hurt you or Raven again. I couldn't," she choked out. "I walked in to get the baby and that man was going to… I saw him. Standing over Raven. I had to stop him. I just had to stop him before he..."

And that's when I made the decision that changed our life forever, Ladybug.

There comes a pivotal time in everyone's life when they will be tested beyond measure. When their back will be flung up against a wall and they will have to face a decision that could either change, or severely alter, the course of the rest of their existence. And no matter how much you try, you can never plan for it. You can't say, "Well, I'd do this" or "I'd do that," because until faced with whatever it is, you have no idea what you'll do. For me, in that split-second of time, my test was awaiting my answer, and for once, without any dithering or uncertainty, I knew what needed to be done.

"Put the gun down now. On the bed," I ordered Mrs. Grant. "Take Raven. Get in the truck, and go back to the house. Clean her and yourself up. I want you to get rid of the clothes and the baby's blanket. Whatever you do, don't let Pop see you. Burn your dress and everything else you two are wearing, but not today. Bury it all for now, in the woods by the cabin, cover it up where nobody will find it or go looking for it."

"But what will I say to Pop?" she asked pleadingly, still in shock. "I've never lied to him before."

"Don't tell Pop anything, do you hear me? Make something up. Wait. I know. Tell him I decided to stay over. I needed time to rekindle my relationship. Make up anything, but whatever you do, nobody can ever know what happened here. NOBODY! Nod that you understand me."

"But, Terri, we have to call the police. I just killed two people."

"No, YOU didn't. I'll take care of this. Promise me you'll take care of Raven no matter what happens. PROMISE ME!"

"But, Terri!"

"PROMISE ME, PLEASE!"

"But—"

"There is no 'but.' Not this time. As God is your witness, just promise me, please!"

She nodded solemnly, still in a daze, unsure what she was making a commitment to.

"PROMISE ME! Say it."

She nodded, eyes cast down. Reluctantly agreeing, still too stunned to argue back, she choked out, "I promise, as God is my witness." For Mrs. Grant, it would be the hardest promise she was ever forced to keep.

"You need to trust me. Go straight home. Now. You and Raven. Go back. And no matter what happens, no matter what anybody says or does, you made me a promise in front of God. Do you understand? Now give me the gun," I demanded.

Mrs. Grant gingerly held out the gun, squinting with confusion.

"Whose gun is this?" I asked, taking the gun away from her before she shot anyone else.

"Pop's. I took it just in case. He keeps it in the glove compartment."

"Are you sure? Does he always keeps it in the glove compartment?"

"That man was going to hurt Raven, Terri. I couldn't let him hurt Raven."

"I know, I know… Does Pop keep the gun in the glove compartment—all the time?" I needed confirmation.

"Yes, I think so."

"SHIT! You think so? Okay."

I checked and saw two rounds left in the chamber. "Take Raven and go."

Mrs. Grant took you in her arms, but she couldn't stop glaring at the carnage, so I yelled, "NOW! GO! Get the HELL OUT OF HERE! Please."

"I can't leave you here. I need to call the police. They will understand. This is my fault. I'll tell them, I'll explain."

"No! Don't call anyone. You have to listen to me and do as I say. Take Raven home with you. I will take care of everything here."

"But how? I can't leave you..."

"You need to trust me," I pleaded. "Like I have always trusted you."

I watched as she grudgingly strapped you into your car seat. I can still remember the way you refused to let go of me, screaming, "Mama, Mama" as I forcibly pressed you into Mrs. Grant's arms. Your tear-streaked face peering out the backseat window, searching for me.

And then you were gone.

In the backyard, Carl's worthless hound continued barking, wildly jumping, but thankfully still chained securely to the fence. My mind was racing. I had to cover up the crime. Trying to think up ways to throw off the police, I bolted outside with a dirty plastic bowl from the sink and collected as much fresh, mushy dog shit as fast as I could. I was careful, making sure not to get too close to that motley, fire-breathing beast who kept pulling at his chains to get at me. Once back inside, I opened the fridge and grabbed a bottle of ketchup and pancake syrup too. Don't ask me why—who thinks straight with two dead people lying in the next room?

I wiped down the gun like I'd seen done on television, as well as any area in the house I thought Mrs. Grant could have touched coming inside. Then I began throwing dog shit, ketchup, and pancake syrup everywhere near the bodies. On every single door handle including the front door, coating every surface I could find, including Carl, my mother, and the gun. Then I rolled Carl onto his back, using my foot as a lever. His dead weight made budging him easier said than done. Once finished with him, I dragged my mother by her arms into the room, turned her over as well, laying her bloody body next to his. With the now goopy, tacky gun in my hands, I fired one last time between Carl's splayed-out legs, purposely pointing at his balls, making sure the gun residue was now on my hands.

Fighting off waves of nausea, I gingerly placed the gun between Carl's legs. Covering my already stinking body with the sticky, warm blood from the both of them, I frantically scanned the room to see what else I should do. I immediately made up my mind and pulled the blankets and pillows from my bed, tossing them haphazardly around the room, making doubly sure to sufficiently cover them in blood and crap as well. By then, the waves of nausea that had been welling up inside of me won out, and I threw up all over the dead bodies—the cherry on the cake.

I honestly contemplated emptying the fridge of all its condiments, creating a regular visual smorgasbord of revulsion, but exhaustion overtook me. In spite of this, enough time had gone by, leaving me somewhat confident that the police hadn't been alerted. I sat in the kitchen on a stool instead, and waited for about an hour, giving me a chance to clear my head and collect my thoughts.

When it felt like the right amount of time had passed for me to safely take my leave, I left the house of horrors and began my journey. I trudged first through the surrounding woods as slowly as possible to provide Mrs. Grant more than ample time to return home. She needed to get both you and herself cleaned up and settled before the spectacle of turning myself into the authorities commenced.

The adrenaline that had kept me pumped and moving up to that point had all but dissipated, but surprisingly, so had my anxiety. As insane as this sounds, while plodding through the woods, the peacefulness and openness of my surroundings allowed my mind to bounce off the strangest collection of topics. Random thoughts and indiscriminate pondering filled my head about stuff I've read or heard. For example, did you know that adrenaline is a hormone? I read how it's secreted by the adrenal gland when a person gets stressed, angry, or frightened.

I began to wonder if the hanging leaves above in the trees knew when their time was up. Did they have a clue as to when they would fall to the ground, and if so, did they fully comprehend how detachment from the branch that helped nurture them meant certain imminent death?

I even thought about how, in all likelihood, this final walk alone would probably be the last time I would hike these woods. The last time I would hear the crunch of dried leaves beneath my step and feel the free, clean air sweep gently across my face.

A rush of complicated, mixed-up thoughts rushed through my head. Despite what I had just witnessed and willingly participated in, I distinctly recall thinking at the time how weird the mind works.

It was sort of the way my mind would behave when Carl would corner me. He'd be on top of me, pounding away in his sick, demented little world, as my mind would switch off, whisking me into protective mode, sending me blissfully elsewhere. Off I'd be sent, transported far away, gone, someplace else, thinking up all kinds of really obtuse, strange stuff until he was through with me. Believe it or not, despite the fact that I was hiking through the woods covered head to toe in blood, ketchup, dog shit, and pancake syrup, I remembered feeling liberated. Exhilarated. Free from the terror Carl had been permitted to perpetrate upon me, and also from the horror my mother had so cruelly inflicted upon me all those years.

During the rather long and arduous trek, I concocted my story. My plan was simple—I'd keep my mouth shut and wouldn't say much of anything. I'd stay as quiet as possible and try to muddle my way through the inevitable as best as I could. I find it's the lying and scheming that can foul you up more than anything else. It gets you busted, and frankly, after a while all the lies become impossible to keep straight. You're bound to mess up, become confused, and I couldn't afford to let that happen. I wouldn't let Mrs. Grant take the fall for killing those two worthless pieces of shit, and for what? Protecting you, my baby girl, like a real mother would and should? She saw you were in danger and never hesitated for a second, Raven. She wouldn't let Carl do to you what he had been allowed to do freely to me. She did what my real mother failed to do.

Mrs. Grant did what she had to do to protect my baby. There was no way in hell I was going let the judicial system put this sweet soul through a legal maze that endorses, by proxy, filth like Carl and Winnie to exist and commit unspeakable atrocities unimpeded! I would not allow her to be humiliated or punished for standing up to MY abuser, something that should have been done long ago. To hell with that!

There was no evidence of my past rapes. Besides, I knew Pop wouldn't have been able to live a single day without her. As tough as he pretends to be, his heart remained unfaltering in hers. No matter how cute, old, and innocent she may have appeared at the time, they would have thrown away the key just like they have done to me.

And in truth, you needed the two of them in your life more than you did me, Raven. I was, and will always be, damaged goods, marked as the wounded and walking dead. I owed them both my life, and as far as I was concerned, the time to pay off that debt had arrived.

Once out of the woods, I knew it was only a matter of time before I was going to be arrested, charged, and found guilty of the murders of Carl and my mother. I planned on freely admitting to the killings, but decided to plead not guilty because I didn't feel remorse. I also planned, if pushed, to explain how I did them, and the world, an enormous favor by getting rid of those two worthless pieces of scum. I hoped that these outlandish kinds of statements would keep the police focusing their investigation in my direction, and never suspect what had really transpired. At all costs, I had to protect the Grants and keep you, my baby girl, safe. Not the brightest plan, but the only one I had.

Finally, when I reached the edge of town, I said a little prayer to the man upstairs, apologizing for what I was about to pull. I ambled across the road like I was walking to my doom. Heading toward the old town church, I plunked my weary ass on the steps, waiting for the extravaganza to begin, and I didn't have to wait long. After about ten minutes, I saw the preacher turn the corner, holding a bag of groceries. At first, he didn't acknowledge the apparition covered in blood sitting on his steps, but as he neared and began to climb past me, he did a double take. From the corner of my eye, I saw his face drain and his brow scrunch up. I suppose the gruesome scene failed to completely register, because all at once, his head turned in my direction as he took one long, pensive look and sniffed—and then it clicked. Never in my life had I seen a preacher hightail his ass to a phone as fast as that one managed to do. He was quite impressive, actually.

Minutes later, a barrage of sirens could be heard blaring off in the near distance. A crowd of onlookers began to assemble, keeping a safe distance. I continued to remain seated, bracing myself for what was to come, and I certainly wasn't disappointed.

At first, the stench from the dog crap caked all over my person made even the most hardened and seasoned officers cringe. They approached me apprehensively, guns drawn. I would have laughed, but I was scared shitless. Get it? Shitless? Sorry, gallows humor—"gallows," as in, the prison. I'm on a roll tonight.

Okay, let me reel in my hilarity.

Since I wasn't putting up any resistance and was obviously off the wall, the cops called for an ambulance. Within minutes, I was strapped to a gurney and unceremoniously carted off to the psychiatric unit where

I was immediately cleaned up, thank the Lord. I despised being covered head to toe in that disgusting, nasty goop. I couldn't wait to shower, but to present the full effect of my performance, I had to pretend smelling like a dirty diaper didn't bother me in the slightest. As if it was entirely reasonable to be covered in dog shit and pancake syrup.

At the hospital, I was placed in an examination room and handcuffed to the hospital bed with two armed guards standing outside my room, not entirely sure if the police presence was for my protection or theirs. Nevertheless, while I underwent testing and observation, I assumed the rest of the squad was dispatched to the crime scene.

After weeks of endless question-and-answer sessions, a myriad of tests and examinations, I was deemed mentally competent to stand trial and hauled off to the county jail with the rest of the losers. From there, I was dragged in front of a judge who assigned some recently hired legal aid attorney to represent me. This guy had almost no court experience. He was still wet behind the ears, but it didn't matter. I was broke, he was free, and I was going to be found guilty anyway. "C'est la vie."

My interview with the detectives assigned to the case was entertaining, if not surreal. They each took a turn asking me every way under the sun, if and why I killed Carl and my mother. What was my motive? Had I planned the murders in advance, or was it in the heat of the moment? Why did I move the bodies around? Why the dog shit, ketchup, and pancake syrup? What was the significance of that? I grinned, smiled wide, but remained silent.

Then the detectives decided it was time to take a different approach. They started asking a bunch more questions about a host of irrelevant topics. Do I like sports? What's my favorite food? Am I hungry now? Can they get me something at the deli when they go out? You name it. Anything to get me to trust them, open up, and become chatty. But I had nothing to say.

It hadn't taken long before the detectives became frustrated with the continued lack of deference or appreciation I had for their well-rehearsed police shenanigans. "Buddy, buddy, let's be friends" turned into yelling matches and threats. They started telling me how hard life was going to be for you with a mother locked up for the rest of her life. How foster care would swoop in to take you away if I didn't cooperate. How once locked up, I could look forward to being raped day in and day out. But then I was told that if I cooperated, they would, of course, put in a good word for me and have me sent to a "nicer prison." Yep, all kinds of scare tactics were employed to worry the crap out of me. In truth, I almost wet my pants a few times, but nothing they threatened or did was enough to make me waver or recant.

Prompted probably by a perverse mixture of mutual exhaustion, aggravation, and occasional boredom, I do admit to once in a while busting chops. I retaliated by making the officers believe that I was finally going to open up and tell them what they wanted to hear. Instead, I'd relay some dark, sick, and highly inappropriate joke—just to freak them out.

I did whatever I could to avoid any and all thoughts that reminded me of the real reasons why I was sitting under arrest in a police station, being accused of double homicide. Instead, I practiced focusing on the hate and traumatic events in my life that led up to what had transpired. The constant, disruptive nightmares that never went away and would keep me up at night, causing my body to shake uncontrollably and break out into a clammy sweat. How I was forever in a state of morbid hyper-vigilance, waiting for the inevitable attack, and the disillusionment and inability to feel love or happiness. Except for Diarmuid and the Grants.

I kept this running dialogue in my head as they continued to drill me, reminding myself of how quickly I could become angry or irritable, and thinking about the constant battle I fought between what I knew was the right way to react, as opposed to my body's way of lashing out to self-protect. After a while, an emotional numbness gratefully washed over me, mentally allowing me to drift off to a place inside me where no one could ever find or hurt me again.

In jail, I followed my keeper's instructions explicitly, short of refusing to talk other than to say my name. I did, however, do a lot of nodding and double thumbs up. Eventually, my keepers, tired of playing games by this time, left me in my cell to rot while they continued to build up a rock-solid case against me.

The media did their considerable part to have me convicted. The reporters had a field day expounding on what they thought happened in the most sensationalized way imaginable. I ignored all of that regurgitated claptrap too, maintaining my resolve to keep my lips zipped, only participating enough in the legal scrutiny to keep the police convinced of my guilt.

However, I would also like to thank the media for their due diligence, because apparently, my ready-made, psycho-media reputation and infamous notoriety caused the other inmates to leave me the hell alone, collectively deciding I was obviously a new, special brand of degenerate, as well as a certifiable looney-tune. Trust me when I tell you, "crazy" has its perks.

Because I demanded to plead not guilty, my attorney asked for a trial by jury. Granted. The trial lasted a hot minute since I offered up absolutely no defense other than my opinion that I shouldn't be found guilty based on the fact that the two dead individuals were slime and human excrement. My attorney begged me to reconsider. He wanted to have me committed as opposed to jailed, but I wouldn't hear of it. During the psychological interviews, I flipped the script, coming off as highly intelligent as I could—well spoken, non-emotional, cordial, but remarkably clear thinking. Hannibal-Lecter witty.

Refusing to defend myself helped the wheels of justice to spin frantically unimpeded. However, my Academy Award-winning performance of, "I'm Crazy, So Watch Me Burn" wasn't convincing everyone. On the second day, right before the court reconvened after lunch, I overheard the two detectives who had been stuck with my case, discussing me.

"Something's off."

"This again? For Christ's sake!" Detective Catalano was sick and tired of this same stupid conversation. He couldn't wait for this case to be over with.

"Wadda you want me to say? This case has always bothered me. I know, I already know what you're thinking—she confessed," whispered Detective Roberts, staring straight ahead. "But that doesn't mean she did it."

"Are you kidding me?" Catalano started doing the finger countdown. "One—she was found covered in dog shit and blood. Two—gun residue was found all over her hands. Three—she described the crime scene to perfection. Four—SHE CONFESSED, and then five—she has adamantly refused to defend herself in any way, shape, or form. What would you call that?"

"False confession. Staged attempt to cover up a crime?"

"Give me a break. I've been working homicide for over fifteen years. I think I'd know a false confession if it bit my ass in the dark, and that crime scene was anything but staged. What we walked into that day was evidence of a demented mind unraveling. Plain and simple."

"I don't know...something about her demeanor gives me the feeling there's more to this case, something we missed."

"You're reading too much into her so-called demeanor. The woman's a certifiable nut case."

"Okay, then explain the old lady trying to confess," challenged Roberts.

"The old lady? Seriously? Talk about a false confession! Listen, we've been through this a hundred times. You think for one hot minute that sweet old little lady who's never even been late returning a library book all of a sudden could commit the sickening and over-the-top, gruesome nightmare we walked into? Are you freakin' kidding me, or what? Come on already. Think about it—it was obvious the old lady was just trying to take the blame for Stone. Everyone we interviewed confirmed the old woman was the nicest, God-fearing individual they knew. Enough."

"Yeah, well, something's not right with this case. I can feel it in my bones."

Agitated, Catalano smirked and shook his head. "All you feel in your bones is arthritis, now, shhh. They're starting."

For a week or so, I was paraded into the courtroom, filled with spectators hungry for blood. Although I knew the Grants took turns coming every day without fail, I refused to allow myself to make eye contact with either one of them. At this point in my life, their opinions of me were the only ones I cared about. I knew Mrs. Grant would use any opportunity to imploringly stare into my eyes and soul and beg me to retract my plea. She tried everything to get me to allow her to break her promise to God. After finding out she had failed to get attention from the police, I assumed correctly that my attorney would be next—but I beat her to the punch, giving him strict instructions to ignore any cockamamie story she told him. I explained to him what I thought she was up to, and to take anything she had to say with a grain of salt... Nothing more than the overprotective ramblings of a sweet old lady.

While in the holding cell with nothing but time, I took the opportunity to write the jury a scathing, bitter note. I didn't have anything against the police, who were doing their job, and I didn't particularly have a problem with the judge or lawyers, either. But the jury was a whole other animal. I disliked that collection of bastard dipshits the most. I guess it was their dirty, sneaky, leering, snooty stares, like I was an anomaly or something. I don't know... I tried to ignore them, but there was twelve of them and only one of me.

During my trial, I'd occasionally glance up, pretending I could read their useless, docile faces as they sat all upright listening intently to the prosecutor as she systematically laid out her whole case against me. I despised the way a small number of them stole cowardly side-glances at me, unwilling to look me directly in the eyes. So damn smug and contemptible. Sitting all high and mighty as if they were somehow better than me. I caught a few rolling their eyes while others shook their heads in disgust. Some fidgeted uncomfortably, while others brazenly gazed at me with repulsion. There was one woman in particular out of that whole worthless batch of jurors who had balls, I'll give her that much. This witch never took her beady, judgmental eyes off me, as if she was trying to figure out if I was human or not.

Out of all the lawyer and detective interrogations, it was only the jury's haughtiness and attitude that almost caused me to cave in and speak up. Sure, I knew I was going away, probably for life—I set it up that way, but who the hell were they to sit in judgment of me? They really pissed me off!

By the third and final day, I wanted to march right back in the courtroom and declare in no uncertain terms where the whole lot of them could shove their inevitable conviction. I almost whipped out my letter of declaration, demanding to be heard, until I was led back into the courtroom to hear the verdict. That's when I caught a quick peek of Diarmuid sitting way in the back, completely mortified and lost. One glimpse at his face was enough to cause the mounting, angry vibrato inside me to fizzle away into nothingness.

I had no intention of making this situation any harder on him or the Grants than it already was. His face was pale, disbelieving. I suspected Diarmuid hated me like all the rest did, so I kept my fat mouth clamped shut and just stared ahead, pretending not to care anymore. Barely listening to the judge jabber on, sporadically winking at a few jurors, and once, just to be vindictive, I even blew that one evil, snooty, staring bitch a kiss. You should have seen her recoil in her chair. Hilarious.

The trial took no time at all; it was exceptionally brief. The decision to render a guilty plea took all of twenty minutes, and I suspect most of those minutes were spent back in the jury room preparing coffee. They couldn't wait to have me convicted. Of course, they weren't to blame. It certainly hadn't helped that I refused to offer up any information in my defense. However, what my frustrated lawyer and the judge, and what the jury failed to appreciate fully, was that I had no problem with being found guilty. That's what I wanted under the circumstances, of course. It was just that I wasn't going to plead guilty. I would never plead guilty, but I didn't expect them or anyone else to understand this subtle, convoluted distinction.

I was found unanimously guilty of first-degree murder with depraved indifference, and given life imprisonment without the chance of parole. Within the week, I was cuffed, assigned a number, and thrown into the back of a prison bus, and then made a permanent guest of the beautiful state of New York.

And that, my daughter, was that.

CHAPTER 24

HIDDEN LIES

KENDAL TURNED THE CAR into the hospital's parking garage, wishing to be any place else, still uncertain as to how long of a visit she could manage. Her aggravation was barely skin deep. Over and again, Kendal played different scenarios out in her head. She was not entirely sure whether it was best to either confront Dermot head-on, or remain totally silent and pretend like nothing happened. She thought about dropping a few not-so-subtle hints to nudge him into finally opening up about how he actually felt, but Dermot and subtlety had never fully meshed. Either way, the time had come for real answers, before she developed a full-blown ulcer or committed murder.

Carrying an overnight bag filled with a few of Dermot's toiletries, a pair of slippers and his bathrobe, Kendal entered the elevator distracted, pushing for her husband's floor. As the elevator doors closed, her apprehensiveness increased. She was uncertain if Dermot would try to play dumb, his usual ploy if confronted, so she made sure this time to bring a little insurance policy—Terri's letter.

Heart beating forcefully in her chest, Kendal used her shoulder to push the thick, wood-laden door quietly, poking her head inside. On the bed, she found Dermot staring at the ceiling, face damp, fresh tears streaking down his face. Hearing the door creak open, he promptly used the crumpled-up tissue in his hand to wipe his face and nose.

"Hey, Love, come in, please."

Kendal approached the bed, standing close, but not close enough to touch her husband. "Have you been crying?" she asked. Dermot rarely ever cried.

Dermot's voice cracked. Clearing his throat, he waved her to bring the chair closer to the bed. "I need to talk to you. Please sit."

In all the scenarios Kendal had thought up, she had never anticipated Dermot would initiate the conversation. Kendal placed the bags on the floor, slid a chair over, and sat, not sure how to react. Before she had a chance to utter a word, Dermot pleadingly reached out for his wife's hand indicating to place hers in his.

"I haven't been entirely honest with you all these years."

Here it comes. Kendal braced for heartache.

"I've never done anything to purposely hurt you, but I've kept something locked away, hoping that over time, it would disappear on its own—but it hasn't."

"Dermot—"

"Please, Kendal, let me finish. Then when I'm done, you can ask me anything you want, and this time I promise to tell you everything."

Kendal pulled her chair closer. She had never seen her husband like this. She wasn't sure what to make of it, and was frightened now to hear the truth she had been wanting, and wishing for, for so long.

Dermot cleared his throat and began to speak again, almost in a hoarse whisper. "For years, you've been trying to get me to open up and tell you what happened to Terri and me, and for years, I blocked you out. I need you to believe me when I tell you that I wasn't attempting to hide anything I did that was wrong. I was just tryin' to hide the feelings I thought I could make go away if I didn't think or talk about them. Obviously, that didn't work." Dermot's eyes filled again with tears.

As her pulse raced, shoulders tensed, and one leg bounced up and down, Kendal's breath quickened. Was her husband about to tell her that all this time, all through their marriage, he had been in love with Terri? She lowered her gaze, unable to make eye contact.

Dermot continued. "Look at me, Kendal. I need you to look at me."

Kendal looked up, lips press together, eyes glassy, waiting for the hammer to drop.

"Terri was my first love—I guess you could call it puppy love. Up to that point, I hadn't felt certain emotions, never experienced what love was or wasn't, and never knew what to expect. And, well, Terri was more experienced than me. The talk was she'd been around, and I knew that, but when she was with me, she was different. Not like what everyone was saying. At the time, she seemed like she felt strong about me too, and soon, I guess, you could say we were going steady. I thought I was in love with the girl. I thought she loved me too, but then she turned up pregnant with some other guy's kid, and well, you know the rest of that."

Kendal nodded, so far Dermot hadn't told her anything she didn't already know.

"So, this is the part I never told you. I didn't want to hurt you. You've been the best wife a man could ever ask for."

A single tear slid from Kendal's face plopping onto her lap, but she didn't dare break eye contact.

"I've always felt guilty about not helping Terri when she got into trouble. I let her walk away; I heard she got thrown out of her house pregnant and was living on some farm. I was so angry with her for cheating on me that I pretended not to care what happened to her, but I did. Sometimes I even wished she'd lose the baby." Tears cascaded down his face, but Dermot continued.

"Then I heard through the grapevine that she'd given birth to a little girl, and I vowed never to talk about her again. I wasn't sure if that was true or not, and I didn't care either way. By this time, you and I were already together, and I didn't want anything to go wrong between us. I didn't want to take the chance that you'd walk out on me, too… So I never spoke about her, even though you'd try to fish for details."

Kendal winced. Dermot was right; she had relentlessly fished for details, desperate to know what her competition was. Squeezing her husband's hand, they both shared a knowing nod and smile.

"So, I forgot about her. You and I had our life, and she had hers, until she went postal and killed her mother and stepfather, and it was all over the news. You remember?"

Kendal nodded.

"Right? It was disgusting—she was covered with blood and dog shit. Shooting up her parents in cold blood. I couldn't believe it. Couldn't believe how wrong I'd been about her. Couldn't for the life of me understand why I hadn't seen Terri for who she really was all that time. I never told you this, but I almost offered to marry her, even though she was pregnant with some other guy's kid. What stopped me was the way she treated me, the way she turned her back on me, like I never mattered, either. Like I was just some jerk she was just using. Terri made me so angry. I wished her dead."

Dermot started to sob harder. Shoulders racked, Kendal stood up, leaning over to nestle her husband's head soothingly into her bosom.

Sitting at the edge of the bed, swiping a tissue from the box, Kendal gently wiped away Dermot's falling tears. She tenderly rubbed his head and patted his back, giving him the opportunity to get out all the pent-up emotions he'd been carrying locked up for years. *This can't be helping his heart,* thought Kendal.

"I went to the courthouse the day Terri got convicted. I had to see for myself if this was the same person I had fallen so hard for. She, of course, didn't know I was there. I purposely sat in the back, out of sight. The place was packed. The prosecutor stood up and started talking about Terri and all the wacky things she told them. The whole hearing was sickening. It was as if the prosecutor wasn't even talking about the same person I knew, and not once did Terri open her mouth to defend herself. She just sat there, glaring straight ahead, as if the whole thing was some big joke or something. Do you know, I actually saw her blow a woman juror a kiss! I don't get it. None of this made any sense. It still doesn't."

Calmer, Dermot shook his head, leaning back on his pillows, indicating he had more to say. Kendal tensely sat back down on the chair, leaning forward to catch Dermot's every word, unsure where this conversation was heading next.

"When Terri got convicted and thrown into prison, I remember being glad," admitted Dermot. "My anger was so irrational and childish, still nursing the hurt over some supposed lost love. Ridiculous really, but I never dealt with the anger. I was too embarrassed to talk about it, I guess. I didn't want you to think I was a jerk, or that I still loved her."

"You should have spoken to me."

"I know... But I couldn't. At the time, Paddy was a little guy, and you were pregnant. I didn't want to bring up anything to upset you. It seemed that whenever Terri's name got mentioned, you'd get all fired up, hounding me and questioning me like I had done something wrong. It's just that ..."

"It's just that what, Dermot? Tell me. Get it all out, because I'm sick and tired of this elephant in the room between us—the so-called 'taboo' subject. Every time I've tried to draw it out of you, you clam up and shut me down. I'm done with it. Say it! Say how you still love her. How you wanted to be with her instead of me."

"That's not true."

"Bullshit! Say it! Be a man for once and tell the truth!" Kendal was trying to modulate her voice, but her pulse was racing, words were flying, and she desperately wanted to have this out once and for all.

Dermot inhaled deeply. Taking his wife's clenched hands in both of his, he soothingly protested, "It's not true. I never did Kendal. I swear to God."

Dermot would never admit this to Kendal and hoped God would forgive him this one lie. No matter how many times his wife forced the issue, he'd never utter those words. He cared about his wife way too much to ever hurt her in this way, nor would he jeopardize his marriage more than he already had. "It's just that when I heard Terri had killed herself, all the anger and bad memories came back, but honestly, that would have been it if…"

"If what? Don't stop now, spill it already!" Kendal shouted, bracing for the worst.

Dermot assumed Kendal was going to flip out when she heard what he had to tell her. "It's just that Raven, Paddy's girl? She's…well, you're not going to believe this."

"Dermot!"

"Okay, okay… She's Terri's sister. I just found out."

Kendal's face froze, registering only confusion. "Raven? Our Paddy's Raven?"

"Yeah."

"The sweet girl who comes over our house Raven?"

"Yeah."

"It can't be, are you sure?" Kendal demanded.

"Of course I'm sure."

"I don't understand. How do you know this?"

"Paddy let it slip. Yesterday. He doesn't know about my history with Terri of course. When he came back from visiting Raven all upset the other day, I asked him, "Hey what's up with you?" He started telling me about Raven being all upset about her sister committing suicide. I never even knew she had a sister, did you?"

"Of course I didn't!" Kendal snapped.

"Okay, well me neither. Now, the other day, when I heard on the radio about Terri, I didn't put two and two together yet, why would I have? Right? But then I asked Paddy when the funeral would be for Raven's sister. This was when he dropped on me that Raven drove over to the prison to pick up her sister's belongings and that her sister committed suicide! I couldn't believe it!"

Kendal sat stunned. Dumbfounded, she never would have anticipated the conversation taking this direction. Not in a million, trillion years. Dermot continued.

"Then Paddy tells me Terri wrote Raven some long, deathbed letter. Supposedly, Raven is at home right now, reading it and losing her mind, getting mad at Paddy, and, well, the rest of the pieces just fell into place."

Kendal remained motionless, unable to fathom how the sweet girl Raven was in any way connected with that devil woman Terri.

"I don't know," muttered Dermot. "The thought of Paddy being with Terri's sister got me so upset I—"

"Had a heart attack," countered Kendal flatly. *I knew all along that miscreant was somehow to blame,* and now Kendal had all the proof she needed. *How I loathe that woman.*

"Yeah, I know it makes no sense. I shouldn't have let myself get so worked up, but it caught me by surprise. The doctors said I have been carting around high blood pressure and some plaque build-up in my arteries. Anything upsetting could have caused it, it just so happened to be this." Dermot sat back, exhausted. His pallid face appeared more at ease now that he told his wife everything. Almost everything.

Kendal leaned back in the chair, unable to fully comprehend all of what Dermot just dumped on her, combating waves of mixed emotions. On the one hand, she felt a sense of relief, no longer haunted by Dermot's emotional baggage, but on the other hand, she experienced fury at having to go through round two—this time with Terri's ghost. Both polarizing emotions were vying for a position.

All these years Kendal had been so sure that Dermot held a torch for Terri, assuming his lack of communication had meant he wanted to be married to Terri instead of her. Now, to find out that all along he had been just too humiliated to admit that once he was so naïve to have had such strong feelings for a girl who turned out to be a monster. A murderer.

Kendal couldn't believe it. All this nonsense could have been cleared up years ago, but no! Dermot had to have a heart attack to bring the discussion back up to the surface. And now her son, her Paddy, was in love with Terri's younger sister and all this time, nobody knew. This cruel, ironic quirk of fate was troublesome to say the least, and Kendal wasn't sure what to do next.

Terri's ridiculous love letter Kendal carted around and kept hidden all these years no longer held any power or sway. Now, it was nothing more that some last-ditch, feeble attempt at clutching back her husband's attention, but Terri had been thwarted. Kendal could easily dispense of the letter finally, once and for all. However, dealing with Raven would prove to be an entirely different state of affairs.

CHAPTER 25

AS DEATH DAY APPROACHES

Terri

Less than two days left before Death Day

IF TIME COULD ONLY stand still, Terri would have been able to exhale, but the days were spinning way out of control while the nights grew heavy with dread. Terri's mind rushed, plagued with irresolution. The desire to compose a list of what was left to finish was curtailed by necessity. No use taking any clumsy, uncalled-for chances. She had come too far and was way too close to the end to screw it up now.

Terri's last few nights had been aggravating, to say the least. Unfortunately, a large portion of her time had been spent fending off Martina's advances, along with counting the stashed pills, cleaning the cell, and throwing a few unimportant items in the trash without drawing any unwarranted suspicion or attention. The rest of her meager belongings were systematically sifted and sorted through as she methodically packed the items she wished to keep and piled the rest into neat stacks. The order Terri surrounded herself with brought a sense of calculating stillness that she required more now than ever.

Surprisingly, Terri felt little urge to relish or soak up the last remnants of the living experience before her set demise. She felt no sudden urgency to catch a glimmer of her last rising and setting sun, nor did Terri relish every morsel of food. The longing to die and be rid of the confines of her prison overwhelmed her so, that she constantly had to remind herself to be patient and stay the course, no matter what.

The small stack of cherished photos under her pillow, which were rubber-banded together, would have to be destroyed. They were Terri's one Achilles heel and only connection to reality, her daughter, and to the life she never had, but desperately wanted. As much as Terri hated the thought of destroying these relished treasures, she had to, unable to take the chance of them falling into the wrong hands after she could no longer protect them. The prison was notorious for thievery and perverts, willing to jerk off on any pretty face they could get their hands on. Every last photo would be shredded and tossed. Terri decided it would be one of the last tasks to undertake before the end.

Nothing in life or death is ever easy. Martina had inadvertently thrown a monkey wrench inside the efficiency of Terri's plans. Instead of allowing Terri a peaceful exit, Martina upped the stakes and dramatized what could have been a simple business relationship. Instead, tensions ran high between the two women and turned most taxing.

Martina was losing her mind, allowing her nerves to center on her imminent release and cloud her better judgment. To hide her nervousness, Martina lapsed into a reactionary and highly aggressive, pushy behavior. She senselessly reverted to base carnal lusts, all of which Martina utilized to satisfy her destructive urge to self-sabotage.

For days now, Terri consciously sought to ignore the sexual overtone of Martina's hungry touches, avoiding her as best she could. Terri deliberately let pass the mounting trail of sloppily dropped hints and lust-filled innuendos. For the most part, avoidance worked until Martina's gauche attempt at cornering Terri in the shower stall.

Terri was ready. She had caught sight of Martina watching her as she headed to the showers, anticipating Martina's scheme. Just as Terri pulled the curtain closed, Martina fell for it, slipping through behind Terri and wrapping her arms tightly around Terri's waist seductively.

"Can I help you?" asked Terri flippantly.

"I think you can," murmured Martina, hot, bothered, and ready to pounce.

Terri spun around to face Martina. "Not here. Too chancy," Terri whispered urgently, trying to sound legitimately concerned. "You can't afford to get caught."

"It'll be fine, trust me." Martina was fired up and not getting the message. Letting her towel fall to the wet tiled floor, Martina reached out to grab Terri again, but this time, Terri made her move first. She clutched

Martina by the throat, forcibly shoving her violently back and pinning her to the wall.

With eyes wide open and filled with panic, Martina gasped for air, scarcely able to breathe yet too scared and frightened to call out for help. Terri leaned into Martina, pressing her wet, naked body close to hers and purposely enunciated each syllable in her terrified face, "I. Said. Not. Here."

Terri enjoyed the terror on Martina's face and knew she had her just where she wanted. Neck still clenched, Terri murmured, "Are you hearing me now?" Martina rapidly blinked her bulging eyes to take the place of nodding her head to indicate she understood clearly.

"I won't tell you again," Terri whispered. Then she proceeded to loosen her grip slightly. Still deathly afraid, Martina, with hair drenched and matted across her face, stood shivering and immobilized, unsure of what to do or say next, so she waited.

Terri had been inside long enough to know how these jailhouse hook-ups played themselves out. One wrong move and Martina would be back on top and in control. Terri wasn't about to let that go down.

Now, to make Martina swoon and obey, Terri gently cupped Martina's wet, full breasts. Then with her tongue, she ran the tip down the length of Martina's slightly bruised neck until she heard her groan in hungry pleasure. Terri then forcibly parted Martina's panting lips with her tongue until Martina, now fully engaged, began to reciprocate, grinding her body in response. But Terri understood the game and continued arousing Martina until she knew for sure when enough was enough. As soon as Martina became completely submissive, Terri whispered dismissively, "Now get out of here."

"Don't stop, please, Terri," Martina begged.

"I'm done with you. Get out of here. I'll let you know when I want you."

Terri knew she was taking a big risk playing the dominant role with such a strong personality, but if she didn't, Martina would walk all over her, and the demands would only increase.

Martina didn't appreciate being dismissed and began to protest until she caught Terri's facial expression turn twisted and vulgar. Martina instantly chose to keep her trap shut, willingly subdued with the promise of later.

"Be ready," ordered Terri, practically throwing the soaking wet towel at Martina. Then Terri opened the curtain a crack, peeked out to make sure the coast was clear, and practically shoved Martina out, naked and dripping. A few inmates waiting for their turn saw the end transaction, but were smart enough to pretend nothing unusual had just occurred. The typical back and forth banter, smirks, and jokes didn't happen. Nobody wanted to be the fool who crossed Martina, or Terri, for that matter.

Although ravenous, Martina played her new steamy role to perfection, perfectly content to slip out of the shower stall undetected by the guards and instantly into a stall of her own, hot and deliciously bothered. Terri closed the curtain and continued to lather up, satisfied that this little steamy episode had bought a timely reprieve while hoping not to be around for the next curtain call.

CHAPTER 26

DISCLOSURE MOUNTS

THE GRANTS REPEATEDLY TRIED to contact me, sending sealed notes through my attorney. They generously offered to tap into their life savings, begging me to let them hire some expensive lawyer instead of the newborn representing me, but I adamantly refused. As I said, it would have been a waste.

Mrs. Grant came to the jail, tried to visit me on her own, only to be turned away. I knew damn well what she wanted me to do, and that was never going to happen, so I refused to put her name down on the visitation list. I wasn't trying to hurt her... I missed her and Pop dearly, but staying out of contact was imperative. I couldn't take the chance that Mrs. Grant would break down and confess yet again. I assumed Pop suspected the two of us were hiding the truth, but as stubborn as Mrs. Grant was, I was ten times more so.

I know the promise she made was killing her, and keeping the truth from Pop was a lot to expect, but what was done was done and there was no turning back. No matter how much she wanted to, I couldn't let her take the fall for this. I wouldn't let her. Making her solemnly promise to God had been the smartest move I ever made, and probably the only thing I had going for me to make her comply.

You have to understand, Raven—her and Pops were the best, most honest, loving two people I had ever known in my life. In my darkest hour, when I was homeless, pregnant, with no one to turn to, they didn't hesitate to take me into their life, into their home. Mrs. Grant did what she had to do to protect us—YOU—and I wasn't going to let the law lock her up and throw away the key because of me. I wasn't going to let twelve jurors who knew nothing about her decide that she was guilty of murder, like they did me. Besides, I already knew you would be in good hands, I never had doubt, and if I had to stay in this place and rot to death, at least I had that in the back of my mind to help keep me strong.

For many years, knowing you were growing up into an amazing young lady sustained me. It kept me going when all I wanted to do was not wake up to face another tedious day.

That doesn't mean I haven't had regrets, because I did. Tons of them. Missing you, not being able to watch you grow up. I still believe with all my heart that I had been right, you know, about leaving you in their care. Under their wings, you grew into the most beautiful young woman with a promising future ahead of you. Don't squander it.

I was okay with all the aloneness and dispossession until I heard the word from you in your last letter that both Grants had passed away. When they died, so did my resolve. It crumbled. I don't know how to explain it. There was no longer a reason to be in here. Life for me became purposeless.

I'm tired, Raven.

I did my job. I kept up my end of the bargain.

You're grown, you know how to take care of yourself, and you most certainly don't need your nutty sister who is, in fact, your mother—the murderer—hanging around in the back of your mind. People get funny about stuff like that, as you will undoubtedly find out for yourself, should you be foolish enough to share. I suggest you never do.

This is not living, this life stuck permanently behind bars, with no chance of ever leaving, and nothing to look forward to. Nothing left to relish, nothing left to plan. A person can't exist like this forever. I know I can't do it, and I don't want to do it. The truth about what happened that day dies with me. My only chance of freedom is in a casket, or in a cheap urn if you have me cremated. It doesn't matter to me what you decide. In all honesty, if I can't be buried near the cabin, then what they do with my remains is superfluous.

Do you believe people have a soul? I do. I'm counting on it actually, and hoping that by the time they cart my body away my soul will be long gone, and if there is a God, hopefully to a better place.

And by the way, Raven, don't feel compelled to tell my story, no need to clear my name—I don't care much anymore. The time for me to leave this place is drawing near. I no longer have to protect you from the truth, or Mrs. Grant from the noose. Only the lies are left.

Let history take care of itself for a change.

CHAPTER 27

DEATH & LIES

"**NEMO MORITURUS** praesumitur mentiri—no one on the point of death should be presumed to be lying."

Terri had specifically requested for the sealed letter to remain closed until after the entirety of her letter had been read. Raven honored Terri's request, but now the sealed envelope remained the last vestige to a painful, closing saga. After all else that had been disclosed and discovered, Raven couldn't imagine anything else Terri had to say would have the power to shock, but this was a wager best left untaken.

Paddy had called, explaining how his father's hospitalization meant longer work hours. Between the job and his family, he wasn't sure when he'd be able to make it back over. Raven again told him that she completely understood, and to take care of what he needed to do, not to worry. The truth was, Paddy's absence permitted Raven the time and space she needed to work things out in her head, and make some final decisions of her own.

Raven was anything but fine. All that she thought she knew was now mere supposition. Her personal history was nothing but an outlandish, tall tale concocted by two women desperately in need of protecting the other. Raven wondered if these two even had the ability to distinguish truth from an invention, or was everything just one big lie? And what about Terri's alleged false confession? Did she plead guilty to protect her and Mrs. Grant, or was it more out of some deep-seeded guilt? Or was it Terri's heroic attempt at making up for past transgressions?

These past few days had been a rollercoaster ride of epic proportions, leaving Raven clenching the railing, trying desperately to hold on—but her grip was loosening. Her mother's letter to her might have been nothing more than a last feeble attempt to feel vindicated for the heinous crimes committed, but if innocent, why then not fight the case? Why not be exonerated and cleared of a crime she now claims not to have done? Why go on to commit suicide?

And then the doorbell rang.

Startled and certainly not expecting anyone, Raven jumped up to peek through the bedroom curtain, stunned to find Mrs. McMahon of all people, standing on her stoop. Other than Paddy, no one from his family had ever been to her home before, so it came as quite an uncomfortable surprise to see Paddy's mother there now.

"Coming!" Raven quickly glanced in the mirror, *Ugh, I look disgusting, damn it*. "I'll be right there."

Kendal stood on the porch, dreading the conversation that had to happen. Inconspicuously taking in her surroundings, and picturing a time long ago, when Terri would have been the one answering the door instead of her sister.

"Oh, hi, Mrs. McMahon. Please, come in." Raven opened the door wide, grateful she had taken the time to tidy up the place the day before.

"Thank you," replied Kendal as she stepped inside. "I'm sorry to barge in on you like this, but I needed to speak with you, alone."

Raven wasn't exactly sure why Paddy's mother was here. "May I take your coat?"

"No, I won't be staying long, thank you."

"Is Mr. McMahon all right?" Raven asked, anticipating something terrible had happened. Anxiously she started blathering again. "I spoke to Paddy this morning, and he told me that he was doing much better. I would have come by the hospital myself, but Paddy told me there was nothing to do there except be in the way, and well ..."

"He's doing much better, thank you for asking. The doctor assured us he'll be released from the hospital once all tests are completed, and his medications are stabilized."

"Oh, that's good... I mean, great! That's great." *Oh, God, shut up, Raven!* "Please, take a seat."

The two women made their way into the living room. Raven quickly swiped up all her mother's papers in one swoop, bringing them in a pile to her bedroom. "Sorry for the mess. I've been going through paperwork, trying to sort things out," she yelled over her shoulder from down the hall.

"Yes, I heard. I'm... Deeply sorry for the loss of your sister," replied Kendal awkwardly. "Paddy shared your heartbreaking news with his father shortly before...he fell ill."

Raven sat down and nodded, kind of surprised Paddy had shared with his father anything about her situation, but it made sense. Paddy and his dad were close, and he probably just needed someone to confide in after how crazy she'd been making his life. "Thank you. It's been a lot to deal with, especially after losing both my parents so recently."

"I can imagine." Kendal studied Raven's features searching for a familial resemblance to Terri.

The room fell uncomfortably quiet.

"Where are my manners? Would you like something to drink? Coffee? Tea? Water?" asked Raven, anxious to fill the awkward silence.

"No, thank you. I'm fine. I really can't stay long."

"Of course... Umm, you wanted to talk to me about something?"

Kendal had come to see Raven without Dermot or Paddy's knowledge, hoping that she could persuade Raven to do the right thing, and leave her son alone.

"Raven, you are a very sweet girl. Paddy is fond of you, but under the circumstances, with you losing your parents, and then your sister committing suicide, well, we think, his father and I, that it would be best for the both of you to take a breather. Go your separate ways before somebody else gets hurt."

Fond of me? End our relationship? "I don't understand. Do you mean break up? Did I do something wrong? Did I offend you in some way?"

"No, we think you are a very lovely young woman, but we feel strongly that for Paddy's best interests, that he concentrate on his family's needs and the business. His responsibilities will have to increase as a result of his father's current health situation."

"But why? I still don't understand," confessed Raven, utterly confused. "I would never get in the way of Paddy's obligations to his work or his family."

"Yes, well, you may not think so, but Paddy hasn't been himself recently, and this relationship between the two of you is nothing more than an unnecessary distraction. Paddy may not realize it now, but as his parents, we think this is what is best for our son."

"I see," Raven whispered. "Does Paddy know you're here, telling me all this?"

"No, and I'd like to keep it that way. Just between you and me. Paddy doesn't always know what's best for him, but I am his mother, and I know what he needs better than anyone else."

"But I love your son, Mrs. McMahon."

"Love isn't always enough Raven."

"Paddy loves me, too."

"He thinks he loves you too, but Paddy's too young to know what real love is," Kendal admonished. Trying to maintain her calm, she took a deep breath. "Raven, you have a lot on your plate, and you need time to get everything back in order, and so does Paddy. He doesn't have the time or energy to be picking up the pieces of your shattered life along with his."

"What? What do you mean by shattered life? What exactly did he tell you?"

"Let's not play games here, Raven. We know you were adopted, the Grants were very nice people, but your sister was…a murderer, who, if I'm not mistaken, killed your real mother and father. We're not trying to blame you for who your family was or wasn't, but at the same time, it's not the kind of emotional baggage we want for our son."

"So you think I'm 'emotional baggage?' All of a sudden I'm not good enough for your son? Is that what you're implying?"

"Take it any way you see fit," snapped Kendal, abruptly standing up, ready to take her leave. "I'm asking you nicely; stay away from my son."

"And if I don't?" challenged Raven.

Kendal couldn't believe the nerve of this defiant girl, cut from the same rag as her sister. "You say you love my son, then think about him, think about his future. Do what's right for him instead of being self-serving and self-centered." Kendal headed for the door, pulled it open, and turned with one more parting zinger. "Do what's right and leave my Paddy alone, Raven."

Seconds later, she was gone. Raven remained seated, tears streaming down her face, not sure whether to be angry or offended. At the same time, she couldn't help but understand where Paddy's mother was coming from. She obviously loved her son. Raven never questioned her loyalty or motivation. Apparently Mrs. McMahon worried about what kind of influence she would be on Paddy now that she knew Raven's less-than-desirable pedigree.

Raven had a difficult time blaming Paddy's parents for not wanting a murderer's sister as their son's girlfriend or wife. Imagine if they found out Terri was really her mother! That piece of news had barely sunk into Raven, no less anyone else.

Raven was grateful she hadn't had a chance to disclose the whole sordid story to Paddy, and now she wasn't sure she ever would.

How would Paddy have taken the news of his mother's visit, she wondered. Had his mom been acting totally on her own accord, or had she been doing Paddy's bidding, as well? Raven checked her phone. No missed calls.

* * *

Dermot...

The conversation had gone unexpectedly well with Kendal yesterday, mused Dermot. He had half-expected his wife to storm out of his room again, throw around a few hurtful accusations, or at the very least, demand from him some sign of marital allegiance. Instead, all she did was listen intently. Finally opening up about Terri, and now the strange twist of events with Raven being her sister, had been difficult, but not as difficult as keeping the subject guarded and closed all these past years. Dermot had to wonder to himself why he hadn't trusted Kendal more with the information. A lot of the animosity and misunderstanding could have been avoided had he been more forthcoming and honest—not just with her, but with himself.

Before Kendal had headed out, she and Dermot mutually decided to have a sit-down with Paddy to try to encourage their son to open up about his feelings more. They'd have him discuss projected, long-term plans, and in turn, attempt to gauge whether or not he considered Raven an integral part of his life. At this point, the concerned parents both assumed she was. However, before Paddy made any permanent life decisions, they had hoped they could sway him from taking the plunge with Raven. Dermot thought that conversation would be fraught with tension, assuming Paddy was hell-bent on marrying this girl.

Dermot felt pulled. He honestly really liked Raven as a person, but an awkwardness had been created as a result of her relationship to Terri.

Now his son's emotional well-being was in question. How could his son possibly have a normal life with a young woman whose childhood has been so tainted by dysfunction, turmoil, and loss? Damaged goods, but would Paddy listen? Would he trust his parents to steer him toward a better decision? Would Dermot have listened to his parents had they approached him about Terri years ago? Probably not, and therein lies the real issue.

Enough already of the hospital, the machines, the lousy food not fit for livestock, and the constant bloodwork the doctors seemed to order done every few hours. Time to go. Dermot felt a sense of relief to be heading home tomorrow, finally released from his invasive, semi-purgatory. Time to get back to work, to living, and most of all, to his family.

* * *

Paddy was exhausted, physically and mentally. Besides his father's noticeable absence, the shop was short staffed. One guy was out with some stomach flu, and the other mechanic was on vacation visiting family and not expected back until next week. Fortunately, most of the long-term customers had already heard about Dermot's heart attack—living in a small town, word travels fast. So compassionately, not many exerted pressure on Paddy to get their car work done immediately. Paddy understood enough about human nature to know that this level of communal bigheartedness would only last for so long. His father's expectation that the shop would keep up with demand despite any disruption was legendary.

As assumed, Paddy would step up to the plate, take the responsibility, and make sure the work got done—just like his father had done, and his father before him. He knew better than to indulge in excuses. Failure to do one's best would not be acceptable. If Paddy knew his father as well as he thought, he knew that every decision made moving forward, and every job performed in his dad's absence would be under heavy scrutiny. Paddy remained determined not to let his dad's trust down. Eventually, and now maybe not as far into the future as initially assumed, Paddy was going to have to run the family business pretty much on his own. Now was as good a time as any to get a real taste of what would be expected of him.

CHAPTER 28

DRUM ROLL, PLEASE

THE ACCUMULATED STRESS of the past few months had finally made its home in Raven's soul. Weighed down by a combination of hurt and condemnation, Raven moped around the house for the rest of the day. She felt unmotivated to do much of anything, above all, finishing the last few pages of her mother's testament. Raven resented the caustic intrusion of Terri's letter and the manner in which she chose to end it all, but inexplicably, Raven continued to answer the call to read obediently.

Paddy's mother had shocked Raven. She had never before treated Raven in this manner or anything close to it. Her visit, along with her harsh words and cold demeanor, caught Raven completely by surprise. In the past, Mrs. McMahon had always been perfectly polite, generously kind, and exceedingly welcoming, going out her way to set an extra place for her around the family table. As a matter of fact, meals with the family had been her idea. Raven, who was struggling to define her relationship with Paddy, now seriously questioned whether or not a future together was even possible, despite the sudden hostilities and overly protective concerns apparently stemming from both his parents.

Raven didn't necessarily fault Mrs. McMahon. As Paddy's mother, her reaction was perfectly understandable. She would do whatever she believed was in the best interest of her son. At the same time, being blamed for being genetically related to someone the McMahons considered less than desirable didn't seem quite fair, either. The whole mess stank.

At this juncture, Raven wasn't being straightforward with Paddy, leading him into believing there was the possibility of something more permanent ahead. She just didn't know. So much to think about, she wasn't sure how to handle Paddy, their relationship, her mother's entire life story, and now this. With no one to talk to or seek advice from, Raven sank into a level of turmoil and sadness she had never experienced before.

Raven wished for her former, uncomplicated life to return, a time void of the lonesomeness and foreboding she currently experienced, a time when she had a supportive foundation, parents who adored her, and a future not clouded by uncertainty. A few minutes later, the phone rang. Unable to summon up the energy to scoot over and answer, Raven let it continue to ring until automatically switching over to voice mail.

"Hey, Rave, it's me. Listen, work is crazy over here, and on top of it, I'm short-staffed. By the time I get done tonight, all I'm going to do is go home and crash. Sorry, I won't be able to stop by again, and thanks for being so understanding. Talk to you tomorrow, bye."

Paddy. His voice sounded drained, distant, but sincere. Conceivably, his mother could have been acting only on her own, maybe with the support of his dad, but not necessarily with Paddy's endorsement. The message he just left sounded as if he was unaware of her stopover. In theory, that should have felt more reassuring. Instead, Raven felt obligated and forced to continue a ruse. Raven wanted to feel angrier, but in reality she knew that his mother's visit had only served as the catalyst she needed to either declare her undying love for Paddy once and for all, or as the final recognition that theirs was only a relationship of convenience and security, at least on her end. She now knew that love and *to be in love* are parallel emotions, which never cross or meet.

* * *

Terri…

Do you remember at the beginning of my letter, or maybe I wrote it more in the middle? I can't remember. The part in my tale of woe, when I told you how I sent Mrs. Grant home to get herself all cleaned up after the murders and to get rid of any evidence? Yeah, well, I left out a big piece of the story, probably the most significant part.

You see, Raven, after Mrs. Grant left with you, I remained back to think up a slew of creative ways to botch up the already pretty gruesome crime scene. My only goal was to make damn sure only I would be the one found guilty. Okay, this part you already know. That was the PG version of events, but there's more.

Oh, you may want to sit down for this one. Should you decide to remain standing, so be it, but I would strongly propose you make sure that you're alone. Also take a peek around and make sure there isn't anything hard you can smash into or knock yourself out with on the way down. Just a friendly suggestion.

Moving on.

A few minutes after I watched you both leave, I had to work up the nerve to relocate the bodies. For some reason, those two crud buckets had to lie next to each other to symbolize their communal demise. I have to tell you, touching dead bodies is revolting. Nevertheless, it had to be done. I searched for anything to help me prop the two assholes up, scoot, or even roll them over with, but I was drawing a blank. In hindsight, I have, of course, thought up thousands of better ways, but again, I digress.

I know I claimed I worked on Carl first, but that's not exactly the truth.

I dragged my mother into the room first, and boy was she heavy, and well, dead. As I pulled her alcohol-vein-filled legs I had to keep fighting back my urge to retch, all while continuing to struggle. Drag and stop, pick up, and then, finally, once in the room and approximately where I wanted her to be, with my feet, flipping her over. When she limply rolled over, I screamed. The expression on her face was horrifying! Spooky! Nothing but an expressionless glare permanently melded her features. Even the dull light of life in her blood-shot eyes remained missing. All that remained was ghastly and wickedly frightening.

So next up was Carl. After my mother, Carl should have been a breeze, right? But when I bent down to flip him over to move him closer to her, I thought I heard him moan.

"AHHHH!" I jumped back and banged into the wall, scared shitless!

Carl was still alive! I don't know how, but that prick was still somehow breathing. My knees began to shake involuntarily. Instinctively I thought I should call for help, but that made absolutely no sense since I was right in the middle of trying to stage a double murder. Just my luck to have one of my corpses still breathing.

Pacing up and down the hall, I wasn't sure what to do next but I kept popping my head back into the room to see if Carl was still making any sounds. I was kind of waiting for that creep to sit up and holler, "Gotcha!"

Nothing.

Maybe I was hearing things…perhaps the moan had been nothing more than my very overactive imagination.

I continued to pace up and down the hall, back and forth, hugging my stomach, shaking, cursing, and still trying to fight back building waves of nausea. I remember feeling so frustrated, pissed that I couldn't even do this right! The absurdity of the situation only got better when I started crying and shouting a bunch of brainless stuff. Stupid, angry, off-the-wall stuff—

"You bastard, die already!"

I even had the audacity to start praying to God, like we were partners in crime, in cahoots together, begging Him to do His part and help me cover up the crime. I know, I know, totally an inappropriate request; and honestly, I know that now, but at the time it seemed entirely plausible.

My anxiety shifted into high gear. What am I going to do? Oh, God, make him die. Please make him die already. What does it take to kill this piece of garbage? Tell me what to do.

Then I crept back into the bedroom, as if by tiptoeing I could better hear him grunt or moan, and noticed the gun lying on the bed. Just sitting there, like an answer to my prayers. I scurried over, wedged my way between the bodies and bent over and picked it up. Rubbed off any prior fingerprints again, checked to see if there was any ammunition left in the chamber, and felt relief wash through me when I counted two more bullets. My prayers had been answered, or so I believed at the time.

I decided to check again, for posterity, just to see if the creep was still breathing or had a pulse. I honestly didn't want to touch him, but what choice did I have so I tentatively placed my two fingers on his throat near his artery. I didn't feel anything, so I pressed harder, this time actively searching for the artery again. Shit. Faint, but still hanging on.

I took one step back, aimed right at his balls, and fired. I shot the man's balls off.

His body slightly lurched and convulsed, so I pulled the trigger again, but this time I hit his thigh and blood spewed and bubbled out. If Carl wasn't dead, he would be shortly, I told myself.

All my bullets were gone. There was nothing left to do except create the mess I told you about. All that was true.

So, in actuality, in the end, I was just as guilty of murder as Mrs. Grant, if not more, because I enjoyed it immensely. And to be perfectly honest, killing Carl, finishing him off the way I did, was pure justice. You have no idea how much I hated and detested that man; how much I loathed his invasive touches, cringed at his lingering stench, and how to this day I still wake up at night in a cold sweat, reliving the attacks of his pawing, and his threats.

So here we are, you and me. I must say, I don't have many absolute beliefs in my life, but I confess there is one that I have faithfully clung to and discern as truth. For one to proficiently write, one must read, but in conjunction with reading, one must also live. Living is the juice that feeds the creative process; the underpinning of experiences and thoughts meshed together to form a multitude of feelings that can then be transcribed into a collection of words and descriptions, explanations, or testaments. These last few months, I have made a concerted effort to live through my words to you, writing down each sentiment and emotion until I emptied the well. Every single word, no matter how large or small, was integral. Each word like a drop of affecting water, pooled together, made to lay bare on sheets of writing paper for you to consume and house in your well of memories and soul.

I have done everything possible to use my remaining time wisely, carefully fulfilling my last obligation to you with the truth finally on my side, and the annoying, whirring sound in my head has finally vanished. After all the years living in this mental fish bowl, the promise of perpetual silence is welcome. I am excited to exit this ride. I would tell you I'd write, but we both know that isn't going to be possible. Not this time.

Now, my well has run dry. I am emotionally threadbare. Finally, and blissfully, empty. Satisfied that the next time I close my eyes, it will be with a purpose. No more toxic droplets of experience to forcibly squeeze out, no more choking feelings to dredge up and reveal, no more hidden truths to strip bare, and no more secrets or lies to uncover. All except one—I have one more secret to turn over and expose, and then, and only then will it morph into the truth.

This is the hardest of the lies I have kept secret because it is the only lie I have loved and cherished. This was my treasured lie, my secret hidden inside me and only me. There is not another single soul on this planet that knows of my secret's existence. Once I tell you Raven, you will be instantly transformed into its keeper, protector, and finally, its undertaker. This information will have the power to either imprison or free you, but only you can decide which fate is yours. I am only the dispenser now. My time has come to an abrupt end, and I have no more to share. My love for you was my oxygen, but my life's experiences have depleted my supply. There is no more I can impart, no more I can consume, and so my dearest daughter, Raven, without further ado, I bid you a final goodbye.

Be the writer of your story, your history, and your experiences. Allow your life to splash color upon your every movement and thought, and permit your heart the freedom and ability to strain and sift through each with decorum, humility, and empathy.

Live strong, live true to yourself, and don't take any shit from anybody.

Drum roll, please… You may now open the envelope.

The Fateful Envelope...

The plain, sealed envelope had held Raven's adoption papers and her original birth certificate along with a small clipped note that read: "I NEVER meant to deceive you."

In the spot allocated for father's name: Diarmuid Padraic McMahon

Diarmuid? Wait, what? I thought Carl was my father?

The room began to spin. The walls started to close in on Raven, and every fiber of her being froze. Had she not been already sitting, Raven would have surely passed out, but instead, she bent her head in between both knees, panting rapidly, trying to regain some vestige of mental clarity.

Get the f—this can't be true. Raven grabbed her cell, frantically texting Paddy one single question:

What's your father's name?

Time stood still. Panic and dread left her entirely immobilized, unable to do anything but grip the cell phone and wait for Paddy's reply.

Pling.

"Why?" replied, Paddy.

"Answer me, please!"

Pling.

"Dermot."

"Legal?"

Pling.

"Guess."

"I'm serious!"

Pling.

"You're seriously weird <3."

"Paddy, please. What's on his birth certificate?"

Raven held in her breath, phone gripped tightly, willing it to bring forth an answer. Seconds felt like an eternity.

Pling.

"Diarmuid Padraic McMahon, why?"

* * *

Three individual granite headstones procured their rightful and prominent places on the small incline. Together, they were nestled discreetly behind the cabin, situated comfortably back from the curve of the slope, but still overlooking the stream. The clearing of the immediate land around the cabin had taken time, but Raven was determined to make sure each final tribute had its proper placement and direction. She had come to the decision that each headstone should remain as near to the stream as possible. For Raven, the stream water symbolized a quiet place of reflection. Its hypnotic effect epitomized the power of manifestation.

While no actual human remains lay buried amongst these somber markers, these symbols served as both a remembrance as well as a definitiveness. For Raven, this memorialized the parts of their lives that linked all four of them intrinsically together, now and for eternity.

Raven refused to indulge in any displays of pomp and circumstance to commemorate their passing. All three souls would have detested such a boorish display. However, buried incredibly deep beneath the ground rested a metal box, only slightly larger than an average-sized shoebox. This unique metal container required no key since it had no lid, no hinge, and no opening. Sealed with the intention of keeping the contents inside eternally locked away, each corner firmly welded shut.

The metal box had nothing purposely decorative adorning the outside apart from the carved initials **T.A.S.** However, the inner recesses of this miniature metal coffin encased years of accumulated letters and cards, news clippings, a lifetime of painful secrets, and all documented past indiscretions. Every last truth had been hidden inside. The culmination of dreams deferred and every forbidden decision, which had dictated the terms of Raven, Terri, and the Grants' collective fate.

The final determination to bury this select collection of painful history instead of thrusting the lot among the flames had been a rather simple one. For Raven, too much of her life had already been destroyed. The conscientious decision to no longer allow this world to devour a further portion felt like the right thing to do, despite the accumulation of untold secrets and lies. By burying the box near the cabin, Raven returned to the earth that which it bore, in the same place that collectively held importance and promise.

The ominous spring skies above boasted a gathering of weighted, gray rain clouds. High, gusting winds began to pick up momentum and strength. The canopy of whipping, tall tree branches caused even the most tenacious leaves to beat violently to and fro, creating a soft whistling resonance in the air, which accompanied nature's impending threat.

Anticipating the looming downpour, Raven quickened her steps, fleeing inside the cabin just in time. Chilled raindrops angrily pelted every available surface. The steady beat of the heavy rain against the windows was deafening, but the warmth and dim candle light of the cabin delivered a welcoming refuge. Paddy, the consummate protector and provider, had made sure Raven's cabin was kept amply supplied with more than enough wood, split and neatly stacked, and strategically sheltered from the elements. Bolting the door shut behind her, Raven tended to the already lit fire, stoking the flames and adding another log or two.

It was hard to believe three months had already passed since Terri's death, the day Raven's world began to silently implode. It marked a painful and wrenching period when cyclical mourning gave way to eventual regeneration. So much had transpired since then, and while admittedly not everything had healed, each vexatious day survived better than the last, and for that much Raven remained grateful.

What had not survived was her relationship with Paddy. Raven could not deny that there were times when she immensely missed the closeness they had once shared. But now they were nothing more than distant friends.

Raven had loved and adored Paddy. In many ways, she still did, but the day she opened her mother's last remaining letter permanently sealed the course of all future decisions. The secret that last letter contained was too big, too menacing, and entirely too damaging. The only viable solution had been to cut all remaining intimate ties and allow the healing to commence, all while burying the past to keep its power to destroy safely contained. Without her consent, Raven had been appointed as the new secret keeper, the guardian of a legacy gone awry.

Paddy also missed the closeness he had once shared with Raven, but there was little left that he could do to convince her to reconsider. Their relationship stayed amicable enough, but the realization that Raven was no longer in love with him still cut deep.

Raven's breaking it off with him shortly after his father's heart attack did little to rekindle his strained relationship with his parents, in particular with his mother. Paddy had become inconsolable, lashing out angrily when Raven, under duress, finally disclosed to him about his mother's unpleasant visit, using that as her excuse to call off their relationship. He pleaded for Raven to reconsider, *to give him one more chance... To ignore what either of his parents thought or wanted; he could,* he told her. As a last ditch attempt, Paddy begged Raven to marry him, but she would not be swayed. Exceedingly hurt and dejected, Paddy reluctantly left Raven alone.

Right or wrong, Paddy adamantly blamed his mother for Raven's abrupt change of heart. A rash of hurtful words volleyed between the pair while final ultimatums were declared. Broken trusts mounted until all parties retreated, licking wounds, but not necessarily defeated. While the ties between mother and son had been severely damaged, the permanency of antagonism was still unknown. Dermot had tried to reach out to his son to explain his mother's actions, imploring him to show his mother compassion, but by then it was too late. The haunting legacy of lies and deceptions had won over a new set of victims to feed off of.

Despite the fact that Raven hadn't necessarily appreciated the visit from Kendal, she refused to hold Paddy's mother to task in the way that Paddy continued relentlessly to do. Raven knew better. She knew the real truth. For everyone involved, time would eventually be the greatest of equalizers.

Regardless of the decision, Raven's heart felt as shattered as Paddy's, if not more. But she forced herself to hide her true feelings. She knew in her heart that one day Paddy, just like Dermot, would make some other woman the perfect husband. It just couldn't be her. Not any longer.

Inside the cabin, the flame of the burning logs gave off a warming and welcoming glow, while outside, the rain continued to pelt violently against the windows. Taking a deep breath in, she knew there was one more hurdle needing attention. Raven reached out and swiped the pharmacy bag off the table and marched straight for the bathroom, determined to get this damn test over with. She had put it off long enough.

Not all that proficient at following directions, Raven was relieved to find out the kit included excellent diagrams. "Easy enough," she murmured.

Once the deed was completed, reading the results meant waiting a whole forty-five agonizing seconds.

Tick, tick, tick, tick... "Come on already," she anxiously whispered, legs shaking nonstop.

Tick, tick, tick... No, no, no, no—God, no.

She had her answer.

Never had Raven despised the color pink so much as she did in that moment.

She leaned over the sink and cleaned her hands, grabbed the towel, and pressed it firmly to her face. She began to sob uncontrollably. The pregnancy test result confirmed Raven had an arduous decision to face, similar to the path her mother traveled years ago.

Placed in an untenable position, inducted grudgingly as the latest keeper and protector of secrets, Raven reluctantly accepted that she alone would bear the brunt and weight of the consequences of her choices, not totally of her making.

FOR DISCUSSION

1. The novel is called *Secrets That Find Us*. How does this title reflect the story?

2. Why do you think the author chose to use Terri's undelivered message to the jury as the starting point in the novel?

3. During the trial, Terri became preoccupied with her hostility towards the jurors as opposed to anyone else in the position of locking her away for the rest of her life. This included the judge, the prosecutor, her attorney, and the police. Was her resentment justified, or was she simply deflecting and lashing out?

4. Terri explains to Raven in the letter, "I wasn't born a murderer." With the dysfunctional childhood Terri had growing up, she understandably grew into an angry and bitter woman, yet, one still strangely in need of validation from the one person left in the world who still cared about her. Do you agree with Terri disclosing her past to Raven the way she did, or was her method merely cruel and selfish?

5. Terri purposely made a bona fide, disgusting mess out of the crime scene in an attempt to deter detectives from finding out the truth. Did it work, or was had the combination of her theatrical admission of guilt, the fingerprints on the gun, her intimate knowledge of the crime scene, and her bizarre behavior following the crime become enough of a reason to accept the crime at face value and nail her case permanently shut?

6. Did you agree with Terri about taking the blame for the crimes committed by Mrs. Grant, or should she have had faith in the justice system to work out all the particulars? Knowing what you do about Terri's abusive past, if you had sat on that jury and Mrs. Grant was being tried for the crimes instead of Terri, what would your verdict have been?

7. Mr. and Mrs. Grant had been a close couple. Did Mr. Grant suspect his wife was involved with the murders, or do you think he assumed, like

everyone else, that she was innocent, only confessing out of her motherly love and protectiveness toward Terri?

8. Terri assumed Carl fathered her baby up until the day Raven was born. However, besides putting Diarmuid's name on the birth certificate, she never tried to make contact with him until after being sent to prison. What do you think motivated Terri to keep this particular secret, and was it only hers to keep?

9. Why did Diarmuid change his Irish name to the English equivalent, Dermot? Do you think it had anything to do with his relationship with Terri, or his need to start his life over with Kendal?

10. It was only after Terri received her life sentence that she finally decided to reach out to Diarmuid—but his wife, Kendal, blocked her attempt. Why did Kendal feel threatened by Terri? Was there something else in that letter that made Kendal so hostile and afraid? Should Kendal have given the letter to Dermot when it arrived, or was getting rid of it the best option? In Kendal's place, what would you have done?

11. Wrong place at the wrong time— What would have happened if Terri had refused to visit her mother on that fateful day? Would Winnie and Carl have given up on trying to extort money from Terri, or would they have continued to hound and threaten her until something just as awful took place?

12. Terri frequently describes prison life to Raven throughout her missive, claiming to do so because she wants Raven to clearly understand the dismal life she can no longer endure forever. Is Terri's motivation based on looking for Raven's absolution and forgiveness for committing suicide, or is she just venting and complaining?

13. Despite being in a maximum-security prison, inmates procure many illegal items and substances, as well as sustain many illicit relationships. Did the level of ingenuity and resourcefulness inmates used to cope with their surroundings come as a surprise?

14. Initially, Terri is able to easily manipulate Martina unwittingly into supplying enough pills for her to eventually overdose. At some point, Martina becomes dissatisfied with the agreed compensation for said services, and demands sexual favors instead. Terri becomes sadistic and calculating in response. Was Terri using learned survival skills, or was she so damaged from life behind bars that cruelty has become an acceptable behavioral alternative?

15. Burying Terri properly was Raven's sole motivation for searching through Terri's legal papers. Disclosure of the letter could have easily been missed for years, maybe even forever. How differently would Raven's life have been if she had in fact found Terri's letter years later and not when she did? *What if* Raven had already cemented her relationship with Paddy by that time, even started a family, and then found Terri's letter?

16. One of the novel's themes is the destruction caused by hidden secrets, half-truths, and the harboring of past hurts. With this said, Raven has an important, life-changing decision to make. Will she or won't she keep the baby, and if she does, do you think Raven will repeat history and take the secret of the baby's paternity to the grave?

The *secrets that find us...*

If you enjoyed

SECRETS THAT FIND US,

Here's a sneak peek of

AS ONE DOOR CLOSES

By Sahar Abdulaziz

PROLOGUE

LIFE HAS AN UNCANNY WAY of tying up a host of loose ends. Not in the neat, all-creases-matching, hospital corner-to-corner kind of way, but in a cloudy, murky, uncertain mish-mash collection of what ifs, could haves, and a busload of should haves kind of way. But what happens when all the magnificent stars in the heavens, and all the resolute planets in the galaxy, agree to simultaneously align? What happens when the glorious birds of prey in the sky and the steadfast worker ants of the ground all decide to ally? And more intriguingly, what happens when the settling of old hurts and scores becomes so alluring, so certain, with the whispered promise of everlasting, as to lure with it a collection of hardly surviving, barely functioning, scattered, and damaged souls together once again? As one door finally seemed to close tightly shut, two others flung wide open, and the darkness of life's most protected secrets and haunts invited the crippling unknown to bask once again in the glaring, naked light.

—Skye

CHAPTER ONE

BASKING IN THE EARLY QUIET of the cool but still lingering late, hazy-mountain summer morning, Zoe, only feeling barely half-awake, mechanically sipped at her all-too-sweet, pre-diabetic hot tea. Taking in small, quick sips, so as to not burn her tongue, she obtained the pleasure of feeling the welcoming, soothing heat envelop her and quiet her worn-down body, calming what was left of her shattered nerves. After a long, exhausting, and emotionally challenging day yesterday, an arsenal of strong caffeinated tea would have probably been a smarter choice than just sipping at a singular yet convivial cup, but since intravenous tea had not yet been invented, her lone, oh-so-sweet cup would simply have to temporarily suffice.

Death—the so-called greatest of equalizers. *Yet, I feel guilty that I'm not the least bit sad that he's dead. Something about the man made me feel uncomfortable, —hesitant.*

Zoe continued to stare out of her kitchen window in a daze, eyes looking at everything around her, while not really focusing on any one particular this or that. Lately, she was had been finding it increasingly difficult to concentrate and often found herself standing with arms crossed over her chest, eyes gazing, and mind off daydreaming.

Pennsylvania summers, especially those in the mountain areas, are usually on the short side. Maybe not technically, but they certainly had the ability to leave most inhabitants feeling that way. Tepid temperatures reign in the region, for the most part, with a few serious hot spells mixed in for sport. That's when fans and air conditioners are blown at full force as if Armageddon itself is approaching. Then boom—within a day or a two, the green, vibrant leaves on the lofty collection of mountainous trees begin to turn a sensational burnt yellow mixed with deep orange hues, laden with shades of brown and rich reds. Spectacular fall foliage, closely resembling tourist postcard photos, marks the seasonal passage of time in the Pennsylvanian mountains.

Zoe loved her home in its picture-perfect setting, nestled comfortably with enough space so as not to see her neighbor's business or they see hers. She especially adored the wide array of multihued fall foliage, a living kaleidoscope of eye candy, an enchanting place each year when local folks intuitively begin to hone their latent pioneer skills. They start nesting, chopping, and gathering corded, seasoned wood with a bit more diligence, if they still haven't done so.

When the last stubborn remnants of emptied backyard gardens are turned over—beds tilled and prepped for the following year's most welcomed crops—life slows down. Leaves are not usually bagged on the mountain, except perhaps in small, modern, gated communities, but for the majority of neighborhoods where forest is permitted to live in harmony with homeowners, leaves are raked, gathered in large piles, collected on oversized tarps, and then systematically dumped into large composting bins or forested backyards to once again become nature's fertilizer.

Zoe most admired most the way the magnificent old oak trees around her home towered everywhere. Once full, green, and luscious, they now seemed to haphazardly drop their leaves, intuitively closing down shop for the pending, brisk, and often especially harsh winter months ahead... and there would undoubtedly be many of those to contend with. Winters on the mountain can could be brutal, sometimes stubbornly lasting until the end of March or later, teetering toward the end of April before spring is eventually permitted to commence sprouting. The land then reveals its promised hidden bounty and effervescent treasures.

Zoe affectionately regarded Pennsylvania mornings on the mountain as nothing short of invigorating—oftentimes chilly and sometimes downright cold until the heat of the sun began to make its comfortable presence known closer to noontime. That's when the warm rays would heat up the land and its inhabitants. Until then, a light sweater would have to do.

But no amount of nature-inspired beauty or foliage would ever prevent the seasons of Zoe's life from turning their next inevitable corner. Zoe was turning the big five-oh in a matter of only a few days, and the prospect of this particular looming number was starting to stir up in her a slew of mixed, and oftentimes, skewed emotions. Sure, people liked to joke that the alternative, which was death, was a whole lot worse, but seriously...what exactly did this superficial number fifty signify, and why for God's sake did it seem to have such a hold on her the way it did? She had to wonder to herself if the number actually symbolized something to her personally. Or was it a societal bookmark, which signified for her looming ruin for her? Damned if she knew.

As far back as Zoe could still remember, when she would hear someone admit publicly to being fifty years old, that number generated an automatic young-person's-reference-code alert: old, ready to meet the maker…and without saying as much—invisible. "Invisible" described her recent feelings to a tee how she was starting to feel most of the time lately. She despised how invalidated getting older made her begin to feel, mocking her, reminding her that life wasn't everlasting. Now, with an approaching five-zero birthday, she was in the same old boat, facing the same number delineation, and she couldn't stand it. Zoe cringed, visualizing the smirks on the faces of the younger, instinctively self-absorbed crowd who most likely would now lump her in with the old folks just as she had done at their age. While admittedly she was no spring chicken, and certainly no longer addressed as a "miss" but a "ma'am," being treated as invisible was probably the worst possible outcome.

Just like an old cow on a farm, Zoe was beginning to feel as if her turn to be "put out to pasture" was on the close horizon. In the mornings, her body was had started to ache in the mornings in places and ways she didn't know existed. In the valleys near where she lived, the grass and meadows were turning an off-white, straw-like consistency, much like the coarse, hard-to-manage hair on her head.

The cultural attitude that worships youth and beauty remains narrow-minded toward those aging and those already aged, and frankly, that scared the shit out of Zoe. She never wanted to visualize herself as a social pariah or worse yet—helpless. Some days, when she had had a restless night, waking up in pools of cold sweat, pillow matted to her face, and her hairline soaking, she found herself becoming forgetful, clumsy, and struggling through simple tasks. The bluish, thin veins and age spots that she remembered on her grandmother were now beginning to become more pronounced on her own hands, as well. Tragically, no amount of expensive miracle hand cream seemed to make the least amount of difference, except that she smelled oh-so-expensively good.

The last of the now shorter summer nights had recently become stunted and a good deal cooler—what Zoe affectionately referred to as "sweater weather." Animals large and small who inhabited the mountain instinctively knew the real deal, as well. The daytime skies, in accordance with nature's demands, began to gray earlier, only sanctioning the sun's intense heat to be doled out in small, select increments. Sensing the changing seasons, the animals earnestly began preparing for the scarcity of available food. Armies of gray, furry, and often assertive squirrels would be the first to go ballistic, gathering up hordes of fallen acorns, on a mission to finding appropriate and often forgotten hiding places, while lumbering black bears lazily would feed on whatever goodies they could forage for—including some of Zoe's unsuspecting neighbor's left-out garbage pail, fortified with nothing but a weak, pliable lid. All were fair game, and a great reminder for Zoe, who made yet another mental note to buy a new pail with a more secure lid. She loathed being the one left to clean up the stinking mess her furry neighbors all too happily left behind.

In the aftermath of the dark evening air, clear- blue skies filled with flocks of magnificent birds that could be heard and seen heading south, flying in perfect formation, and landing periodically for a rest on either some tall oak trees or old telephone-pole wires before continuing their controlled journey to the promise of warmer winter abodes. Between their endless hunting and mating rituals, those few hardy breeds of bird that toughed it out and chose to remain through the mountain winters, spent their autumns aggressively reinforcing their nests with pieces of twigs and discarded garden strings. Zoe deeply envied how the social order of the animal kingdom ran like a well-tuned engine. Not so much in the human domain, where basically it was a free-for-all where anything went.

The shocking news of her father-in-law's sudden death turned yesterday entirely upside down and inside out. From what little Zoe understood so far, he had made it semiconscious and barely alive to the hospital via ambulance, suffering from what the ER doctor described as a rupturing cerebral aneurysm in his brain; this. It then turned quickly into a second, and much more intense, fatal stroke. He died before making it into surgery.

Once the hospital phoned, all previous plans for the day were, of course, immediately placed on hold as her husband Gavin sped off to the hospital. As usual, Zoe, who had a hard time saying no, especially to her husband, was unwittingly nominated for the bleak task of making all the necessary phone calls to Gavin's family members, all of whom she barely knew despite how long they had been married.

Still, if truth be told, in total there weren't very many calls to make by virtue of the fact that most of Gavin's family members weren't exactly on speaking terms with one another. This made performing the current uncomfortable chore placed on her shoulders unusually difficult to handle. So, Zoe took a deep breath and another swig, or three, of her tea and set out to make each individual phone call. Part of her had held out hope that at least one member of her husband's family would be so kind as to offer to make a phone chain or better yet completely take up the job where she left off, alleviating her—*the married-into-the-family person*—of this extremely awkward responsibility, but that never even came close to happening. No big surprise there.

Before placing the first call, Zoe, the list maker, mentally prepared a small, simple script in her head, trying to figure out the best way she could convey the most relevant information in the most painless way possible. She had tried to explain to Gavin that it was probably a bit premature to make all the calls in the first place, considering there wasn't a whole lot of pertinent information to share at this point other than that the man was dead. However, Gavin was adamant, so she reluctantly acquiesced as she usually did. What else was new?

Besides, now wasn't exactly the prime time to quibble with him, so to make her life easier and make the calls go smoother, she developed a straightforward, no-fail plan: call, sound as sincere and appropriately soothing as possible, drop the news, and hang up. Simple enough, right? Zoe figured this would be the best course of action to take since in all likelihood she would probably be dealing with people feeling and expressing a wide gamut of highly intense emotions—everything from grief to despondency and a mixture in between, which would only be normal under such circumstances.

So, she played around in her head with a few delivery scenarios, but each time she tried them out, they all sounded too contrived and insincere. Part of her just wanted to blurt out, "Hi, this is Zoe, Gavin's wife. Just wanted to let you know your father/uncle/brother is dead. Um, and that's all I know for now, so like, yeah, as soon as I know more…I'll call you back? Talk to you soon. Ta-ta."

However, by the fourth phone call it became absurdly apparent that anything close to displays of grief or sadness were not going to be of any concern in the slightest since the responses she had heard back thus far from Gavin's clan were more akin to orating a political treaty with shifty tribal alliances. She felt like they were all on some crazy deserted-island game show with one vote left to determine who would remain and who would be kicked off the island. So much for heartache and family despair!

"Will so-and-so be coming?"

"Did you call so-and-so? What did he/she say? Are they coming, because if they are, I'm not!"

"Are you sure he's really dead?"

"Who did you say died?"

Then there was the particularly catty "How did you get my number?" response that came from one particularly spiteful cousin of Gavin's who sounded peeved and put out by what she considered the unsolicited and unexpected interruption of her well-established morning routine and cookie-cutter life.

But the best line ever came from Skye, one of Gavin's sisters, whose only stoically curt reply right after hearing Zoe's well-oiled speech about her father just kicking the bucket was, "Finally—indisputable proof there is a God." Zoe, slightly embarrassed and confounded, had no planned response for *that* reaction except to nod like a spaz and silently chuckle in agreement.

Over an hour and a half later, Gavin finally had a chance to give her a quick call from outside the emergency hospital examination room where his dad still lay. He described in hushed, hurried detail to Zoe all the craziness that was happening all around him in the emergency room, starting off with the ambulance that almost backed up into the wall of the receiving bay. Then Gavin went on to tell her about the homeless drunk man with yellowing, bruised arms and filthy fingernails who, while propped on a gurney in the hospital hallway with an intravenous needle inserted into his arm, tried to accost him, stinking to high heaven of a sour combination of alcohol and urine.

"Damn stinking, dirty-ass imbecile almost pulled his disease-infected needle out of his arm as he tried to swing off the stretcher to grab at me, probably looking for a cigarette or his next drink!" he yelled, ranting irately into the phone. "I'm so sick and tired of these selfish parasites on society always looking for an easy handout."

Zoe rolled her eyes the same way she had done most of her marriage when Gavin got on his self-righteous soapbox. Trying at this point to reason with him or offer any solace would only be met with more yelling, so why bother?

Then Gavin went on to describe the extensive, bureaucratic paperwork he still had to sign off on. Sounding exhausted and overly irritate, Gavin, who naturally specialized in being excessively callous in the face of catastrophe, was apparently overcome by the added strain, so he subconsciously began to further incriminate himself by wondering aloud as to how the whole funeral/hospital thing was going to get paid for. "I hope to God Dad had some life insurance policy. I don't know how we're expected to financially cover this mess," he complained. Zoe listened with her eyes staring at the ceiling, knowingly remaining mute and unresponsive to her husband's tacit, uncensored, cold-hearted comments.

Next on Gavin's agenda, he explained to his still silent wife that he was to head directly over to the local funeral parlor to make whatever necessary arrangements so *the body*—that's what Gavin "sensitively" called his own father, *the body*—could be picked up from the hospital morgue and properly prepared for burial. Once that was done, he continued that he was off to the cemetery to buy a plot, unless of course the funeral parlor could arrange that, as well. He wasn't too sure what the protocol was. Strangely, and arrogantly in Zoe's opinion, Gavin hadn't even bothered to consider that he should first contact his two sisters and/or his ailing mother to find out whether or not any of them wished to be a part of the plans and decision making. Zoe almost felt the desire to point out this egregious oversight to her husband, but instead, she decided to keep her mouth shut. Zoe learned long ago not to bother meddling in Gavin's family affairs. She just let him deal with them the way he wanted, no matter how wacky it seemed to her.

"Were you able to call everyone on the list?" Gavin barked abruptly at her. His attention became noticeably diminished as he tried to cup the cell receiver with his hand for some added privacy.

In the background, Zoe could detect a clamor of voices sounding like nurses preparing for a shift change. She thought she heard someone say, "I smell like urine and vomit. I can't wait to get home and get cleaned up." As the noises drew closer, Zoe assumed it was probably the nursing staff flitting in and out of Gavin's father's hospital room. While faint and hard to clearly hear, it sounded to her as if they were trying to discreetly gauge by Gavin's responses when best to move *the body* to the morgue and start the cleanup and room preparations for the next critical-care guest.

"Yes, I made all the calls you asked me to," was all Zoe had the heart to reply. The whack-a-doodle details would come later.

"Okay, great. Thanks," Gavin hastily replied back. He was obviously distracted and anxious. "As soon as I get any more information, I'll call you back." And with that, he clicked off before waiting for any response. Typical Gavin.

During their marriage, Gavin had explained to Zoe that his family did not make it a common practice to observe long, drawn-out, "fancy" funerals, Gavin's code for expensive. Therefore, it came as no surprise when that evening Gavin curtly pointed out to her, "No long procession of shiny black limousines, overpriced floral arrangements, or wreaths, music, religious formalities, or long good-byes are going to be required. One pine box, a few guys to help carry it, and we're good to go."

That was yesterday, and today was already the funeral. Zoe, of course, had to make a whole new fresh round of calls last night to the same disagreeable bunch. She dreaded the insufferable, forced exchanges, but this time she hadn't even bothered with sounding even remotely melancholy or consoling. *Again—why bother!*

Slumped at the round kitchen table, still wearing her crumpled camisole nightgown, Zoe continued to indulge in her morning tea ritual one blessed sip at a time while knee deep in personal deliberation. While she felt exhausted beyond recognition, her feeble attempts at procrastination were only a trifling, temporary fix, especially given that she still ultimately knew what and whom she had to face today... *No mere human controls time,* she thought to herself, *me included.*

After placing the now empty mug on the table, Zoe absentmindedly slid her strong, sinewy hands down to her pleasantly plump thighs and began to squeeze at the excess skin, a habit she had begun when her body decided to expand and jiggle. Zoe scrunched her face, grimacing with repulsion when she finally couldn't help but notice what she was absentmindedly doing. Looking moodily down at both her thighs made her inwardly groan, especially with how the clumpy cellulite just seemed to congeal and crinkle up in lumpy-like pebbles reminiscent of curds of cottage cheese. *When the hell did this happen?* Certainly, her legs were once considered one of her best body parts—always an enviable given, a sure thing, one of her hottest attributes. Why, oh why were all these mega-gravity-stricken body changes happening to her so quickly and so thoroughly? Sagging chin, the telltale signs of a turkey neck forming, arms that hung and wobbled, spurts of uninvited gray, wiry hair that had a life of its own, and now this!

Pulling her robe closed again as if she held the evidence of a crime, Zoe knew full well that she didn't have time today to ruminate over what used to be her body. However, that did little to stop her from once again leaning back slightly on her high, ladder-back, wood chair and letting her mind race back and forth in futile, solitary conversation. *Wasn't it just yesterday when I was a young, vivacious woman, not necessarily beautiful in the conventional sense perhaps, but definitely desirable?* she reflected to herself with dissatisfaction. She remembered when she was just setting out into the beckoning, wide world, readying herself to face and conquer all kinds of exciting life choices and decisions. She had just graduated from high school, invincible and fresh, excited to take the next major step toward the altar of beckoning success...basking in the promised, exotic splendor of the impending mysteriousness of womanhood, and setting the victory marker in the sand for others to aspire to and lament over.

Ironically, it was just a hiccup ago when her forearms didn't involuntarily wag in the wind without an accompanying breeze at least. When her crown of glory in the form of her long, thick, brunette locks were actually still pretending to mimic a shade other than gray. The slight, but certainly obvious, muffin top forming over her beltline made her want to gag. She wondered if her squishy belly made Gavin want to gag, too; he never kissed her there anymore.

Zoe could remember a time not all that long ago, when the creased and set laugh lines around her mouth actually marked true emotions of sadness or disappointment, not just the furrowed lines that now naturally lined her aging mask and sagging jawline, making her appear just perpetually pissed all the time.

What am I morphing into? she lamented under her breath. *How did this sum total of yesterdays accumulate into this uncharted, unknown, and kind of scary new world?* This incredibly daunting and foreboding emotional trash heap of life experiences set forth in unmapped motion that no one around her, as far as she could tell, had yet been able to navigate any better than she has thus far.

Zoe was sick and tired of being subjected to everything these days that shoved youth in her face—from television, to movies, to advertisements, and commercials. Newsstand walls were filled to the brim with endless rows of magazine racks displaying Botoxed, plastic, aging beauties, airbrushed and tweaked until barely recognizable, who were now the expected societal norm. Fashion books declared what was in and out, while exercise gurus with flat six-pack stomachs and to-die-for thighs marketed their wares with the promises of ageless beauty and toned, rippled biceps. Popular music went out of its way to speak to youth, flaunting sexual overtones and gyrating bodies. Where oh where among these glossy hipster magazines and endless rows of how-to books were the hands-on, friendly manuals for women who just wanted to do nothing more than enter into maturity in a way that didn't leave them feeling indiscernible and socially invalid?

How could it be possible to feel so incredibly accomplished one minute, on top of the world, ready at an instant *to be all that you can be,* and the very next, kerplop! Down for the proverbial count! IT'S *NOT FAIR!* she reflected. As women, we are left gasping for breath, haphazardly doing the doggy paddle of life, while the carefully contoured landscape of our female world comes swooping in, ready to crash and burn as soon as the visible, physical facade of our youth becomes a collection of indiscriminate, irrelevant passing days. *Oh, crap, Zoe—that's super deep!* she scoffed to herself.

Thinking back on her life over the years, Zoe credited the official start of her personal and physical downfall to soon after she married and began to birth her brood of children. For over a decade, her days and nights blended together until they became indistinguishable, a time-capsulated period in her life, which now she forever dubbed "The Numb Years." A time in her life when sheer daily existence and an occasional rare hot shower became her new set of norms as opposed to the exhilarating odyssey she thought it was supposed to be. *When did my life take a drastic swerve off the proverbial numb cliff? And who helped push me over…or was I a totally willing participant?*

Stunned to find herself trying to fight back a suffocating lump growing in her throat, welling up from deep down inside, Zoe once again warily pulled her robe a bit tighter around her pleasantly plump waist as her eyes glazed over and welled up with tears. Fighting back the mounting urge to indulge in a good, all-out cry fest, Zoe sniffled and swallowed hard. Luckily, the house remained uncommonly, but oh-so-blissfully quiet. Zoe took this rare opportunity to continue to bask and indulge in her own thoughts, even for the fleeting, treasured moment or two.

Weekends were cherished during the summer months since they tended to allow for these kinds of momentary lapses of perpetual demands being hurled in her direction. At least until the demands of the combined stomachs of her family members made them collectively rouse from their sleep in search of sustenance, or until the grating phone began to blast. *Well, it's not nearly as bad as it used to be,* she thought. Not like back in the days when there were six people to cook for, making mealtime feel more like a soup kitchen. Now, with two children grown and out of the house, leaving just two teen squatters left, mornings were a bunch more relaxed and less strained. Nowadays, everyone in the house woke up with barely enough time to eat, much less to visit, grabbing anything quick to shove in their mouths and then rushing off to do whatever it was they needed to get accomplished, leaving her with an empty feeling she couldn't quite put a finger on yet. The "nest" wasn't yet empty, but it sure felt that way.

Maybe it was the lack of continuity of coming together as a family, sitting around the long, aged farm table breaking bread, swapping comedic anecdotes, discussing pressing family issues and parental concerns, laughing, and on occasion, even hurling insults and arguing together. However, now with the children all growing older with obligations and plans of their own, and the family numbers rapidly decreasing within the home itself, dinnertime had become more like a forced performance, designed by Zoe to make her feel less guilty about all the times she was too busy to sit and eat. Nowadays, meals were a collection of easy-to-throw-together foods, cooked or assembled and left covered for her family to just grab and gobble. Not the most satisfying…

Whoa. Zoe violently shook her head incredulously. *Less guilty? Wait, wait, wait—wow. Now where did that just come from? Look who missed the women's liberation movement and fell into crazy!* Zoe was shocked at herself! She then resolutely stood up, trudged over to the stove to pour another cup of hot tea, and grabbed a few tea biscuits out of the can she kept hidden for such emotional emergencies.

* * *

Zoe forlornly could still recall a time in her life, not all that long ago mind you…well, sort of anyway, when all she desperately wanted with all her heart and soul was to be an artist. As a young woman, she was a bohemian at heart, wearing long, sewn jean skirts to school with flip-flops, peasant shirts, and her extra-long, braided, thick auburn hair cascading down her back. Her earrings were always big and always spectacular. Her long, delicate, swanlike neck housed a nice assortment of colorful, homemade beaded necklaces, while soft leather strips of all sizes and shades casually adorned her thin wrists. Every item of hers became a piece of her personality, exploding. Her body was her canvas. Long vines of elaborate flowers were carefully drawn with henna on her arms and legs. Even her slender fingers and clear-painted toes boasted a collection of silver rings decoratively placed.

While Zoe colorfully ornamented her body in order to transform it into a walking, breathing piece of art, she kept her makeup at a sparse minimum. Besides playing up her stunning, light-green eyes with a little brown kohl, she didn't need to do much more back then to accentuate her innate beauty. Her perfect, white teeth and dazzling smile stood strong on their own. Her youthful, flawless skin glowed a naturally warm, kissed-sunbeam, light brown, and her fine, willowy legs made her appear as if she glided into a room rather than merely walked.

Always considered a wild, free spirit, Zoe reveled in anything creative or mildly crafty. She was the sort of child who utterly despised receiving a board game or a doll as a gift, but if given a new set of colorful markers or watercolors and some real art paper, boy oh boy, was she in all her glory! Her mother, who was more like her own secret kindred spirit, would inform anyone willing to listen to her complain that with Zoe in the house, an empty pad of paper was just not safe. On the sly, however, her mother always made sure copious amounts of paper and a constant, steady supply of pencils or any other art supplies she could finagle on her very limited budget were made available for her "little artiste."

Zoe's father, on the other hand, a more cerebral and analytical kind of personality, did not share at all in Zoe's artistic pursuits and leanings, relentlessly prompting his daughter "to land." That's what he called it—*landing*—as if she was such an incurable space cadet that he needed to remind her constantly to join the rest of the world here back on Earth.

But Zoe knew her dad to be a good and honest man, for all his haranguing, who was loyal through and through. A man who neither minced his words nor bantered for the sake of hearing his own voice, but always had a kind shoulder to lean on in times of duress. A man who honored his children through the loyalty, devotion, and unwavering respect he showered on her mother. Theirs was a love story that many never experienced or thought really existed except in romance novels; and while her father deeply loved and adored his baby girl, he worried constantly about her "ditzy" personality. He was relentlessly concerned that it would eventually lead her down dangerous paths, compromising the future and upending the happiness he so deeply wanted for her and worked so hard to provide for all his children to experience in life.

Her father was also an extremely traditional man, and didn't much appreciate how his only daughter refused to dress herself in a manner he considered proper, choosing outlandish outfits better suited for some "hippie pothead chick," like the kind he saw portrayed in movies and documentaries about Woodstock. What made him more troubled was the fact that he earned a respectable enough living, certainly more than enough money to make sure his family lived and dressed decently. So why, for heaven's sake, his daughter continued to dress like she was some psychedelic, homeless bag lady was beyond his narrow comprehension. It was a bone of contention that caused many an argument.

Thus, after she had graduated from high school, instead of letting her follow her passion for the arts, her father used his arsenal of emotional blackmail to persuade his daughter to study something "more practical, something—anything—more potentially lucrative." Not sure what to do exactly that would be enough to please him and at the same time not totally depress her, Zoe opted to become an elementary school teacher. She figured that her love for being around young children, coupled with the opportunity she hoped that she would one day have to also spread her love of the arts through the eyes of impressionable young minds, seemed like a good compromise. And let's face it—at the same time, becoming a teacher would make her parents proud, particularly her father, who hopefully would finally be lulled into a numb complacence and permanently get off her aching back.

Elementary teacher, while not exactly glamorous, seemed at the time like a win-win concession. However, when Zoe was in her second year of college, hating every single minute of it, she met her soon-to-be husband, Gavin, who was also a student at the same college. Unlike Zoe, Gavin was a thoroughly serious student, and *totally hot*. Tall, lean, but oh-so-muscular, sporting a very sharp, closely trimmed mustache-beard, and always impeccably dressed. Zoe could hardly keep her lovely, green, almond-shaped eyes or her hands off him.

Openly flirting with Gavin was clearly out of the question. He seemed like the self-assured type of guy who was used to unsolicited attentions being draped on him from the female persuasion, so coming on that hard and strong would have just turned a guy like Gavin off completely. Zoe sure didn't want that to happen! However, it sure didn't hurt any that they had a nice amount of mutual friends in common, making being in the same place at the same time socially acceptable. Zoe smirked to herself while floating through these memories.

Made in the USA
Middletown, DE
21 November 2022

15653166R00139